D1131660

GOD'S WORLD
IAN WATSON

Carroll & Graf Publishers, Inc.
New York

Copyright © 1979 by Ian Watson

First Carroll & Graf edition 1990

Carroll & Graf Publishers, Inc.
260 Fifth Avenue
New York, NY 10001

Library of Congress Cataloging-in-Publication Data

Watson, Ian, 1943–
  God's world / by Ian Watson.—1st Carroll & Graf ed.
    p. cm.
  ISBN 0-88184-574-4 : $17.95
  I. Title.
PR6073.A86306   1990
823'.914—dc20   90-31723
                                                    CIP

Manufactured in the United States of America

For all history is in some measure a fall of the sacred, a limitation and diminution. But the sacred does not cease to manifest itself, and with each new manifestation it resumes its original tendency to reveal itself wholly. It is true, of course, that the countless new manifestations of the sacred in the religious consciousness of one or another society repeat the countless manifestations of the sacred that those societies knew in the course of their past, of their "history". But it is equally true that this history does not paralyze the spontaneity of hierophanies; at every moment a fuller revelation of the sacred remains possible.

Mircea Eliade, *Shamanism*

CONTENTS

Part One

IN HIGH SPACE

A*

ONE

THIS TIME, WHEN Peter and I make love, we unmask the port-hole. Dousing the cabin lights, we float in the pale gloaming. We touch, we kiss.

Outside is High Space: a grainy, mottled sea of trembling, incoherent half-light. Brighter kaleidoscopic whorls well up and die back in that twilight sea, as though they are the distorted, prismatic images of actual stars out there. But they are not that; the ship's instruments cannot translate them into patterns corresponding to stars. At times they appear like ghostly images of our own ship, probability echoes trying to suck us back down again into normal space. Perhaps they're simply the product of atoms sloughing off the hull, particles scattering away through the boundary of the High Space field, becoming mountains of virtual mass in our wake before they cascade back among the ordinary interstellar hydrogen.

"So far from Earth, and so close to ourselves," murmurs Peter, with a royal purr. Freckles stipple his upper reaches (I chart their chiaroscuro with outspread finger tips) as though nature couldn't make up her mind whether his top half was to be white or amber. In the vague glow of High Space all these freckles tend to merge, while his legs, bare of freckling, seem magnified, stockier and plumper than they really are. He's quite short, and wiry. A curly red-head.

"Yet how far, Amy? We can measure our own closeness far more easily. This way—"

From our long, free-fall foreplay of tongues and toes and fingertips we are borne gently down upon the waiting bunk.

Or rather, here it is that we bear down by choice. For in High Space a strange, subjective sort of quasi-gravity comes into play. As we are drawn to each other by intense desire, so we gather a

11

local force of gravity in ourselves. It pulls and holds us against each other as though we are about to be fused by natural law as well as inclination. Only extremes of feeling trigger the effect—and its opposite, if hate or rage is the feeling: an actual repulsion, a thrusting away.

So the tethers of the bunk rise towards us, Indian rope trick style, as we sink down. Peter catches hold and tugs impatiently. Will we never reach our goal? Time is stretching out now, teasing us. At last the tethers wrap round us softly. We squash the bunk, we squeeze each other.

So he slides inside me: slow dance of swelling tissues, hot muscle, nerves aglow, *glissade douce*. We are dense with this. Our joy winds us together slowly like twin rubber bands of nerve fibre which seem as if they can never reach a snapping point. Ours is snail-love: the slow mutual twining of molluscs. In this sliding world we move only by muscle waves, snails both of us, his love dart lodged beneath my mantle. The love-making of snails is very beautiful.

Outside in High Space the whorls bloom and dissolve back again into the formless modality of pre-Creation: fingerprints of our ship's transit, perhaps. My fingertips press into Peter's flesh meanwhile, his into mine.

Our twin orgasm, later, expends the quasi-gravity in a slow shockwave detectable throughout the ship, tugging vicariously for a while—we know well!—at the rest of the crew. There may be smiles of complicity later on, perhaps a grimace from cold Jacobik who deserves no first name. (Could he ever have been a product of love?) The others can sense that it was us, rather than René and Zoe, say; there is our signature, our flavour in the gravity pulse . . . Oh, we're all very much together on this journey.

When we finally drift apart, in free-fall once more—in detumescent space—Peter remasks the porthole while I illumine the little cabin softly, rheostating the lights to half-strength.

Despite the size-constraints imposed by the ellipsoid of the High Space field, here is a private place. Private space guards us against the conflicting subjectivities of High Space, and makes me wonder again (as a good cultural proxemicist): what is the irreducible distance between people? What unconscious

12

forces still resist the equalization of all humanity?

One wall of my cabin is decorated with a photocollage of those extraordinary events whose origins we now fly to discover: the God's World broadcasts—those temporary appearances of angels and avatars who came into existence and departed from it again. Here are the photographs: actual snapshots of God's messengers. I brood on them. Can one film an illusion? A durable, solid illusion? How solid and durable must an event be to be classed as real rather than imaginary? These angels and avatars hovered precariously between the two categories—though not so the chariot they brought for us; that remains, amidships.

Peter claps his hands. Here am I wool-gathering before my photographs! So easy to lose track of time, where time is ours to construct. How long have we been *en route*? Forever—and no time at all. Clocks tick on, yet they are only clockwork toys. True time depends upon our attention. Yet a shared consensus still exists by and large: the average of all our attitudes. In this same steel hull we contrive to coexist.

Peter bowls a ball of clothes for me to catch, my blue jump-suit unravelling slowly in mid-air, arms and legs inflating, offering me part of my stencilled name, lest I forget: AMY. Briefs detach themselves and hover: a white butterfly.

Acrobatically we dress. Pulling on the magnetic boots, we click gently to the floor. Now AMY DOVE faces PETER MUIR, not loving snails but two crew members of Earth's first starship—which is Earth's only in superstructure. Myself, psychosociologist. And him? Call him parahistorian: chronicler not of profane but of sacred time, of events that occur outside history, in faith, legend, shamanic rites; cartographer of the 'Other'. When we first met it was fairly obvious that he was the obverse of my coin, and I of his. For I charted the extent to which we can still remain 'other' to one another in an increasingly homogenized world, and my basic yearning must always have been for that lost human *terra incognita* which he was pursuing, in fossil form, on the sacral plane: by way of the idea of some lost Golden Age of direct communication with the sky, with the beyond, to which we had all lost the key. Which is now so suddenly and alarmingly restored to us . . .

"If you really love someone," I suggest, "any baby you make

13

together isn't 'yours-and-mine' or 'yours-or-mine'. No, it's a
fusion. It's the impossible fusion that you can't actually reach on
your own, by yourselves." A third side of the coin of 'otherness':
the unity of lovers?

He grins roguishly. "We don't do so badly."

"We aren't *one*, though. Our baby would be that one. I think
that's why people have babies, really. To be fused forever, even
though they can't experience it directly. When we get back . . ."

"When?" The word puzzles him; he has to recollect its
meaning.

"That baby would be the sum of ourselves: the sum of our
relationship, wouldn't it? Yet he or she would be somebody else,
quite separate from us—a mere *relation*!" He groans at the play
on words, which is—I admit—pretty ludicrous, and even un-
intentional. Words! So clear-cut and definitive on the one hand,
yet on the other hand so foggy, dissolving into other words, even
into their very opposites. With such words we try to express all
the connexions and disconnexions of the world. Perhaps words
have to be that way or we should see no connexions at all, or
alternatively we should be cast adrift in a sink of consciousness
where everything melted together indistinguishably. As it is, we're
poised in between total connexion and total disconnexion. I click
a few paces across the floor to kiss him. Connecting.

"What will he look like, Amy? Or she! A perfect fusion
would have to be a hermaphrodite, wouldn't it?" Chuckling, he
licks his lips, tasting my love. "It's better in High Time, isn't it?
Making love, I mean. We're that much nearer the fusion of I and
Thou . . . And then the fusion bomb goes off, tickling them all
up and down the ship! And so, we fly apart again."

"Please don't joke about *those*." I'm offended. We may not be
carrying fusion bombs but we do have our quiver of thermo-
nuclear missiles—ten arrows tipped with five kilotons apiece.
To me that is abominable. Yet the avatars spoke of war in
Heaven . . .

"I didn't mean those, love. I wasn't thinking."

"No, but Jacobik does, at every moment."

What will that baby of ours look like? The genetic roulette
wheel should have a fine spin, matching Peter's short befreckled
redness to my own ampler, more exuberant limbs (for I overtop

14

my love by almost a head; though my breasts are quite tiny, really, little cones); to my own tumbling jet-black curls (monkishly cropped for zero gee, alas), my brown eyes flecked with green, my copper-tan skin: I have Irish in me, and Bengali too . . . and am always predictably a little in love with myself, after love . . .

"I'm hungry. Let's go and dial a meal. We'll watch the others smile at us, if anyone's about. Race you?"

A race in lightly magnetized boots is an exaggerated, ridiculous fast walk of pumping elbows and quickly planted flat feet; one must be careful not to leave the floor. We could float, we could fly; but this is funnier—our private game.

So: click, click, click, we sprint in stylized sloth along the corridor, past closed doors. Quasi-gravity tugs at us once, unbalancing us. René and Zoe? Yes! We know, we know. Their signature is in the pulse. Today (what does 'today' mean?) our couplings have coupled, almost. Maybe we inspired them. We wink, we chuckle. Conspirators.

TWO

A TAPE RECORDER stood on a long mahogany table, spools slowly turning. Behind the vast gilt-framed mirror on the wall perhaps a video camera was filming me; maybe a team of psychologists sat there unseen, observing every gesture, every tic. My chair wobbled slightly and was placed too far out in the enormous room, isolating me; however I sat composedly, concentrating instead on the minute interactions of collaborating nations, brought together by the mystery and threat of the God's World visions. Through the tall, heavily draped windows, on the other side of the Rue de Rivoli the trees in the Tuileries gardens were still leafless. A cold scudding shower blew from the north; a forlorn electric *camionette* with striped red awning unfolded was attempting to sell hot *crêpes* to passers-by. Piebald pigeons pecked and scuttled near it.

I shook my head, just once, to toss my curls aside, indicating the faintest impatience with the questions, outweighed by friendly tolerance of the questioners, aware that the ritual was necessary.

"Proxemics," I told my multinational interrogators, "is the study of how close people come to one another—how close they *can* come, psychologically. Cultural proxemics is more; it's the study of how closely human cultures can converge in a highly integrated and homogeneous world. Or whether there's an irreducible core of cultural diversity. Society functions like the stars," I smiled, offering them a bit of astrophysics that I had off pat. (After all, we were talking about going to the stars.)

"The pressure for diversity—for which you can read radiation pressure—balances the convergent pull of the huge solar mass. Where these two balance, you have a viable sun. Where diversity wins out, you get explosions, novae, a tearing apart. Where convergence wins out, you get that collapse inwards upon itself of a

16

neutron sun. Every atom is stripped of its difference from every other. Every irregularity is erased. Worse, you can get the black hole from which nothing will ever emerge. Humanity might be heading that way culturally. Though, of course, the inward collapse —the sheer density—may provoke an explosion in its turn, an outburst on a different energy level: a new fusion explosion in the core. Maybe the God's World broadcasts should be seen in this light—as a sort of resurgence of mythical thought, a resurgence of the 'Other'." (I was annoyed by that 'sort of'.) "I believe it's a useful viewpoint . . ."

"But there *is* an objective machine, Dr Dove," insisted the Chinese interviewer. "An actual piece of alien equipment was transmitted here."

"In which we must participate with our . . . souls, to make it carry us anywhere. Why *now*, at this point in time? That's the question I put to you." Yes, turn the tables on them!

In High Space, where time has ended, to be reborn only when we reach our destination, I remember that world where history had become too much for us. Every moment had become instant history, a matter of recorded data to be sorted and ordered as soon as they occurred. The foreseeable future would consist only of extrapolations from this mass of data—portending the death of our culture? Culture had ceased to recreate itself at every moment. Now it merely accumulated itself (just as the mass of humanity accumulated itself!), and no alternative cultures were in view. I'm remote from that world now, seeing it through the wrong end of a telescope, receding and diminished. In any case, that world had passed away already. The 'Other' had returned with a vengeance, erupting from elsewhere. It was an emergence which I greeted with as much joy as fearful surprise . . .

"Of course my background influenced this line of thought!" (A background which was all on record. But did *I* understand my own record? This was what I had to sell them—or, in the case of the Chinese interviewer, provide a self-criticism session about . . .)

"One of my grandads was a Bengali, a Hindu who'd emigrated to London. He married an Irish girl who'd lapsed from her faith.

My other two grandparents were Finnish and Brazilian; he was an engineer and she was a Kardecist spiritualist. They were lovely people. We all lived—three generations—in this huge house. A family commune. The grandparents used to make up hybrid stories to amuse us kids: Krishna and the leprechauns, you know! After a time this began to worry me. It seemed as if they were throwing away something precious—the totems of the tribe—on anecdotes, so that we could all live together smoothly. It seemed so richly textured and, well, up to date on the surface, but I got to wondering how much of themselves they were all giving up for adjustment's sake. They all gave so much to the common pool.

"Well, you pour water into a bathtub and let it stand for a few days, and it looks completely settled—but it isn't settled at all. The original currents are still there days afterwards, even though you can't see them.

"I began to think, if you pour people together so that they've got no choice but to mix—in a pool of nine billion, do you see? That's why I started in on this line of work. And it also seemed to me that humanity must have had a primitive sense of identification with others and with nature once upon a time—a kind of collective soul rather than separate individualities. Civilization only began when you got differentiation: a sense of diversity, of the existence of the 'Other'.

"Wars and hatreds came from this, but the chance of cross-fertilization too. That's what powers civilization. But our history is growing stationary and locked. Our culture is all together again, and *all alone* because of this. Can it be that these avatars from God's World are symptoms of a new upsurge of diversity: of a rebound, of the 'Other' welling up again psychologically? Where can that 'Other' be found nowadays? Only out there, among the stars! You don't really need to send an *alien* anthropologist—not that any such person exists! You need someone who senses these currents—senses how they can be played on and manipulated."

"Nice commercial." A certain General Patrick Sutton pursed his lips. "These forces are extremely destructive. Destabilizing, hmm? All the religious groups claiming the avatars as their own personal revelation; that's desirable, is it?"

"You speak as though this is simply a psychological event," repeated Chen Yi-piao doggedly. "Do you think we have collectively imagined the High Space drive into existence? Why should you be thought fit to travel to a far star, if it is only to study the irrational in mankind?"

"Because the 'Other' *is* out there. It must be. It reaches out and touches the hollow where the 'Other' was, in us. It fills it. It gushes into the empty reservoir. This may be how we were able to perceive these messages at all: because of our need for them! God's World—whatever it is—has reached into the subconscious context of man. It's a lost context. And now it restores that context abruptly in a world which has no place for it, no social structures adapted to it. Suddenly it becomes objective: in the form of tangible apparitions. The transcendental has come back into our lives. Mystery, strangeness, the numinous, God. That's the form this 'Otherness' takes when it flows in now. The unused symbols are still latent in us."

A certain André Navarre scribbled a note and passed it down the line of faces . . .

Rain stung along the Rue de Rivoli. Electric Citroens and Peugeots passed silently, wipers performing interrupted harmonic motions, bearing citizens whose lives had all been interrupted, some of whom were terribly afraid, affronted in their bourgeois myth by avatars of Christ, Mohammed, Buddha. Solid men of civilization, managers, they were being manipulated by something out of their control which couldn't be tamed in tidy convenient token rituals while the life of the real world went on without revelation; they had been touched by something from outside, manipulating the religious consciousness.

A van with red slogans painted on its side cut in. *'Bouleversez le Monde!' 'La guerre des anges aura lieu.'* 'Turn the world topsy-turvy.' 'The angel war is *on*.' Drivers hooted angrily; they wanted to ram that van.

Here in Paris one should feel safe! The God's World broadcasts weren't visible north of the 44th parallel. Maybe that was one reason why this panel was being held in Paris. One might thus prevent something from eavesdropping. God, in a word: *deus absconditus*, who had recontacted humanity from an alien star . . .

19

THREE

Captain K calls another meeting, summoning everyone personally by interphone. (In vain merely to post notice of a meeting amid this personal timelessness.)

K stands for Kamasarin, Grigory Arkadievitch. Half-Russian and half-Mongol, and a General in the USSR Kosmonaut Corps —though styling himself plain Captain here—with years in military and astronautical parapsychology research, he is a 'sensitive'. Consequently he keeps a foot firmly planted in both camps aboard ship: the rationals and the psychics (wickedly abbreviated to *rats* and *psychs*).

Built like a champion wrestler, a lion of the steppes, is our Captain K: a man of severe merriment and a gracious though tough politeness (of courtesies to opponents on grassland wrestling fields). In his broad ruddy wind-chapped Asiatic face, under a bullet haircut which would render him bald were his stubble not so jet-black, are set mesmeric eyes.

As usual, the meeting (or encounter group, or metascientific rap session) occurs in the mess room. Most of us soon have our butts stuck fast to the adhesive chairs. One or two simply float, albeit not far off the deck. Lese-majesty it would be to float up above Captain K's head; though, as mercury slides up the thermometer, this may happen if opinions hot up. Peter brings two tubes of tomato juice from the autochef as the last stragglers drift in. (They make a point of rubbing sleep from their eyes.) We pretend there is vodka in the tomato juice.

A crew list for starship *Pilgrim Crusader*:

Grigory Kamasarin (USSR; Captain)

rats	*psychs*
Col. Neil Kendrick (USA; computers & communications; 2nd in command)	Heinz Anders (W. Germany; astrophysics)
Col. Gus Trimble (USA; astronaut-engineer)	Salman Baqli (Iranian IPR; planetology)
Maj. Ritchie Blue (USA; astronaut-pilot/navigator)	René Juillard (France; biology)
Maj. Natalya Vasilenko (USSR; astronaut-doctor; life-support systems)	Zoe Denby (USA; comp. religion)
	Sachiko Matsumura (Japan; linguistics)
Dr Li Yu-ying (China; biochemistry)	Peter Muir (Scotland; parahistory)
Mme Wu Chen-shan (China; historiographer/commissar)	Amy Dove (England; psychosociology)
Jacobik (Czechoslovakia; weapons systems, deserving no first name)	

So you see, the punch, the hard technology is entirely in the hands of the heavy rationals, American and Soviet, with Chinese support. (Except of course, for Kamasarin's hybrid role; but he is loyal.) The political trigger fingers are orthodoxly Christian, or their orthodox Marxist antitype : bedfellows in defence of established history. We psychs, who hold the ship in High Space by our presence, are only supportive scientists, really. We may be the batteries that sustain the flight, but the switchgear is in other, harder hands; and if the ship travels the slower for that, so much the worse, so long as it travels.

We visualize High Space as a huge pyramid, apeing the pyramidal shape of the alien drive itself—the higher step you are on, the closer you are to the other side. So we psychs leaven the flight; we make it rise. We're the horses in harness, pulling the royal chariot along (albeit horses much deferred to in our whims). No doubt we should arrive much sooner without the drag of the rat contingent, yet this is a political crusade as much as a pilgrimage, and besides, without rational stabilization the flight might enter a fantasy domain—for we are, in a very real sense, imagining our journey's progress; it is a journey through, *by virtue of*, imagination.

Affectionately Peter slips his arm around me, and I fondle him. Dr Li stares frostily at us—pretty creature, as tormentingly sexless as a jade figurine of herself.

"Maybe it is your *pleasure* that delays us," she hints. "Maybe it holds our journey back. You wish it not to end."

"Your disapproval delays us, dear lady," smiles Peter. Li stares up at the clock ticking on mechanically, bearing no relationship to the time that any of us feel. According to that, we are at Day 41, Hour 13. To me it feels no longer than the day before yesterday since we left. It is always the beginning here.

"Fine way to run a ship," remarks Li, not looking directly at Captain K but criticising him nonetheless. Captain K appears infected by our joy, however. René and Zoe are holding hands too, exchanging enchanted glances.

"There must be amity aboard," pronounces our Captain: his order of the day. "In one sense this is a journey of love."

"Love?" snorts Jacobik, the hatchet-faced. Slightly built, really, starved in his boyhood; bony-nosed, witch-chinned, with dark eyes which never seem to blink—as though somebody has cut the lids off them. He is thinking of his missile bays and lasers. His fist firms. "Love? After what they have done to our civilization? That clock tells lies. We've been flying forever. We'll never get there!"

"Do we send a warship to worship God?" asked Salman gently. (Yes, the meeting has begun. The subject, invariably and as always, is ourselves, our attitude to the voyage and to the apparitions broadcast to the Earth.)

"Did they say anything about worship, though?" enquires Captain K, deftly balancing both sides of the argument. "We are summoned. It is a crusade to the holy places. Yet who occupies them? Who besieges them? Why are they holy? Anyway, we aren't heavily armed against a whole world that can project solid images across the void. And *they* set those size constraints, not us." He smiles distantly at Peter and me. "It is more of a children's crusade."

"We all know what happened to *that*," sniffs Wu. *Comrade* Wu: small, dapper, too tight-skinned for her forty-five years to have left a single mark on her. One thinks of her as Madame Wu—she has such autocratic presence. Alongside sexless biochemist Lady Li, the Chinese have sent as orthodox and historically adept a politician and diplomat as one could imagine: diadem of a mandarin Marxist court.

From her throne, she denounces us.

"We are being thrust back into childishness aboard this ship—into infantile gratification and superstition—just as *they* would thrust our whole culture back, into childishness. I'm surprised at your talk of love, Captain Kamasarin. You grow infected with this"—she gestures at René and Zoe, Peter and myself—"this euphoria which loses touch with time, with history, with Earth's true situation. Making love is only like drinking a glass of water. It is a materialistic need." (And this is a set speech.) "To raise it to the level of a spiritual power that speeds our ship along is another part of their same trickery. Even if the drive does seem to work that way, *still* we must not trust it."

"Actually, it's more like a hallucinogenic drug experience," suggests Natalya the flaxen-headed, of the turned-up nose. "It lasts much longer, but isn't quite so drastic. Though it does have its troughs and its crests. These tricks of quasi-gravity, the dissolution of time, the paranoias and ecstasies. We shall all return to normality when we re-enter normal space. We must simply tolerate the constant dissolution of one's sense of reality till then. Apparently it's our ticket through interstellar space. So let us tolerate it rationally. As indeed you do."

Peter fidgets; Peter disagrees. "It seems more like the original shaman flight to me—a flight to knowledge." (To each it seems what they themselves are.) "We're going up into the sky like the shaman of old, back when there was free communication between all men and the Beyond, before we lost touch. Only, we're flying in a steel ship, rather than on a bird's back . . ."

"We still call 'em birds," grins Ritchie Blue, our farm-boy astronaut, least offended of the rats by the psychic component of our voyage, perhaps since he was once close to nature, if only from the cab of his Dad's grain harvester.

Wu looks offended, but Kamasarin nods understandingly, his mind (I imagine) on the last few seeds of the dying Siberian shaman magical tradition, barely a memory in some centenarians' heads, painstakingly gleaned from among the Tungus, the Rein-

23

deer People, the Yakuts, the Mongols, and replanted by the paraphysicists outside Novosibirsk.

"Costly ticket," grunts Gus Trimble. "A trap." He speaks in crossword clues, in anagrams; as though wishing to say something else, only he doesn't know what. He sweats: a meaty man, with padded hips and butt that fail to emulate Captain K's sculpture of muscle.

"Why should it be a trap?" asks Peter angrily. "If they had simply bombarded the world with inexplicable visions and quasi-beings and had *not* come through with the High Space drive so that we can follow them up—well, we might justifiably feel paranoid. As it is—"

"They're manipulating human history," Wu interrupts. "They destroy the very essence of history—which is human practice, human action. That's why Colonel Trimble rightly speaks of a trap." (Though actually she spoke of it first. But such is her diplomacy. Or cunning.) "He senses this accurately. Whereas *he*"—a finger pokes out at Peter, and with her other hand upon her hip she is a teapot with a scalding, scolding spout—"*he* brags about primitive shamans. Is that to be our astronautics from now on? You see how the God's World broadcasts rob us of our really noble, authentic human dreams by seeming to make archaic, obsolete religious dreams come true! It's pitiable that we should fly on a hand-me-down broomstick fuelled by super-stition. The fact that it will not work without 'psychic' sensitivity is the real trap."

"If it *does* work," sneers Jacobik. "If we really are going any-where. If we can return."

"Ach, the probability of our arrival goes on rising," breaks in Heinz Anders. "At least, most of the time it does. As to return-ing, we will find that out. One would hardly go to so much trouble to maroon fifteen humans light years from home." (Would one?)

"Pitiable," repeats Madame Wu, still pouring tea, "that our history is seen by many now as guided—however evasively—by emanations from another world. Most pitiable of all that the artefact we have found—the main drive of this ship—suggests to these same people that our whole technology is merely the feeble rediscovery of some ancient, star-guided wisdom." Her lip curls

24

on the last word. "It diminishes man. *That* is the intention of the trap. That is why we carry our weapons with us—not because they summoned us to some vague contest."

"Those missiles are hardly planet-busters," regrets Jacobik, as though a planet-buster exists. In his dreams, no doubt it does! "Tactical stuff. This ship's too damn small. Come and fight, my little ones—but don't bring your catapult, just bring a wooden sword."

"Perhaps," says Wu, "the trap was waiting to be sprung all these centuries in the Gobi desert, instead of being projected there overnight. Perhaps the broadcasts all came from the pyramid machine itself? Perhaps that has been recording and assessing human activities for a very long time? We hardly understand its workings, do we?"

"That's a new point of view," allows Captain K. "Yet it's hardly supported by the geographical cut-off line of the broadcasts."

"With the pyramid found near the very boundary? I've been giving a lot of thought to this of late, Comrade Captain. The High Space pyramid may be much more complex than even we suppose. It did 'grade' the candidates for the mission. It is," she speaks bitterly, "responsive to human thought patterns. Some would say to some numinous sensitivity. Why shouldn't it soak up human thoughts world-wide?"

"Some ancient traditions do suggest a centre of, well, power somewhere in or around the Gobi," recalls Zoe, our priestly negress. "There was the legend of the Kingdom of Shambhala, north of Tibet. An invisible redoubt of magical wisdom was supposed to exist somewhere there. Are you suggesting that this tradition was based on the presence of some kind of psychic sponge-*cum*-time bomb—which some people, Tibetan lamas, for example, were aware of?"

"A mind bomb," echoes Captain K, with one slight change of wording, as if to lead Wu and Zoe on. "A psychic projector? A sort of God machine, switching on periodically?"

"To keep us all in thrall, in ignorance!"

"No," frowns Ritchie Blue. "The thing was custom-built to take us to the stars. Well, to one particular star."

"Just how," Wu asks him, "is it known out by 82 Eridani that we have achieved sufficient know-how to lift it into space and build a ship around it?"

"Extrapolation from our radio output?"

"They didn't contact us by radio, boy," snaps Trimble. "Their approach was a damned sight more direct! We might have been under surveillance—*mental* surveillance, deep down. Maybe that pyramid, maybe something else. I guess some of us—and it could be a whole lot of us—have been growing sort of opaque to that surveillance for some time now! Our third eye has shut up shop. We've been getting a sight too rational for their liking." He glares bullishly at us psychs.

Captain K flexes his arms, stretching strong fingers out. "We must arrive in agreement and amity. I believe it is good to talk out our differences of opinion like this."

And quite suddenly I see the truth behind these meetings. It's as though I've read his mind, for the thought leaps fully formed into my brain, and it does have a 'flavour' of Grigory Kamasarin attached to it as surely as there's a flavour of whichever lovers are responsible, in the surge of quasi-gravity that tugs our bodies but touches something too within our minds. That thought is that the authorities on Earth, who have fully confided alone in Captain K, hope that we fifteen human beings, in constant proximity to the activated High Space drive which 'registers' at least half of our number intimately, will somehow achieve a collective insight into the true nature of the alien device. The thought is that we shall measure its essence by collective parallax from all our various viewpoints, some of which are safely opaque to it. That's why he condones—no, *encourages* the fusion of love-making, over and above the presumed speeding of the flight. He hopes that we shall somehow fuse into a consensus mind—if only for a moment, if only in someone's dream!—and perceive the real purpose. We are a flying laboratory of ourselves, as well as being pilgrims, crusaders, scientists, whatever; and of course, who better than Grigory Kamasarin to run it?

I stare at our Captain, till Peter grows restive at my inattention to himself. Captain K sits invulnerable, a distant smile on his face.

While Jacobik launches into some revolting gratuitous anecdote about flaying people alive and about executioners sticking heads back on their victims with glue behind the guillotine . . .

We listen to the sadistic ravings of the Czech as though hypnotised by a snake. What is this doing to our probability of arrival? Yet no one cuts him off. One is free to say anything at these meetings. Let him vent it all out of his system; let him get it off his chest. I'm scared, though. He's a madman. He must have been under huge restraint before, to fool the panels. This side of him has only betrayed itself now in High Space. It's as Natalya says: paranoia, hallucination, dissolution of reality threaten us constantly. Oh, let love conquer them!

Much as I would prefer to stuff my fingers in my ears, I realize after a while that he, astonishingly, is uttering poetry—rendered into English so that we can all appreciate it. Even if it is a poetry of death and torment, which alone speaks to his twisted soul.

"King Herod alone," he sings,
" loved you pure white babes
above everything else
and ordered you to be set free from life
Give thanks therefore to your saviours."

27

FOUR

THE YEAR 1997: the millennium was a little early. On the other hand, maybe Christ was really born in 3 BC? And what did time matter anyway: this was revelation—the end of secular time . . .

It was Easter Day in Jerusalem. In the dingy cluttered Church of the Holy Sepulchre, to a crowded brawling congregation of Roman Catholics, Copts, Greek Orthodox and others, in the chapel that contains the empty marble-lined tomb of Jesus, there appeared a radiant angel—a tall shimmering creature of golden light. Rapidly it resolved itself into more tangible bodily form, naked but for a loincloth, with wounds in the wrists and ankles and a deep gash in its side.

"Come to God's World in the Heavens, for I am the Son of God," it told the exalted faithful (variously heard in English, Russian, Greek, and even in Latin by some clergy). "Come to the holy places in the sky, where there is no death—" So saying, the being vanished.

Before news of the miracle had spread into the nearby streets, let alone around the world, by the Wailing Wall close by appeared another—or the same—creature of golden light. For Jewish pilgrims it resolved itself into a tall, white-bearded, white-robed figure, heard by most witnesses to speak in Hebrew, in the prophetic perfect tense—the tense for a future event of such certainty that it can be spoken of as already accomplished. "You have come to God's World. You have climbed Jacob's ladder. You have crossed the years of light—"

As this figure vanished in its turn, in the Noble Enclosure of the Moslems beyond the Wailing Wall, in the bright and beautiful mosque of the Dome of the Rock from which Mohammed is said to have ascended to Heaven, leaving his footprint behind in solid rock, a third glowing angel appeared, becoming a black-bearded

28

man wearing kaftan and turban, with a scimitar by his side. He planted his foot in Mohammed's footprint and called out in Arabic, "Come to God's World, come to success!"

As the world spun on its course that Easter Day a whole series of manifestations came and went: a mere shaft of light at Lourdes—but a robed Christ figure who endured for all of five minutes on the terrace of the hilltop church of Bom Jesus at Congonhas in Brazil. (Here the first photographs of an apparition were shot. Standing amidst the remarkably lifelike soapstone statues of the twelve apostles who look out across the valley, it invited an ecstatic crowd in Portuguese to visit Heaven.) In Salt Lake City appeared Joseph Smith's angel, and in Mexico the Virgin Mary . . . and some hours later at the Great Shrine of Ise in Japan, amidst the cypress trees, materialised the Sun Goddess Amaterasu. And on, across South-East Asia and India, avatars Buddhist and Hindu appeared at holy places, completing the circuit of the globe in Mecca as a golden angel floating above the black-draped granite block of the Kaaba, calling out to circling pilgrims the same message: "Come to God's World, come to success!"

Even in China an ancient warrior figure coalesced out of light in the Square of Heavenly Peace and fired arrows of light towards the horizon.

Northern Europe, Canada and the USSR, excluding its Asian southlands, were alone unblessed . . .

Over the next few days, as people flocked—and inevitably trampled over each other—to these places of witness, the apparitions gained in duration and solidity, as if they actually borrowed strength from the increasing numbers who saw and heard them. Already it was apparent that they spoke to the ear of each faith (even to atrophied faiths) and presented themselves to the archaic not the modernist eye. It was apparent too that the apparitions tracked around the world in a systematic scan from numinous node to numinous node, remaining below latitude 44° north.

The composite message of the avatars, given through the lips of quasi-Jesus, quasi-Buddha, quasi-Mohammed—and interpreted a little out of the language of revelation—ran as follows:

29

I am the prophet/angel/messenger/message
from Heaven/the heavens/space
where God lives/where God's World is.
There is a star in the River/constellation Eridanus.
That star is unique/an isolated star.
Your best souls will go to Heaven/will ascend/fly there.
If you die, you will live again, undying.
Now there is war in Heaven/conflict/struggle. Gird your arms
  about you!
Join the Crusade. Bear witness/send witnesses/an expedition.
Send champions/representatives.
Follow the path of the angels/the waveguide of these messages.
The way is open/transport is arranged/a means.
Join the caravan/the drive//yoke your caravan (your craft?)
  to the drive/means/engine we bring you. Hitch your wagon
  to the stars/your craft to the star-drive.
It is high time you came//it is in High Time/sacred time you
  will travel/it is outside space-time/in hyperspace. Ascend to
  Heaven through High Space/the space above/hyperspace.
Look beyond the highest mountains, beyond the roof of the
  world.
There is the instrument of light beyond light.
Bring pure minds to the task//only suitable minds (your wish/
  intention/consciousness) will make it work. (The journey is
  imaginary?)
I (it) will judge/diagnose your best/most suitable souls.
Let some hard (evil? unresponsive?) souls ballast your ship, so
  you will travel more steadily (or slowly?). For all are called,
  both sheep and goats, and all WILL BE chosen in the end.

The 'God's World broadcasts' ceased after seven days, having persuaded many that a contemporary, ecumenical God had sent messengers, or aspects of Himself, to intervene in human history once more to save mankind, or merely to indicate that all religions were equally true. They persuaded many more people of the exact opposite, namely that particular forms of belief had been declared authentic—a situation fraught with Jihad and bloodshed. Others interpreted the messages as overt contact by alien intelligences of a superior order who had been influencing

30

the growth of human religions in the past. A final interpretation, to which 'sane' men clung, was that here indeed was a message from the stars—from a star in the straggling star river of Eridanus —calling for aid and comfort, or at the very least begging for contact and support (if in a somewhat authoritative way); and this message was transmitted in the only way that such contact could apparently be made with human minds—by triggering religious imagery, tapping mythical levels of the psyche (a numinous node in the brain, almost) in geographical locations where the sense of worship was most powerfully imprinted.

The distribution of the broadcasts, with fade-out at the 44° latitude line, appeared to rule out, among nearby candidate stars in that constellation, Epsilon Eridani, since any broadcasts from Epsilon should have blanketed the northern hemisphere (though what wavelength were they transmitted on?). The second leading candidate, twice as many light years from Earth, though even more likely in theory to possess a habitable world, was the star 82 Eridani; and this star was only visible from those latitudes where angels and avatars appeared.

What of the promised 'instrument of light beyond light'? (To be interpreted as 'faster than light'?) To be found beyond the Himalayas and beyond Tibet, yet south of the 44th parallel? Satellites angled their orbits over that terrain in the far south-western stretches of the Gobi desert on the desolate border between Mongolia and China; spy planes overflew, peeling away only at the very border . . .

And so the interviews continued at a guarded, woodland-girt château outside Paris with small groups of candidates, as the Joint Space Liaison Committee shuffled and reshuffled its cards, mixing and remixing its cocktail.

The Chinese woman, Wu, wore an orange badge. So she was not an activator of the High Space drive. Peter wore a green badge, as did I, so we were, and so was the tall black American woman Zoe Denby. We had already been flown into Tyuratam (by night, seeing nothing of the Cosmodrome) and passed the 'psych test'. Now we four sat 'informally' around a circular table in a chandelier-hung room, with Generals Patrick Sutton and Grigory Kamasarin (who, strangely, wore a green badge too) and Chen Yi-piao, drinking coffee.

". . . It *is* a message from the stars," Peter argued (and here perhaps my love for him began). "But not in matrixes of prime numbers or whatever. This is in terms of revelation, vision—in mythological language, burrowing deep into the human psyche and borrowing from that. So we don't have *pi*, but symbols which all rational people believed had been discarded. Yet here they re-emerge in all their devastating pristine force, like an upsurge of repressed material into consciousness. They were never really lost, only overlaid. The 'psychs' among us are still sensitive to this symbolism, you see. The 'rats' are those in whom it's been most deeply repressed and has almost atrophied. But actually it never can. Atrophy, I mean. Not entirely."

"That is how we 'read' the broadcasts," Wu agreed. "They trigger psychic patterns in our minds. So, I will accept that. But what are they really *saying*? That superstition is true. That prayer can bring power. Now that we have the chance of perfection and greatness in our hands, through human *practice*, this is loosed upon us. It is rank sabotage. It has a material origin, and is being used as a weapon of control—as priests have always used religion against the people. Only, these priests are alien ones."

Peter shook his head. "With respect, you're confusing two things. One is a psychic symbolism inherent in man, which gives rise to religions. The other is the use of this strong symbolic language to make contact with us. I'm mainly interested in the old belief that direct contact with the 'sky' was once both possible and practical. It was a numinous thing, but it was also quite pragmatic too. Something in the mentality of early man must have given rise to this tradition. Alas, it degenerated considerably."

" As we grew wiser."

" If it was a capacity of ours, it evolved out of necessity! By now it's been severely repressed. But it's still a capacity of *theirs*. And latently of ours. Very powerful psychic structures must be involved, and to have evolved in the first place they must have survival value, right? They must correspond to something in the real universe. You can't deny that. Now this channel is being used. We aren't fully understanding the message because we don't know what it *should be.* So the shapes appear to us and we translate them into images of Christ and Mohammed—whatever our cultural context is." He paused. "It may even be that we *need* to have this triggered in us."

Time for me to speak up. "We've reached a psychic threshold," I agreed. "The 'Other' has practically vanished from our lives. But now direct communication with the Beyond, in Peter Muir's terms, can resume. How do we adapt ourselves to it?"

"With a new theocracy, perhaps?" asked Wu, sarcastically. "How is it that they know us so well? Our weakest points."

Peter frowned. "I think the answer is that they don't. It is *we* who do not know ourselves. Thus the message is at once comprehensive—millennially so—and incoherent. Don't you see how dominated the world is today by abstract images and symbols? Art, music, have reached a nadir where the symbols only state that they are symbols. They don't refer to anything else."

"Take the dove as a symbol of peace." He smiled at me. (And perhaps his love for me began there.) "Merely because it's white. Which," he smiled apologetically to Zoe, "is another piece of partisan symbolism. Are doves peaceful? If you put two strange doves in a run together, the weaker one will be pecked to death. Sorry, but it's true. Just suppose that there are symbols which really *have* got intrinsic meaning: symbols that correspond to forces in the real universe in which we have evolved in common with other alien life forms? Suppose that this symbol language can be a means of communicating about the really important things which seems *more* natural to some alien beings! So we can contact them on that level. But we have to relearn the language. Rediscover it."

Wu stared ahead. "Symbolism only functions within an economy of thought, and if we aren't careful this is the Wall Street Crash of *our* economy of thought!"

"These messages enter a totemic void," went on Peter. "We've lost touch with the ancient common symbol language, but it's still ingrained in man's psyche. Amy Dove may be right. Why not ingrained in alien psyches too? We do share a common universe."

"Yes, and history has become our captor," I said. "We're trapped in it. The discourse of the world is all abstract data—

data abstracts. Here is a way out into something else. It can be a rejuvenation, a recreation of the world."

"A new time," smiled Zoe. "Really, this is more important than if an alien starship itself had landed here. It isn't merely contact with an alien otherness. Amy Dove's right: this is the renewal of the 'Other' in ourselves."

So we three were in agreement; with Wu as Devil's advocate. Kamasarin's role I did not yet understand.

FIVE

"EQUALLY," MUSES JACOBIK the warrior, "we may be chess pieces in some cosmic game—held in abeyance till now, and now suddenly queened." His finger trigger-itches, and he scratches his neck in a displacement gesture.

Which riles Madame Wu. "That is the illogic of outside manipulation too. Humanity isn't a pawn. History isn't a joke of the Gods. There are no Gods."

"But we fly to God's World," Zoe reminds her.

"Oh, such certainty! As though God sits on a throne there in full view surrounded by his angels. The broadcasts are simply . . . phenomena, to be called to account."

"It's that sort of attitude which slows our journey. It's like hanging a lump of lead round a swimmer's feet."

"Far better lead than alchemists' gold. A more useful metal."

A heaviness is coming over me: a dragging down. Zoe's image has become physical reality in this malleable domain. Terror floods me: fear of drowning from this weight around my feet! Gus Trimble is gasping for breath. He tries to rise, and can't. Floundering, he makes swimming motions in the air. Lady Li is affected too: quivering, like some out-of-favour Chinese concubine wrapped up in a carpet, about to be dropped down a well. Kendrick whitens.

"Let us not forget ourselves," commands our Captain. "If we don't *attend*, we shall travel in secular space, not High Space, and the flight will take centuries."

"Yes, the sin of forgetfulness *is* deadly." Wu admires the pictures on the mess room wall one by one—a Chinese petrochemical complex ablaze with light, the Golden Gate Bridge, the Eiffel Tower. The works of man.

"Dammit," cries Ritchie, "a spaceship that you have to think

35

positively about, or it won't work! I guess I always thought positively about cars, planes, whatever. They *do* work better then. That's plain efficiency, respect for your tools . . ." He trails off. Of course it is much more than that. His interruption is prompted, I do fancy, by tact—tact aimed at allowing our Chinese harridan a graceful withdrawal from something which she plainly doesn't understand; which she *can't* understand, even if superficially she knows it to be the case. Does Ritchie admire her? Is he drawn to *her* by the emotional vectors of High Space? Good God. As what? Stern elder sister? Or schoolmarm?

We're all naked to each other. Currents link us, twist us. Ritchie blushes furiously, stares accusingly at me, then looks away.

"Yet this ship works in an entirely different mode of space," resumes Captain K. "In a different mode of reality. It isn't simply a question of its working 'better' than any starship we could have invented." His gaze falls on Heinz. "There's a logic behind this craft. It's simply not the logic we're used to, is it? Let us think about this; it may help." There's an ecclesiastic, patriarchal tone to his voice now. He summons Heinz to recite a litany to which we must all respond. He requires him to lead us in our orisons.

Heinz rubs and tugs at his black beard. A hirsute fellow is our astrophysicist from Frankfurt. The backs of his hands crawl with hair like a Dr Jekyll in mid-transformation. Short, and squarely-built is Heinz—a Nibelung, not of underground mines but of the blackness of space and the burning coals of distant suns, which are his eyes.

"Refresh our memories, if you please, Herr Anders. The principle of complementarity. We must constantly remember."

"So there exist various ways of speaking about experience, *ja*? Each may have validity. Each may be necessary. Yet they may be mutually exclusive. Well then, the choice we make determines the reality. Whether, for instance, light is a wave or a series of particles. Now it is one, now it is the other. Thought *constructs this*. Time is a construct of thought too. In High Space this is all more nakedly obvious, is it not? Space isn't a *thing*. As Kant said, it is one of the forms through which we organise our perception of things. So we can travel through High Space by organising things differently. Our space drive is a thought construct of other

36

beings, depending upon our psyches for its *modus operandi*. We create the kind of space it uses: the space of, well, almost . . . imagination. Our intention to reach 82 Eridani counts hugely. We must accept this or the drive will not work. Yet we mustn't lose touch with the ordinary physical reality either. Consequently the ballast, if you'll permit the word. The rats."

"Some of us sure haven't lost touch," grins Ritchie impishly, glancing our way, avenging himself (though unvenomously) for my intrusion on his feelings about Wu.

"With the help of the alien drive our senses construct the reality as if we are in a higher plane of the universe, one of unbound thought, not of solid things. Our voyage occurs simultaneously, I believe, but our sense of duration, our *construction* of time determines the apparent rate of progress. Which is why we have to think in terms of a probability of arriving rather than actual distance travelled as such. Without duration we couldn't think a thought from one moment to the next. Possibly, for beings sufficiently advanced such a journey might take no time at all . . . I've been thinking up some equations along these lines."

Dear, bushy Heinz: he gives us a critique of pure space-time instead of a pep-talk. Yet actually this is what at least half of us need. For rats can't travel intuitively, but only step by step. Their fears and reservations make us plod along. They need his scientific authority so that they can relax, and glide . . .

Or is Heinz a Rumpelstiltskin? About to stamp his foot on the deck in irritation at those who are only boringly interested in how fast the straw of ordinary space can be spun into the gold of High Space, and not at all in the alchemy itself or in what High Space might actually be. Easy to visualize him stamping his way through the deck and vanishing out into High Space with a howl, on a private trajectory of his own! Yet no; he is a more accommodating, more self-possessed Rumpelstiltskin than that.

He clears his throat. "We are complementary to each other too, like wave and particle." His head bobs up and down, tugged by the beard. "Some of us have this frame of mind. We accept the new configuration, which is actually a very old one. Whereas you other people resist it fiercely. But if you weren't here this wouldn't be a scientific expedition at all. It would indeed be, as Peter puts it, a shaman flight. I suspect we might be lost in realms of magic that we couldn't control. We should be quite outside the normal consensus universe instead of merely travelling through High Space—and we wouldn't know how to control that magic zone, not yet. Here is our complementarity answer. You are the stabilisers. You prevent the voyage from disintegrating into a dream journey. We don't know how to navigate the space-scape of the archetypes, not yet. Any sufficiently advanced science must seem like magic, because it actually recaptures the magical!"

A pretty speech. Captain K looks grateful. It heals a dawning rift.

"Let us all think about this," repeats our Captain. "Let us meditate about it."

"Let us pray," mocks Madame Wu. However, she concedes. If it works, use it . . .

"Come to God's World, come to success," murmurs Salman, ironically yet respectfully. His faith in Islam remains unshaken in spite of the plagiarism of the Moslem call to prayer by the avatars. Indeed, it seems strengthened by it, though not in any narrow partisan way.

At Captain K's request we all link hands, to let the concentration flow through us all, believers and unbelievers alike. And we all sense, as we concentrate, that we are closing faster on our destination. The probability is rising. For a little while there's such a wonderful feeling of community. Only Jacobik sits aloof amidst us, his paws limp in Sachiko's and Natalya's palms, sniffing the air suspiciously.

While we are all relaxed, he tenses suddenly, and pulls himself free.

Does he anticipate the danger before it strikes?

For this is when the klaxon hoots, destroying our peace.

Bee-bu-bu! . . . *Bee-bu-bu!* The dactyl signal for mass proximity.

Bu-bu-bee! The anapaest code: for damage to the ship!

"We're under attack!" Jacobik shouts happily. And grins.

SIX

So our emergency procedure lurches into use. Captain K is already on his feet.

"Bridge Team to control deck, with me. Blue Team to follow. Other teams next. Bridge and Blue have priority."

"Psychs there? During a fight?" Jacobik's joy is dashed. "It's ridiculous. They'll get in the way."

"I am no psych," snaps Wu. (She is her own team together with Li.)

"I may need anyone to interpret what is happening!"

Quite a contrast to the crisp, polite co-ordination before we activated the drive and entered this semi-subjective domain, where our will and wishes play a part in our very progress! I remember that as a kind of anti-dream, as though the rules of ordinary life operated in the dream, whereas now id, libido and fantasy rule the waking world. We all need to be near the drive now. It offers irrational, magical protection. It will see us on our way.

Pilgrim Crusader is a triangular steel prism with hemispheres that bulge, dome-like, from each rectangular face. These house in turn the hanger bay with its twin shuttle craft, the reactor, and the missile bay. The overall design is dictated by the ellipsoid field of influence of the drive, that strange crystal pyramid set precisely amidships. Aft of it are this mess room and the cabins, with stores below decks. Bulging from the aft triangle of the prism are the tanks of JP-20 and the main jets for normal space flight. Forward, in full view of the pyramid, stretch the combined observatory and control deck with laboratories beneath them— though only the peak of the pyramid with its control faces actually rears through the deck, the main mass being below. Dish

39

aerials and sensors fill in the interstices between the three projecting domes so that all in all our ship resembles a huge model of a strange molecule, with bonding sites cupped open to receive other such molecules . . .

The long viewports of the control deck are all unmasked. Outside High Space bubbles palely, with the usual transient brighter spectral whorls welling up and dying back. We skirt the peak of the alien pyramid—some flying, some stepping magnetically—to blink at the irreality beyond the windows. We're in a submarine deep in some ocean of abstract jelly, with phantom mandala beasts existing for a moment before dissolving back again into essence: fish of the abyss with bodies invisible, only their phosphorescence to be seen . . .

Two fish *are* fully visible, though. Two strange ships hang out there. Near or distant, hard to tell—minnows or whales? They rush closer and then recede again without really changing their size, which is indefinable, rather like the walls of a child's bedroom at dusk, in those drowsy, hypnagogic moments before sleep when images become hallucinatory. *We* shrink before them, then enlarge again to dwarf them. Now they're on Ritchie's scope-screens too.

"Range?" requests Captain K, planted magnetically in the middle of the deck. (Ahab . . . In High Space we're all archetypes—substructures of persons—just as the space out there is the substructure of reality . . .)

Ritchie shakes his head. "Can't get a reading. They're in focus visually but the radar figures are nonsense—hundreds of klicks, then none at all."

One fish is a fat ovoid with crystals girding its waist and rear. The other, a cone with balloons spilling out in ruptures.

"We've been *hit*," reports Natalya, as the red tell-tales blink before her. "Four times. The hull of the reactor bay, control links to engine two, aft radar dish. And we're outgassing Lox from tank D, feeding engine three."

As we look out, two thin red spears of light reach out towards us now, ever so slowly from the alien ships.

"Lasers?" asks Kendrick. "So slow?"

"We can't guarantee the value of C, out there," says Heinz.

40

"We still see according to the normal light speed value inside *Pilgrim*. Here is an area of relatively normal space, englobed by High Space. But out there?"

"How the hell can we see laser light before it arrives?"

Still the red spears grow longer, bending our way.

Heinz broods. "We may be seeing a side leakage from those laser beams, if that's what they are. Analogous to synchrotron radiation. Only, the lasers are exciting the medium of High Space and it leaks the light which we see, travelling at *light speed*. But coherent light—the laser beam—travels much slower. This is essentially an incoherent region. Lasers are retarded light here. I believe the region we're travelling through may actually be rather small. High Space is a short-cut—a shrunk region." He shakes his head. "But our thoughts are a factor in the reality. Our perception is. I seriously suspect this 'seeing' of light."

Captain K cuts him off with a wave. "Maybe laser beams; maybe something else. But we're *damaged*. Why should they fire at all? Kendrick, open all frequencies—hail them. Trimble, ignite engines one and four—give us a push. If light plays such tricks, we'll be hard to hit again once we're not a sitting duck."

"Use rocket engines in High Space?"

"Use them! Or we'll be sliced open."

"How fast do radio waves travel here?" Kendrick is trying to raise the aliens, with no success.

"Maybe they're hoping to communicate by laser?" suggests Salman. "If one was aimed at a radar dish—"

"And at the engines, and the reactor!" snaps Jacobik. "Don't be a fool, don't meddle. They hit us three ways: communications, manoeuvrability, and power!"

"Something is wrong," says Heinz.

"Right!" snarls the Czech. Snarls: I have never seen anybody with teeth bared before. Like a rabid dog. Abruptly Jacobik punches at his laser board, till Captain K shouts him to heel. Incredible indiscipline. But our own thin red lances are already reaching out. Slowly, so slowly.

"You see, those *are* lasers! That proves it." Rabid.

I'm scared; yet it's a dreamlike fear, as though I'm running from something awful yet I know that the awful thing is only the beast of my dreams. Does one really die in High Space as one would in normal space? Perhaps we become part of that amorphous flux out there, still alive in some way. The two alien ships are the watchdogs over this dimension. Now commences a dogfight—a battle of dogs with beaming red eyes . . .

We brace ourselves.

"We have ignition," reports Trimble. Acceleration pushes us back as though retarding us, making matters worse. We waver at an angle, reeds in a streambed. Using skiers' muscles we strain forward to compensate. *Pilgrim* thrusts forward at last, carrying us away from those red lances that are almost upon us. Not lances, now—thin scimitars bending through space as though we're a huge knot of gravity pulling them. But we avoid them.

"Cut engines!" Acceleration pressure peaks, then fades away slowly some while after the switch-off. We slump forward in the air, gradually correcting our posture. Nothing is normal. Those alien fish seem more distant now.

"Cone ship has laid an egg," calls Jacobik. "It's coming at us."

On Ritchie's screen, enlarged, we can see the missile drifting lazily towards us: a tiny sprat darting flame from its tail. We can even see it through the viewports, much smaller—a speck of light.

"Let's hope it's travelling slower than local light," wishes Kendrick.

"I have a firm range," Ritchie calls out. "Eighteen klicks for the bandit ship, seventeen-point-five for the missile. Our High Space field must be acting as a kind of magnifying lens. It's making their ships seem closer than they are. That's a missile, right enough. Not unlike our own. No doubt about their intentions now! Missile range sixteen-point-five, and closing."

Jacobik licks his lips. "Permission to destroy, Sir?"

"The radiation, man!" cries Heinz. "We'll be drenched in X and gamma."

"Permission granted. Do not use lasers. You must use a missile. Programme and fire."

"Captain!"

"Trimble, max thrust. Vasilenko, close the shutters. Easy, Anders. Light radiation seems to be propagating at a very slow rate here. We must assume the same of all radiation."

42

"Missile one gone."

"Wait," says Heinz. "Shouldn't our missile drop down into normal space as it leaves the field? Shouldn't theirs?"

"Missile one on intercept. I shan't let it fail!"

"Shan't, Jacobik? Can you reach out there with your will?"

Acceleration pushes us again, waxing and waning in surges like pseudo-gravity. It isn't true thrust at all, but a reflection of our fear, our desperation to escape.

"We have to match their weapons with the same kind of weapon, Anders," says Captain K, "otherwise we cannot guarantee stopping them. We don't know the rules here. I suspect we're safe unless we get caught in the fireball itself . . ."

So we wait.

"Bandit missile, seven point five klicks. Countermissile, five point five. On target. Cutting scopescreens."

When the screens blank out, we're inside a solid shell with only Jacobik's and Ritchie's green ray tubes keeping watch. Sweat laves Jacobik's forehead and sharp cheeks.

"Fireball! Radar has a double fireball!"

"We stopped it!" We laugh, we cry.

"We're picking up a trivial dosage of X-rays," reports Natalya presently. "Now some gamma. A trifle."

"The radar image comes first, then X, then gamma," says Heinz. "So EM radiation at shorter wavelengths is travelling more slowly than the longer wavelengths—and losing intensity, I suspect! C isn't even constant for all types of radiant energy."

"They've laid another egg. Two eggs," calls Jacobik.

"I have them," from Ritchie.

"Missile two, three gone."

"And missiles use radar guidance! What frequency are the missiles searching on?" Heinz huddles with Jacobik, talking urgently about very long frequencies.

René draws back beside Peter and myself. He rubs his nose quizzically. "This fight has all the logic of a dream, Amy. Maybe we should merely shout at them and they'll go away? Look at Sachiko."

Sachiko is caught up in the abstract yet deadly battle as surely as Heinz has now been by the problem of frequencies. Her slim hands make inchoate warding gestures as though she could deflect those alien missiles with her own palms in an aikido defence.

As a good endomorph, René remains stoutly himself despite the threat. It isn't fleshed out enough to convince him. He's a sensitive but he's also something of a sensualist, and his senses aren't being sufficiently wooed. The recipe for disaster is there before him but he can't yet taste the savour nor breathe the bouquet.

"Who can they be?" whispers Salman to himself, close by. "The enemies of God's World? Those we came to fight?" More than a little seduced too, he sounds, by the thought of holy war.

"Double fireball, twice!" Ritchie calls out exuberantly. He sounds as though he is ordering some jet jockey's cocktail from an invisible bartender. "Uh, radar blips have gone funny, Sir. I'm uncapping the scopes for a visual sighting."

There they are again, swimming on two screens. Have we wrecked them? No, the alien vessels are *changing shape*. The cone is becoming box-like, the balloons are squeezing into tight sausages. The ovoid is altering too . . . It's all wrong.

"Maybe we're just seeing them from a different angle," suggests Natalya. "How can we see anything in High Space at all? If those ships, then why not stars?"

"Because they're using High Space drives too," says Captain K. "Presumably this creates a resonance—a bridge between us. Hence their missiles stay in High Space, and ours too. But no one communicates by firing missiles. Destroy those two ships, Mr Jacobik."

"Four gone, five gone." Jacobik slaps our nuclear darts on their way, while Ritchie caps the scopes. Acceleration surges again, irregularly. We waver, we cling on.

"Renormalise our speed afterwards, Colonel Trimble. We don't know what these velocity changes in High Space may translate into in the normal universe. That may be their plan. The fireworks could be incidental."

"Shit, they've fired a salvo!"

Jacobik's thin smile slips as he stares at his own instruments, counting. "Seven, eight, nine."

"Confirm. Spreading out. Two targeting on our missiles. Others on different vectors."

"Slow lasers," broods Heinz, disenchanted now. "And nuclear

warheads doing about as much harm as hand grenades . . . How punily our weapons perform."

"Hence my remark about fireworks, Anders. Possibly the main effect is sucked down into normal space. I hope we're not disrupting anything."

"You're glad!" accuses Jacobik, driving Heinz away from him with a glare of hatred—which even encompasses Captain K. "You really don't want us to blow them out of the sky. You're dooming us!"

"How could I be?" Heinz recoils, looking puzzled.

"Intercept those missiles, Mr Jacobik. Use the minimum salvo possible."

"Minimum computes as seven. That's all we have left!"

"Double fireball! And again. That's our attack missiles taken out. Seven bandit missiles oncoming. Those slow X-rays can't have cooked their circuits."

"Use all seven, Mr Jacobik. And afterwards, pray."

Jacobik obeys, then stares listlessly at his control board, for his nest is eggless now.

As the tiny double-suns bloom invisibly in High Space, with Ritchie counting off the echoes of the fireballs, something writhes and surges and explodes within. Something discharges in my belly, my abdomen, my sex. There's absurd *relief*. A slackening of tension.

"Did you feel it, Amy?" gasps Peter. To some degree or other we all must have. Jacobik's face is drained of blood.

"A dream," mutters René. "What next?"

As if in answer, Ritchie uncaps the scopes. Four scimitars of red light are cutting in towards us. They're too close. There's no time left to gun the engines.

"We're hit," cries Natalya; and her face reveals astonishment. "No we aren't. Yes we are. There's damage, but it's the old damage. The same sites that were lasered before. I don't understand."

"I do," says Heinz. "We have lasered ourselves. We already did it when the alarm rang, when we were all in mess room. Causality is different here. Cause and effect break down outside. *You* fired our lasers, Jacobik, because your blood's roused and you're fighting mad. We were all getting quite worked up. The

45

beams have looped round us in High Space, and through time too. There are two impact times, balancing each other: after you fired, and before you fired. The effect is the cause of the effect—but the real cause is *you*, my friend. Or," he shudders, "maybe all of us, with you as the catalyst. We've just shot ourselves. Which means—"

"Look at the alien ships!" Peter catches René's arm.

On the scopescreens they're growing larger now, closing in on us from two different quadrants. Still they change shape. The cone is now a prism, studded with four cubes. And the ovoid is a cube, with hemispheres upon it. Ritchie backs off the magnification, and now they aren't closing on us at all, but on each other.

"They won't fire again," cries Peter. "I know they won't. Don't we all?"

René slaps his belly and gufffaws. *"J'en suis certain."*

"He's right!" shouts Heinz. "They're *us*, that's what. They're projections—transformations of *Pilgrim*. Their shape's the same as ours: five linked units each. Topologically it doesn't matter whether those are spheres or cubes or pussy cats. It's a zone of abstract geometry out there."

So the two strange ships converge. So they collide, and pass into each other, becoming one. That one is the mirror image of *Pilgrim*. Rapidly the echo of *Pilgrim* out there shrinks to a vanishing point in the grain of High Space. We're quite alone again.

"So what were we firing our missiles at?" asks Captain K wearily.

"At their *doppelgängers*. Themselves, before they were fired. They exploded in proximity to themselves. I hope we haven't lost much headway because of this." Turning, Heinz marches magnetically across the deck to where the control peak of the alien drive pokes up from below . . .

SEVEN

THE HIGH SPACE drive was an iridescent crystalline pyramid some four metres high. It seemed alive, but in an unknown mineral manner. It seemed that it might have grown up there like a crystal, transmuting the black gravel of the Gobi to build its substance. And it was an object of thought projected from elsewhere, one which formed a sufficiently complex system of *cognita* to endure, apparently permanently.

Russian and Chinese planes discovered the pyramid sitting on a stony tract of wasteland north-west of Gashiun Nor, where Mongolia and Chinese Inner Mongolia ambiguously meet. Small in itself, it registered a considerably larger blip on ground-searching radars, as though a great ellipsoid zeppelin invisibly surrounded it.

Set against one face of the pyramid, up high, was a flat translucent rhombus. Within this plate a pattern of sparkling dots —a star map, perhaps even a coded flight plan—indicated 82 Eridani as the target sun. Since the plate was immovable it merely remained very likely that thousands of alternative courses —thousands of flight plan templates—could be set; or even that this same rhombus could be modified internally to map out other possible flights. (Such as a return to Earth? We do not know that till we re-activate the pyramid, out by 82 Eridani. The knowledge did not present itself. We do not know.)

On a second face, high up, was inset the probability meter, as it came to be known: a triangular orange crystal with a thin green line across the bottom calibration. One sensed that it was so. One sensed much about its workings from being close to it— except *how* it worked.

On the third face was a milky crystal enclosing a tiny pyramid within an ellipse of light. When this crystal was touched, a series of design alternatives appeared one after another within the confines of the ellipsoid: possible starship hulls, as well as some that were frankly not very possible. The effect was three-dimensional. Every tenth hull became too large for the ellipsoid, and broke up in fire. Thus were the size constraints laid down.

The fourth face bore a plate, black as night, with a tiny white pyramid perched on a green ball afloat within. The pyramid fell free of the 'planet', and only when the two were separated by some distance did the pyramid suddenly englobe in its ellipsoid of light. Below, was the activator itself: one simple switch. Again, one knew what it was; the knowledge insinuated itself . . .

Below again, the 'psychometer': a blue panel with a stylized stick figure within—and at the edge of vision hints of other possible entities, squat, rotund, four-legged . . . On either side of the psychometer were shallow recesses with small knobs surely intended to be grasped.

The first scientific teams found themselves learning by a welling up of understanding (so much, and no more) out there in the Gobi in a no-man's-land, while soldiers watched each other and helicopters circled, and the Chinese and Soviet embassies argued (and American satellites resolved in detail what was happening on the ground). Finally the Chinese government insisted on an international expedition. America had the technological edge for producing the starship itself; China's friends of the Iranian Islamic Peoples Republic offered heavy financial backing —in return, it was understood, an Iranian scientist should accompany the expedition, a *Moslem* scientist; while China's Common Market friends, who had spurred the scientific leap forward of the Eighties before the freeze of the Nineties, would contribute too. Russia suddenly endorsed an international scheme, to minimize the Chinese presence on it . . .

"The green line's bobbing up and down."
"Still riding the shockwaves . . ."
Snakes and ladders: our journey takes us across a snakes and ladders board. Now that we've met a snake, we might slide all the way down again. And the snake is ourselves . . . We could oscillate here forever. Or we might suddenly arrive.

48

"Something reached out," whispers Salman, "just as it reached out to Earth. It reached out to disarm us."

Jacobik slumps across his console, *weeping.* Weeping bitterly. I didn't know that he had tear ducts in his eyes.

"It's stabilising at a higher level! It's holding. Oh, we had to unload all our fear and hatred. We had to jettison them overboard, explode them." Heinz beams at Captain K.

Who shrugs. "We're all drugged by irreality, as Natalya says. We hallucinate, we disarm the ship—while the physical constants play dice outside." He moves to Jacobik's side to lay a fatherly hand on the Czech's shoulder while our ex-warrior sobs childishly, impotently, all his stings drawn. "Do you know, Comrade, where I come from they have a saying that magpies in a crowd have more strength than tigers in single file? We aren't tigers any more. Let us flock together, then!"

"Magpies are thieves," sniffs Wu. "What are we really but a flock of thieves—borrowers of alien tools we never made? Nowadays one does not pray, of course. Not yet! One *psychs* the machine, as the jargon goes. The next step will be prayer, though. And on Earth too, as it is in Heaven? As Mencius truly said, 'Heaven does not speak!'"

Our Captain gently reprimands her. "One can only pick one's way through that irreal flux out there by an act of thought and imagination, not just with brute machinery."

"Alas, the mysticism at the heart of the Russian soul." Wu stands there with hand raised, a Chinese Cassandra—of revolutionary Reason. She's too late; the world has already altered. The universe is other than we thought. So she preaches, Cassandra-like, to deaf ears . . . Or is she, rather, that figure poised behind the Emperor's throne, whose duty it was always to whisper in his ear, 'Remember you are only human'? She would certainly omit the qualifier! To be human is enough. And now it's too late for that: the superhuman is upon us from the star 82 Eridani . . .

Yet, blinkered martinet though she is—political appointee, too: historiographer royal!—there's something about her, which Ritchie responds to more deeply than I. But which I do sense. She wears a mask, a very perfect mask, yet it isn't her real face. Even amidst the forced rapports of High Space I cannot see

49

what *that* is. It's as though she has hypnotised herself, to forget herself—a typically Chinese political manoeuvre, perhaps . . . Is that 'real' face of hers identical with the political mask by now? Not quite. There's a faint, yet growing, hint of irony or even sarcasm in her preachings, aimed not merely at us benighted devils but at those preachings themselves, as though she is giving us a covert warning about them, deliberately presenting herself as the epitome of what she attacks: which is blind faith in control of people's minds. She preaches, not just for our apparent benefit, to criticise us (lest we forget), but also to brace her silent, emotionless comrade Li into an even more implausible per-fection. But surely Li is simply a cool-thinking scientist—a lovely neuter who thinks only of biochemistry (assisted by the thoughts of Mao and Stalin), whereas Wu is the demagogue. Somehow, by making herself such a mouthpiece, and such a strident one, Wu suggests that really it's the other way about . . . I don't under-stand her. But there's something to respect.

EIGHT

"BUGGER." PETER SLAPS the screen of the autochef. "Take a look here. What's up with our *Maître d'*?"

René, Zoe and Ritchie have all coincided with us in the mess room; they step or float over too.

```
JERUSALEM ARTICHOKE
ASPARAGUS VINAIGRETTE
CORN ON THE COB
ONIONS A LA GREQUE
BEETROOT
x ICE CREAM x
KALE
```

Ritchie peers. "They're all darn vegetables. Except for the ice cream—and it's run out. There's no meat. I like meat. Why's it putting us on a vegetarian diet? Scared of space scurvy? Not that it knows anything about us! Idiot programme."

"Override it," advises René. "Dial another menu."

"It's hardly amazing that there's no ice cream left," remarks Zoe. "Given the rate at which friend Jacobik's been cramming it down. Not least since you-know-what. Infantile compensation, eh? Cold joys for cold boys."

Peter punches a button.

Appears:

```
JAM PANCAKES
x APPLE PIE x
CARAMEL CUSTARD
ORANGE WHIP
BLINTZES
x ICE CREAM x
KUMQUAT
```

51

"All sweets!" Ritchie whistles. "Something's gone wrong with the housekeeping. I'd better buzz Natalya."

Then the penny drops. "That isn't all that Jacobik's been doing. Look down the initial letters." I trace them one by one. "What do they spell out? Jacobik."

Ritchie bounces back from the wall interphone. He nods disbelievingly. "Sick paranoid. He's screwed up the menu programme."

"Maybe it's a cry for help," says Zoe.

"Yeah, from the gut. From our guts. Christ, has he been indulging in other practical jokes too? He's already lost us all our missiles."

"We *all* lost those," says René firmly. "And a good thing too. A kind of purge."

"A few meals like these and we'll not need purging, friend! I'd better buzz the Captain too. We'll have to check all ship's systems now. Shit."

Zoe is in a forgiving mood. "Jacobik may not be to blame. Just because his name appears here—"

"Of course it's his bloody fault!" I know this for a certainty— as though I've just brushed against his nasty mind, which indeed I do believe I have: momentary contact with a brooding spider. "This is his signature. He's gone *mad*. Oh, he was that all along! But now that's *all* he is."

Jacobik is under restraint in his cabin with an improvised seal on the door. The probability of our arriving has declined again, the green line dropping back down the orange crystal. He giggled like a delinquent child when he was confronted with the evidence. Now we are all in loathsome *loco parentis* to him, and a tiny Jacobik homunculus gnaws away in everyone's mind . . .

Gus wipes his brow. "At least it was nothing worse than the autochef. If he'd had a go at the reactor—"

Kendrick looks furious with Gus. "He couldn't! What do you mean?"

"If the reactor had started—well, over-reacting . . ."

"That's impossible."

Captain K shakes his head slightly at Kendrick. ('Be quiet. Don't go on.') *Strange.*

"Might I suggest," offers Natalya, noticing nothing of this exchange, "since Jacobik is already tranquillised, yet the probability continues falling, that tranquillisation is quite pointless?"

"Is it surprising? He's inside us all!" My head aches with him.

"Maybe he should pass the rest of the voyage completely unconscious? We can feed him intravenously."

Zoe raises her hand. "The voyage will still be vulnerable to his unconscious impulses—all the time then, not merely during sleep. Heinz says that the probability really slipped back"—she waves a dismissive hand at the clock—"a while ago, when he was asleep. When he woke up, the probability steadied."

"In that case he needs to be switched right off, period!" Ritchie bites his lip but there's no way to bite back the words.

"Oh no. He needs to be more alert. He needs to be made more responsible, more aware. He needs to come to terms. Let's stop drugging him and try to *lead* him. Lead him back. He did appeal for help, in a roundabout way. We must give him that help. I can be a friendly listener. You know, I almost became a priest once, long ago."

"Let's feed him ice cream," sneers Gus. "Only, he already ate it all, like he fired all our missiles off."

"He isn't our scapegoat! If anyone is guilty, we all are. As Amy says, he's inside each of us."

"Why should *he* want to arrive, uh? He has nothing to do when he gets there."

"Let me try. A little love and sympathy."

"I ought to try too," insists Natalya. "Some psychotherapy."

"No doubt he should not be so completely isolated from us," nods Captain K. "Yet we can't let him loose either. Still, I worry about either of you being left alone with him."

Natalya laughs. "I can handle myself." Zoe only shrugs; she knows all about self-defence from way back, where she grew up.

"He *is* safely under restraint," points out Wu. "Let him win back his place among us by developing right thinking—by reordering his thoughts constructively." She *mocks* her own words faintly, not looking at Li at all, but speaking to her, I suspect.

And Li, amazingly, reacts. "Yes, he must be conditioned back to right thinking. So we should adopt a criticism-unity policy, a two-wrongs one-good tactic—I refer to the wrongs of religion and psychoanalysis. Mere elimination of the poisonous weed might be harmful to us all."

Beautiful flower Li, with cold seeds of jargon in your heart: mere codes, when it comes to discussing the management of a man (even if it *is* Jacobik) . . . Is that what you're really like?

"Psychotherapy could take months," says Ritchie.

"That's why I'll back my way," smiles Zoe. "He may be teetering on the brink of a—"

"A conversion?"

"—well, of . . . a more positive frame of mind. He's been all negatives so far: a warden of death. How can he possibly adjust if he's kept in a kind of strait jacket? That would drive anybody mad."

"Perhaps both of you should be present all the time," suggests Captain K.

"No, to gain his confidence—"

"The analyst has to operate in privacy," says Natalya at the same time. "He is, as Wu points out, suitably secured."

"Though perhaps group analysis," wavers Zoe—jealous of Natalya?

"Group analysis is what we've been into, all the journey long," sighs Kendrick. "Where has it got us to? Where are we now?"

A question which none of us, of course, can answer.

NINE

IT'S A CORAL morning in Prague. Bells make clonging noises in the air. Amethyst vapours drift up from the waters of the Vltava. The black slug of a barge oozes upstream, twitching a little rowing boat tethered in its wake. Just so does he twitch me along, tethered in his wake . . .

The boy leans on the bridge. He has a catapult stuffed in his back pocket; he wants to pot a pigeon. Or a dove.

"You? How?"

"We're all part of one another, little sister," he grins maliciously.

And I know where I am, as surely as I know—through him—that this is the Prague of his boyhood days. I'm trapped in Jacobik's mind, that has flown home to childishness. He has me. Yet, somehow, now that I really look at him, the grin isn't malicious. Only impish.

"But you were crushed by the tanks, little sister . . . You're very like her, you know. What she would have been. A big brave girl, full of life, full of ideals. My, how you've grown! Life and ideals don't really go together, little sister. Ideals belong somewhere else. Ideals are birds—they should fly off to a place where they'll be happy. Somewhere out of the world."

He looses a stone from his catapult, and a scraggy pigeon flutters brokenly along the pavement, till he gives it the *coup de grâce* with the heel of his hand.

"You bastard!"

He looks hurt. "Don't call your brother that. Don't be horrified, *amie*. I love whatever brings death. Death is the doorway. Death isn't unlovable."

And suddenly I know him. As a sister knows a brother, who is her opposite in every way.

55

This country is a land of the dead, a land fenced in. The tanks have come over the border. The flowers are all crushed by their treads. The only way out is death. He has seen the expressions on the faces of the dead, and on those who are about to die—where it is a look of horrible liberty, almost of licence. The polite etiquette of facial muscles has collapsed. They are slack-jawed, drop-mouthed, spittle-lipped, faces out of control, like masturbating boys in a woodshed peeping through cracks at a sunbathing girl who has slackened, too, the etiquette of brassière straps. The only way out over the frontier is death—whose servant he will therefore be, in minor ways at first, then more professionally, wearing a uniform of the State with all the dour panache of a public executioner. He will rise high—higher than pigeons and doves with their tatty, spurious freedom of the skies and roof-tops—as high as death can be borne. Yet always the horror remains that death might not, after all, be the irrefutable visa; that a committee, a police, a politbureau may preside over death itself, marshalling even the souls of the dead (who will not be dead, but only buried alive), controlling that last freedom.

He reaches in his pocket for another pebble, and finding none, bursts into tears. He bubbles . . . petulantly? No: *heartbroken.* He wept this way after he fired all our missiles and they only cancelled themselves out, did not achieve anything. He's mad. Infantile. He thinks death is an achievement, something to attain —not to overcome.

"We *purged* ourselves when you fired all the missiles," I try to explain to him. (We did promise to help him, after all.) "We couldn't go on to God's World with all that freight of pointless human animosity on board. Pointless, yes! Paltry. It was just plucked out of our grasp, like a nasty toy."

I reach to take the catapult, to toss it over the parapet of the bridge into the misty water of the Vltava; but he clutches it tightly to his heart, almost like a crucifix. As though Christ had been slain by a catapult.

"Pointless? Little sister, it was all our knowledge of death, and what death might be to us! We *need* death as our ally."

"I can't imagine why!"

"Because it leads *beyond.* I shall lead all living creatures beyond! It's *necessary.*" He brightens. "Kiss me, little sister? We

56

belong. You're my other self. I shall search for you forever."

"The hell you will!"

"When a particle meets an antiparticle, they annihilate in a flash of *light*. Let there be this light between us, *amie*. Let us meet in that flash of light. Love meets Death. And they become . . . the pure Light. The God. Through Death. I love . . . but you don't know the language of my love. Kiss me. Annihilate me. Let me be your antiparticle. The tank treads crushed you, buried you alive, but here I have you back again. Let my fingers crush you, instead! I will do the job they cheated me of. Lovingly . . . I'll fight that politbureau of the Dead, if there is one. And I can smell one. It stole my weapons, so that you shouldn't know what a blessing death may be."

Some kind of nasty dream. Just as well I don't remember anything, apart from the nastiness. I don't want to. Something—some healing, soothing element in me—advises that this is best. Something blessèd. Something larger—a wise whale in the sea of general mind—has sieved out the nasty little things that nibbled at me.

Ah yes, I must have dreamt about the phantom battle. But now we're safe. We're purged.

Oh no, we're not. There's still that damned lunatic.

Jacobik is dead, hanged naked in his cabin.

How does a man hang himself in High Space, where gravity is null? By sheer venomous hatred of the ship, and of himself, does he generate surges of quasi-gravity fierce enough to throttle himself in the loops of plastic cable which had formerly secured him to his bunk, his wrists and ankles bound? That cable now tethers his neck to a ceiling brace. His clothes, torn off him, float like rag banners in the air . . .

How acrobatically he must have twisted and turned, to untie the tethers with his teeth! How much in love with death he must have been, for he died ejaculating! Death was his orgasm, and his orgasm was death: a perfect equation which annulled him, adding up to final zero.

"Not so," says Captain K, after we have frozen his body. "I regret to say that he was undoubtedly murdered. The door seal was quite cleverly tampered with . . ." Neil Kendrick nods sourly. "Judging by the manner of his death, I'm led to believe that it must have been a female crew member—unless . . ." He leaves the alternative implication afloat, like Jacobik's corpse, to haunt us. He stares in turn into my face, Natalya's, Sachiko's, Zoe's, Li's, even Wu's; then gazes at the men, too, for good measure. "Somebody let themselves into his cabin. Someone loosed him, though not his wrists or ankles—not till afterwards. I noted the bruises on those."

"He might have bruised them, struggling to free himself," says Natalya dismissively.

"Da, to free himself from death. If he was free, why did he tear his clothes to pieces as a way of removing them? Why take them off at all? Clearly he was still bound."

"He was mad," says Trimble, uneasily.

"Someone seduced him, in his craving and his childish greed and vulnerability."

"This is monstrous," protests Wu.

"Dirty bastard," mumbles Ritchie, bright beads on his forehead. (Meaning Jacobik? Or the unknown murderer? Or Captain K for unwrapping the manner of the crime?) He glares at Salman momentarily, as though he suspects him of homosexual assault or fears something of the sort in himself and associates the idea with the handsome, lambent-eyed Persian. (We are hermaphrodites, because of High Space. How we enter into each other, even sexually!)

"If someone wanted to kill him," says René reasonably, "surely it was simpler to strangle him while he still lay tethered on his bunk? This is a most peculiar way of killing somebody."

"It's symbolic of execution," says Peter. "Death by hanging. Otherwise it would just have been furtive murder. This way, somehow, it's justice. The unconscious mind justifies it."

"Seduced to death." Captain K turns slowly, fixing us all with his glare. "I do not personally know much of these erotic quasi-gravity effects. Only at secondhand. Hmm, about four hours ago, I think . . . No, it must have been longer. Damn this twisted time! There was a tug, a surge. Who was making love *recently*?"

The trouble is, none of us really knows what 'recently' means. No one owns up.

"Love, it sickens me to say, has been used to kill. The little death became the big death."

"Thanatos and Eros hand in hand," nods Natalya.

"What real proof have you got?" blusters Trimble. "This is very harmful—"

"I *sense* it, more than anything. I sense the manner of his death. Bruises and tampered locks are secondary. I know. But I do not know *who*. It carries the flavour of us all. So did that tug of quasi-gravity—recently."

"Yeah, I guess I noticed that," admits Ritchie. "Some time ago. Since I last woke up. I think."

"I too," says Wu.

Some of us are less sure. "I must have been asleep," says Heinz firmly. So must I.

"Maybe we're all responsible," says Zoe. "Though, as with the ghost battle, one person must be the channel—a catalyst."

"Does that console us? Does that absolve the person responsible? As to our peace of mind, though, Colonel Trimble, the probability has begun to rise again. The thin green line creeps nearer to the summit even as I speak."

"*Ja*, it's true," confirms Heinz.

"Whoever is responsible will be even more eager to arrive—as will we all. Yet something precious has gone from the journey now, for me—much worse than the misfiring of the missiles. I bring this out into the open, rather than covering it up as you no doubt would have preferred, for the simple sake of honesty and truth. Irrelevant virtues? Well, they seem to apply here. Let us not feel glad that Jacobik is gone, lest that gladness poison us. Let us genuinely mourn him. And always remember that one of you . . . And to be fair I must include myself in this circle of accusation—"

Why include himself? Surely the impeacher is the one person whom we can confidently rule out? Especially given the grotesque sexual bias of the killing . . . which seems more like a sado-masochistic fantasy every moment. Unless . . . Captain K wishes to suggest that *he himself* might be responsible! Perhaps alone, perhaps in league with someone else, his agent. Who? Natalya—who boasted that she could look after herself? Or Zoe—who offered 'love' to Jacobik? While Li casually spoke of elimination . . .

At this moment—just as in a flash of empathy once I understood how we are all part of Captain K's psychic laboratory—he resonates with me again; then is gone again, gone utterly, blocked off . . .

He is deliberately drawing the poison from the wound in ourselves, into himself. He is acting as lightning conductor to ground the power of life and death which one amongst us has arrogated. In so doing he re-establishes his authority as our real commissar, alone possessing the authority of summary secret court martial and execution. In accruing death and guilt, he distances himself. Strangely, I feel that we have lost him now even more than we have lost Jacobik. What happened to Jacobik was a psychic amputation—and now it is cauterized by Captain K's withdrawal of himself from us. There can be no more killing now, even if a second Jacobik existed, for Captain K is the only one who has such power. Ah, he is a diplomat of the soul.

"Perhaps," says Peter softly, "we have to shake hands with the devil in ourselves, before we can unblock our inner drives. Perhaps it was unavoidable . . ."

Kamasarin silences him. Now he is no longer Captain K—benign, almost avuncular. He is Kamasarin, Grigory Arkadievitch, general and lion. We have all been only children till this moment. But now we strengthen. Yes, we strengthen. All of us.

Part Two

BROUGHT LOW

TEN

At last! Suddenly, ending this hiccup of non-time . . .

A yellow sun burns forth. Thousands of bright stars are preciously distinct in the velvet night . . .

We have only been amoebic and formless till now, without rigidity. Now we crispen and harden in that sun's light, lumps of dough flash-baked by it. From a waking dream we awake to the reality of day. We regard each other—sane, separate, solid individuals again—with embarrassment mixed with relief. We'd been travelling naked all that time without quite realizing it. Now we find ourselves suddenly reclothed—entire within ourselves, no longer leaking subjectivities.

Out there, beyond the unmasked photochromatic viewports, rides a world: a less brilliant double of the sun, shaved by darkness. It is a gibbous disc of ochre, orange, yellow. On the face of that world floats a tiny black spot of moon shadow. We pick out one tiny silvery half-moon, then another . . .

"But it's a gas giant!" exclaims Salman. "We can only be a little under one AU out from that sun. We're right in the middle of the habitable zone . . . There's only a gas giant here. Where do we *go*?"

"To work, ladies and gentlemen," says Kamasarin calmly. "We go to work."

Presently, our instruments are yielding up their results . . .

"Estimated mass of the sun is 0.91 of Sol," reports Heinz. "Give or take. Radius likewise. Surface temperature around 5,100 degrees. So it's a class G5 star—that matches 82 Eridani. Computer confirms the anticipated constellation pattern shift. We're in the right part of space."

"Nothing on the radio bands apart from some natural noise

from the gas giant. Negative on microwave sources." Kendrick frowns. "There's nothing I can interpret as radio, TV broadcasts, radar or other significant power emissions. No one's on the air."

"Maybe they don't use radio. They didn't send the pyramid to Earth by any conventional means."

"Let's hope so, René. Or else, home there's no returning."

"If we re-activate the drive, it might take us right back home. We can't be certain."

Salman has been busy scanning for other planets in the plane of the ecliptic. "We have two more gas giants, out at 5 AUs and 12.5 AUs. This nearby one is at 0.77 AU. So there can't be any independent Earth-type worlds at all because of the inhibition effect. Not unless they're far out and frozen." He purses his lips. "We shall have to revise our planetology, I fear. The sun's radiation pressure should sweep the primeval gases further out, leaving heavy atoms to condense close in. Yet here we have only gas giants all the way . . . Well, this is the first alien solar system we've set eyes on.

"As for the local gas giant, it's in the Saturn league. A bit smaller: 120,000 kilometres diameter at the equator. A hydrogen-helium mixture, very rich in ammonia, methane and carbohydrates—traces of metals too. It's dense and warm—more massive than Saturn, maybe. And of course it gets a lot of sun heat, which should make the weather pretty wild. I'd expect more radio noise from it than Neil says."

"Why?" asks Kendrick sharply.

"Oh, stormy weather on a grand scale. It has eight moons so far. Actually, we're within the orbit of the outermost small moon. The biggest is about Luna-size, with massive cratering and no sign of any atmosphere. Judging from the hull dosimeters the magnetosphere isn't as intense as you'd expect this close in to the sun—not nearly. Radiation hazards in local space are acceptably low."

"Could the gas giant itself be inhabited?" wonders René. "If it's so warm. That would imply a technology quite different from ours . . . Merely because we saw humanoid angels . . . Well, our own minds played a role in shaping them."

Gus Trimble wears a long face, making him seem more be-jowled than usual, as though gravity has already returned and his tissues have slumped as a consequence. "Our current course is taking us sunward, inside the gas giant's orbit. If we leave things alone we'll go into an elliptical sun orbit, bringing us to that hypothetic High Space injection point in another week or so as we leave the giant behind. We've got a problem, though. If we jockey into orbit round the giant, well, unless we can carry out space repairs I don't know that we can get out to that injection point—always supposing there is a ticket home! Not on two engines, with the fuel that's left. Did we waste it in High Space! Yet if we don't go into orbit our shuttles haven't the fuel to get in and back again fast enough, unless they just slingshot round the giant. We'll have to do something about cancelling velocity in the next five or six hours, or else we're just committed to a fly-by." He wipes his brow. "Where to, though? That's unless we find a recharge station parked somewhere round the giant."

Kendrick shrugs. "If there is one it isn't advertising."

Heinz is at the small refractor. "I'm getting another moon—a big one. It's coming out of occultation."

With the naked eye we can actually see the tiny half-disc as it emerges. Ritchie locks in the main scopescreen and magnifies. The gas giant swells rushingly towards us, a vivid yellow fog, striated red and orange and brown. Beyond it, half in day and half in the faintest yellow-ghost night, hangs: a blue and brown world, the blue area mottled with white streaks and whorls.

"That's *big*. That's got an atmosphere. That's our baby," whoops Ritchie.

Salman measures and calculates; before long he has the figures.

"My estimated diameter is just over 12,000 kilometres. That's about 0.85 of Earth's. It's orbiting at 400,000 kilometres." He smiles. "And it has an oxygen-nitrogen atmosphere."

"Still no technological signs," warns Kendrick, who has been watching it too, with his instruments. "If the gas giant was masking them before, I should still be getting readings now. But I'm not. Just the same burst of static . . ."

The child of the giant floats in the open now.

"What we have here," explains Salman, "is a planet-sized moon nearly as large as Earth, rotation-locked to its primary, as

C   65

one would expect. Depending on the ratio of heavy elements in its make-up, the gravity will be somewhere between 0.75 and 0.9 of Earth's. Personally I'd put the figure at the higher end on account of the atmosphere—and the traces of methane are good life indicators."

"Yeah, farting cows," comments Kendrick. "So it's metal-rich without any detectable technology. Paradox. There's been no reaction to our signals."

"We heard you. Now, the moon orbits its primary about once every two and a half Earth days. Rather a long day and night cycle from our point of view! Still, the inclination seems to be only about 11 degrees, so we should expect a fairly equable climate with minor seasonal variations since the eccentricity of the gas giant is so small. The side facing away from the primary seems to be largely water-covered. There'll be very slight irregular tides caused by the other moons."

"Which may be a poor prognosis for life evolving rapidly or to any complexity," says René. "With no tidal intermix to haul life on to land."

"Not necessarily. The rotation-locking could have taken a long time to finalise . . . Anyhow, the main visible consequence of the primary's own pull has been to draw the planet into a distinct pear shape. There's high land on the side facing the primary, as the radar profile shows us. That side's basically highland desert and mountains, with thin air. The other side is ocean with much denser air. Islands, too—plenty of those, possibly volcanic in origin."

"The point is," says Kamasarin, "dare we go into orbit around it for a closer look with no absolute guarantee of return? On the other hand, dare we *not*—when there's no guarantee we can return to Earth through High Space?"

"Perhaps we ought to—" Zoe falters. "Perhaps we should, well, ask the pyramid?"

"You mean pray to it?" Wu curls her lip.

"No, what I mean is, if we all concentrate upon it with this question in mind—well, perhaps the psychometer or something will react? It *does* respond to our consciousness, even if we don't understand how! It costs nothing to try. It has to be in some sort of resonance with its point of origin, doesn't it? Maybe it can . . . well, key us in, now that we're so close."

"Denby has a point," nods Kamasarin. "Maybe we can gain some contact, or insight."

Heinz snaps his fingers. "Another possible pointer. Let's take a look at the pyramid-on-world panel—" He clicks away, pursued by most of us.

"Ach, it's still showing the pyramid isolated in darkness." He reaches out and presses his palm against the panel. "Damn us all for fools! Look!"

Already the symbol pattern is changing. The pyramid shrinks to a point of light. A golden disc appears. A green blip comes from behind it, and tracks across the 'globe' to disappear behind it. A few moments later it reappears. Then the point of light floats up towards the blip and fuses with it. And the sequence recommences.

"It's telling us, in case we're so dumb," smiles Ritchie, "that having left one world we need to get into orbit round another. Instructions for idiots. The blip is our parking orbit."

"No, the blip is something already in orbit. Obviously it's that planetary moon, and the golden disc is the gas giant. Can't you sense it, man? Can't you psych it?"

"Nope. I guess I'm underprivileged. I . . . wait, I dunno. This is crazy. So what became of the other moons?"

"Why show them? Only one moon has life, and it's obvious to any idiot which one it is."

"We still have my idea to try," says Zoe. "The psychometer may double as a communication panel. I'm going down below . . . if that's okay?"

"I shall accompany you," nods Kamasarin. "Muir, Dove, Anders and Baqli: keep watch on the four faces of the pyramid in case there's some reaction up here."

Wu produces a hiss of reproach. But the effect is quite lost.

In:

Bee-bu-bu! . . . Bee-bu-bu!

ELEVEN

ONLY THE WEAPONS board, reduced to control of lasers, stays unmanned.

"Range fifty klicks," reads Ritchie. "Object is overhauling us from ship's south-west, superior quadrant. It's on a collision course. Time of intersection . . . twelve minutes. Echo strength makes it about forty times as big as us."

Stars swirl to a halt on the scopescreen, and are blotted out by . . . a mountain—a rocky mass that glints in the sunlight. Gems sprout from the ragged rock: huge crystals—ruby, amethyst, topaz.

Salman beams. "That's got to be the richest natural agglomeration of minerals I've ever seen! A real pendant for God's neck."

"I think it's ugly." I do. "It's cruel, somehow. Shapeless, jagged—" An irrational feeling? *Whence?*

"Trimble, give us a ten-second burn to take us clear of its path." Kamasarin turns to Salman. "So then, where does such richness originate?"

"I think that dense proto-planets began to form here. So they separated out the richer elements. Evidently they broke up under gravitational stress from the gas giants. Now we have fragments of their interiors flying around the system—in addition to the captured moons. Interesting dynamics at work."

"Ignition in thirty seconds, *mark.*"

Countdown; ignition; a smooth surge of acceleration . . . The scope continues tracking the asteroid as stars move over behind it . . .

"End of burn." We float loose again.

"Goddam." Ritchie gazes at his console. "It's changed course. It's—changed course. Something's *piloting* it!"

The stars are steady again behind it.

"It's still an asteroid," Salman insists. "Perhaps it has been . . . modified."

"Do I give us another burn, sir?"

"It could possibly have outgassed just then," says Heinz. "Though that's stretching coincidences."

"It isn't a comet core," says Salman.

We try a shorter burn. The asteroid also alters course.

Zoe looks round defiantly. "This is contact. Rendezvous. Well, isn't it?"

"It isn't what the pyramid showed."

Heinz swivels the deck-mounted binoculars. "Some of those crystal structures look like . . . what, missile tubes? Or . . . entrances?"

"Seven minutes . . . twenty-five klicks. It compensated for our speed increase."

"Why are we running?" frets Zoe. "Isn't it obvious who they are? The pyramid must have signalled them."

"Can you match radio frequencies, Neil?"

"I'm trying. They don't appear to be transmitting. Doesn't anyone in this damn system believe in radio sets? Or do they hope to take us by surprise?"

"Five minutes," reports Ritchie. "I guess it could be automated. Some of those crystal things could be power cells. An automated rock . . . God, if they ram us—"

"Why should they ram us?" Zoe is quite distressed. "Why must we think so aggressively? That's what went wrong in High Space."

"I'm scared of that rock, Peter. I hate it."

"I've got bad feelings about it too," he admits. "*Why*? Why should I?"

"They might try flashing a light, damn it. Presumably they can *see*. Presumably they have eyes."

"I feel that dislike too," admits René. "Captain, can we blink the lights on this deck?"

"Good idea! Vasilenko, power up the control deck lights to full, then switch off. Give them a one-two-three blink pattern."

Natalya obeys. We blink in the aftermath of alternate brilliance and darkness, while she rheostats the interior lighting back to low and steady.

Easily visible to the naked eye by now is the asteroid: a small, jagged, glinting clinker.

"It's slowing down! I don't see how, but it is. It won't ram us—"

No need, presently, for the scopescreen to pick out details. In another few minutes the mountain hangs out there, two hundred metres abeam, its velocity matched to ours: a rocky mass, salient with crystal tubes and boxes, inlaid with gem facets (powercells, portholes?). Heinz yields to René, who stares through the binoculars at vague black shapes we can all see moving within . . .

A dozen crystal ports spring open. Dark bodies spill out into space, tethered by thin bright cords. The cords shine like silver thread where the sunlight catches them. Quickly the creatures drift towards us.

"God, but they're fearsome looking brutes—"

"Loathsome." That's my word for them!

"There must be forty or fifty of them! That asteroid's a *hive*."

"No space suits that I can see," observes René, overcoming his . . . yes, nausea. "Those exoskeletons must tolerate hard vacuum. They keep their jaws clamped shut. I wonder how large their brains can be? Could they be specially bred for tasks in space? Products of bioengineering?"

They're like giant black scorpions, with eight legs and jointed pincers resembling hands—holding things . . . rods (some of them). And jaws and claws. They're spinning those threads out of their own backsides, spiderlike.

A net of shining threads reaches out to bracket us.

"Beware the Jabberwock, my son, the jaws that bite, the claws that catch! They're Jabberwocks, that's what they are . . ."

"Jabberwockus Dovi," nods René, gripping my arm to calm me. "Or Jabberwockus Columbae? To you the honour, my dear."

"No thanks!"

"They can't board us," soothes Natalya. "All the hatches are power-locked."

The first creature alights on the viewport overhead. Suction pads on six of its ankles stick to the glass, its feet folding out of the way, claws raking. Its two front claws are triple-jointed and serrated along the insides like mantis legs, but they stretch out

70

like arms. The thing is almost the size of a pointer dog. The body is stiffly segmented with an armoured carapace of dark violet, and ends in a purple ovoid spinneret which it holds cocked at right angles, that silver thread linking it all the way back to the asteroid. A sharp ovipositor—or is it a sting?—sticks out beneath. The head is a polished cone on a short armoured stalk—with a stiff moustache of maxillary feelers folded over tightly clenched mandibles. Two glassy, faceted eyes gaze blankly down. I feel sick.

A second creature steps slowly across the viewports, coming from the far side of *Pilgrim*. It settles briefly, its silver thread taut against the glass, then moves on, pulling the thread right round the hull. Others weave their threads around the various protrusions of *Pilgrim*.

"Separately they don't look too intelligent," murmurs René. "But purposeful, oh yes, *that*. I get the feeling that one's a sort of living camera, spying on us . . ."

Ritchie rotates an external camera to bear upon the main hatch. Four of the creatures are standing on it, holding those thin rods in their claws. Suddenly the tips of the rods flare alight. They hold the burning tips to the hatch.

"That's cutting gear!"

"Trimble, give us a five second burn to drag us clear of this."

Gus has only been waiting for the word. He breathes out in relief. "Right! Fifteen seconds, *mark*."

"Decompression in the main airlock, sir," calls Natalya.

"Seal off the section."

"—two—one—zero, we have ignition. Christ, but we're not moving out! We're just turning around that asteroid. It's turning with us! Those threads must be *tough*."

Kamasarin pulls himself into the weapons seat. His hands descend upon the laser board. A rock boils on the asteroid, a crystal facet sparkles and explodes. One of the insectoids flares and drifts away, its silver thread sagging . . . One.

Kamasarin swears softly in some language I don't recognize. He still plays the lasers, as he shouts, "All right, attention! Those are no friends of ours. Trimble, be ready to light the engines. Give ten second warnings over the interphone. All teams except Bridge get down to Stores. Break out the rifles, Blue.

Locker code is quadruple zero seven two. Break out the planet suits, Anders team. Everyone is to get suited and armed. You have time to. They have to cut through the outer and inner hatches and the corridor bulkhead first. Anders team, deploy along the corridor. Beware of sudden decompression. Wu team, cover Anders. Hold them till we can burn free. Ah, I hit another! Denby team, get to the shuttle hanger—they may try to cut through there. Blue team, fetch three suits for us here. Then guard this deck—with Vasilenko inside, Blue outside. We'll seal off. Don't worry, we'll cut free! But go now, everyone, go!"

One last order I overhear as I leave with Peter, Zoe and René (for we four are Denby team): "Neil, reactor code red, preparatory!"

What does that last order mean? It doesn't matter. We go.

TWELVE

A FREE-FALL LAUNDRY room : someone curses, but mostly there are only quiet urgent whispers. These planet suits are much easier and faster to put on than the bulky multilayered space-suits—of which there are only four anyway. They'll tolerate vacuum and cold if need be.

Time slows. We're divers swimming underwater with a single lungful of air. As I dress Peter, and he me, he smiles wryly.

"Does this remind you of something, love?"

"Hell, yes. Will we ever—?" Best left unsaid. I tousle his cropped red curls briefly before I plant his helmet in place and seal it.

We hear Kamasarin's voice over the suit radios : "The TV pickup inside the airlock is still transmitting. Insectoids inside have jettisoned their lines. They're puffing big balloons from their spinnerets—packing out the airlock with them. I think they're building some sort of natural airlock of their own. Another insectoid is pulling its way through. And another. The first four are starting in on the inner door. I've cut about a dozen lines. Try now, Trimble."

"Ignition in ten seconds, *mark*."

We brace ourselves.

"No use."

"Slight drop in corridor pressure . . . Pressure's steady again. That *is* an airlock they built. Continue suiting up, though. They may use gas or spray something. Inner hatch is one quarter through. Anders team, status?"

"Nearly ready . . . Yes, okay."

Ritchie and Natalya already have the weapons locker open. L-27 laser rifles : squat grey salamis with short stock and pistol grip.

c*   73

Now they're both gone, flying, with their rifles—three spare suits opening out behind them into hollow boneless bodies.

"Denby team?"
"Nearly at the hanger."
"Wu team?"
"In place."
"Anders?"
"A glow on the bulkhead. Small hole now, burning brightly. Cutting continues slowly, clockwise."
"Never mind the direction. Fire as soon as you see them. Hold them. I think we've cut about half of the tethers."
"They're refastening one," comes Kendrick's voice. "Look, at ten o'clock."
We four of Denby team cycle through the airlock into the vacuum of the hanger, where our twin shuttlecraft hang cradled side by side, snouts facing the outer doors.
"Denby, open the airlocks of both shuttles. Cover the hanger entrance from inside the airlocks—"
"That door's about to give," calls Heinz. "Ready to fire."
Peter and I pull ourselves into the shelter of *Alpha*'s airlock. René and Zoe have disappeared round the far side of *Beta*. They'll be out of sight of the hanger entrance there. Surely Kamasarin realizes? Ah, but he wants people in the shuttles, or almost in them, in case we have to . . . No, unthinkable. He doesn't dare say so over the open channel. Not yet.
"Blue, go to cover the transverse corridor from the hanger end. Use your hanger airlock as your cover." I'm right. Ritchie is our pilot, *out*. Kamasarin has ordered four people to these shuttles who are psychs—we might still perhaps contact God's World on its own terms. Or does he simply want us out of the way?
"*Achtung!* Door's out. Fire! Fire!"
A woman screams . . .
"They rushed Matsumura," pants Heinz. "They sailed through the laser fire right on to her. One of them is cut in half, but it's still functioning. The silver thread from their arses . . . they're wrapping her. Don't fire *at* her! Hit the doorway."
Sachiko shrieks.

74

"Shut up!" Who's that? Salman? Suddenly the screaming stops. Too suddenly.

"On to me!" cries Heinz. "Wrapping—I can't . . . The sting! Sti—" His voice stops.

"This is Wu. They overcame Anders and Baqli. Insect things are between us and them. Don't shoot there, Li! You might hit people—"

"Bulkhead D will close in ten seconds. Get out, Wu team!"

"Here they come. Die, die!"

A woman cries out. Is it Li? Her cry dies out.

What is going on? Inside the hanger is a horrid frozen peace. The chaos of this blind battle deafens and freezes us. If we keep quite still and don't even move a finger somehow it might disappear. It's only an acoustic nightmare with no visual elements, not a breath of motion to it. We hold our weapons poised like magic wands to ward off the invisible danger. Oh God, and there swims up the image of Jacobik's face, huge, swollen and blue, his eyes popping with pleasure and horror . . . *Why?* A death's head! Image of death. Kamasarin's voice saves me. It's closer to my ears than my own breathing.

"Be silent, everyone! Denby team, board both shuttles. Blue, get in there with them. Make ready to fly. Keep the shuttle airlocks open for"—he sobs, or does he just catch his breath?—"for escaping personnel. You three go now—" He must mean Kendrick, Gus and Natalya. And at this moment the airlock rotates a suited figure—BLUE—into our hanger. I almost open fire. For a moment his faceplate wears the fading afterimage of Jacobik's death-face. I never could be alone with that in this small shuttle, even with Peter by my side. Ritchie flies towards us. Peter cycles the three of us through.

"We can still pull loose," squeaks Gus.

"Go—go! I shall overload the reactor. If these creatures get hold of the pyramid and can use it—! Get out. I stay."

"But you can't overload the reactor."

"Oh yes he can." Kendrick, now. "I already started the sequence. It had to be this way."

"They never told us."

"Would you have *liked* to know, Gus? Get out!"

"Control rods are being withdrawn in sequence. Critical

build-up commencing. Hear this, hear this: any personnel still on board in fifteen minutes will be caught in nuclear fire. Go—reach that moon. God help you all. Sealing the control deck in ten seconds. Out too, Neil." Why does he stay? Captain sinking with his ship? No: the destruct sequence can still be stopped from there—he has to defend it.

Ritchie harnesses himself into the pilot's seat. Quite small is the interior of our shuttle. More than half the space is bulked out by stores, watertank, air cylinders, chem-toilet, mini-autochef, survey instruments stowed away. When the four seats open out, wing-spread, into sleeping couches, no free space is left at all. Ritchie slaps switches with gloved hands.

A squeal. Of a stuck pig? Gus?

A burst of Russian: Natalya . . . calling out what?

"Shuttle *Beta*, come in please," says Ritchie coolly.

"This is René. I'm at the controls. What do we *do*? We aren't pilots. Do I wait for Gus or Neil?"

"Insectoids are heading for the reactor bay," shouts Kendrick, somewhere. "Three, four of them. They must detect—"

Kamasarin swears again in that strange tongue. Mongol? Yakut? "If they realize, Neil! If those things understand. If they sacrifice themselves, as they seem able to do. They might have time to abort it. Pray they can never use the pyramid. Surely nothing so automatic has the spirit to make it work! Yet their guidance mind, if there is one—"

"I'll delay 'em. I'm going there. It'll cost them a few minutes—"

"*Yes*, Neil. Do it."

"Negative, René," answers Ritchie. "There's no time left. I slave you out. Now listen: press the battery master switch. It's red, lower left. It's labelled. Done it? Now switch on your autopilot: the top left, orange knob. Turn it right through ON to REMOTE—"

I can feel, rather than hear, our *Alpha* coming alive.

"Ritchie, someone's coming!"

A single small figure tumbles through the hanger airlock. Immediately it sails out towards *Beta*, the nearer craft. Bad choice: *Beta*'s airlock is round the other side.

"Wu. The insect things are close behind. I'm the only one."

She flaps her arms in flight, realizing her error. Recovering herself without a word, she pitches off the silica tiles of the airframe, rolling up off the deck to disappear behind the shuttle.

"Are both shuttles ready to go?" demands Kamasarin. "I'm waiting to open the hanger doors. They are outside the control deck door."

"No! Wu?"

"*Yes*. I'm in your airlock, *Beta*." The hanger airlock begins to turn . . . (They're not cutting through. They're using its controls!)

"Both shuttles are go, sir."

. . . as the great curve of the double doors splits open in front of us and recesses rapidly into the hull. Cut by the lip of the deck, the bright ball of the gas giant bulges up. Over the left upper quadrant of opening space there cuts a silver thread: one of those tethers. It's in *Beta*'s path. Perhaps. An insectoid hauls itself round the opening—just as Ritchie slaps the release lever. Both of our delta-winged, high-tailed ships leap forward simultaneously—as the creature launches itself across the opening, trailing silver.

Fleetingly: it collides and spins away as *Beta* hits it.

Fleetingly: the carbon edge of *Beta*'s tail-fin hits the thread. The thread stretches, fails to snap. *Beta* lurches to one side, the starboard wing rising high, the port wing dipping at the deck.

And she flies free—downward into the night, angling away from us, deflected. A red tell-tale flashes in front of Ritchie. An alarm buzzes.

"*Beta*? You okay?"

"Think so. Yes. We took a knock. We aren't hurt. I don't know about damage. What do we *do*?"

Ritchie's right eye twitches behind his faceplate. He raises a gloved hand as though to swat a fly buzzing in his helmet.

"I'm cutting the engines now, before we boost too far apart. No sweat. We're leaving *Pilgrim* fast enough. We can coast a while. Okay, there. At least we're headed in the right direction. I'll jockey us over to inspect your damage presently. Then I'll slave your positioning motors to trim the course, and we can lock on again to boost together. Cut your autopilot, will you?"

"Right," hesitantly.

"Let's get out of our helmets to save the air cans."

*   *   *

77

"Will you call *Pilgrim* before the reactor goes? Please, Ritchie. There can't be much time left."

He glances irritably at me. "What for? There are only those insects there now."

"Please. To say goodbye. Even if nobody hears it. Goodbye to Earth."

"A sort of salute?" Ritchie reaches for the radio. "This is shuttle *Alpha* calling *Pilgrim Crusader*. Do you read me?"

The radio crackles, but no one reads us.

"This is shuttle *Alpha*. We're safe. *Beta* likewise. Goodbye. Goodbye."

We sit with helmets off now, to wait the last minutes out, watching the small rear viewscreen. *Pilgrim* and even the asteroid are too far away to see by now, but the explosion will be bright at ten times that distance.

And we wait.

"It hasn't happened," says Ritchie finally. "It hasn't blown. What did Kamasarin say? If those things understand it they can stop it? My God, they did too. Pray Heaven they can't psych their way through High Space!"

"Heaven? This *is* Heaven, Ritchie! Look, there's God's World ahead, sailing in its Heaven. And what was waiting for us? Devils. Filthy things. With stings to stick in us and claws to tear us apart. Things that couldn't communicate. Wouldn't. Didn't bother." (Peter squeezes my glove.) "They were waiting. If Ritchie hadn't got on board none of us would even be here. We're just some specks of dust that blew away."

"The broadcasts warned about a battle, love. We still don't know what that battle is. Maybe the insects are *their* enemy, trying to stop us getting there. Well, they failed, damn it. We got away."

"I don't think we even saw the enemy. We didn't see what directed them. We were just swept aside, right at the start."

"Don't be so bloody defeatist."

Ritchie coughs. "I must get back to René. They'll be going nuts, drifting all alone."

Before long we're staring down at the tail of *Beta*, hanging below us some forty metres off, apparently motionless. The

78

twin port elevons are visibly bent, the outer one badly.

"That sure can't re-enter!" Ritchie laughs bitterly. "Re-enter, eh? When we've never been near that world in all our lives! I guess slaving her down to a landing would be kind of crazy at the best of times. Okay, you three down there, here's what we'll do. I'll line us up, then you can re-engage your autopilot, and we'll get on course for a moon orbit. Once we're in orbit you'll all transfer over here for re-entry. Shit, I mean for landing dirtside. You can't transfer any earlier than that. Too crowded, and we'd run through *Alpha*'s consumables. We'll leave *Beta* parked aloft."

"One little point," comes Zoe's voice. "Just how do we transfer?"

"Oh, life-line. I'll rig it. No sweat, you can pull yourself over with your eyes closed. You'll be weightless. (Maybe they'd better do just that," he mutters to us. "Keep their eyes shut.) Okay, we have six million flicks minimum to travel. That's to the close point of its orbit. The gas giant's pull will speed us up, but we'll have to kill that later on or we'll be coming in too fast to get into orbit. I'll get the approximate path angle and initial velocity out of the computer in about an hour. We'll fine it down with course corrections tomorrow."

"An *hour*?" protests René. "Shouldn't we be getting out of here as fast as possible?"

"Don't worry, Monsieur. We *are* getting out of here, and fast, right now. We have been, ever since we left *Pilgrim*. And one hour *is* soon, you'd better believe it. The computer isn't updated and navigational stars have all shifted. I've got our computer and a Hewlett-Packard, a sextant and a few other things, and what I know in my brain. One per cent difference in initial velocity makes one hell of a difference in flight time. We've got to arrive when that moon's round our side, and at the right speed."

"I'm sorry. I apologize."

"That's okay. If you want to fill in the time, figure out how to use your radar and keep watch behind."

"I am familiar with radar sets," comes Wu's voice.

"You're quite a lady." Ritchie sounds as though he means it.

THIRTEEN

AN IMMENSE RIPE peach, banded pink and orange, gold and chrome, cleft by night. The bright crocus sash around the gas giant's midriff is fringed by a darker bronze braiding. Yet that sash is no portly cummerbund, and its belly is far from serene or autumnal; hurricanes of rushing roiling colour, scallops and shearings of jet-streams and planet-sized spots, are at war there.

To port, our windows are filled by the satellite world we orbit now, below us. Its caul of air breathes a faint violet fog against the black space-horizon.

We rush over barren brown high plateau, waterless and desolate, indented with rugged basins. These old impact craters from earlier times have never been wholly softened by wind erosion. Here the world distends, egg-like, towards its master; here the air is thin.

Ice-fretted, bumpy gatherings of mountains arise, resembling crumpled lace-work or the frosted skeletons of leaves. In reality these mountains are somewhat lower than the high plateau. As the gas giant sets below the horizon behind us, so sinks the land down till eventually we are over cloud-dappled blue ocean. From here the giant world is never seen. Quite a shock for the first mortals of this other hemisphere who first climbed the mountains and saw that in the sky, where it had always been! (If there are mortals . . . Yet there are supposed to be immortals . . .)

Ritchie floats by the airlock in his suit, checking thermostat and gas pistol while I hold his helmet for him. Loops of strong thin wire hang out from his waist. (A noose . . . *Why think of a noose?*)

Fifty metres to port, *Beta* flies upside-down so that both our airlocks face each other across the intervening space.

Down below on the watery backside of the world there spreads

80

a triple ocean, divided by an irregular, inverted 'Y' of archipelagoes. Two of the three sub-oceans, southern and eastern, contain large isolated islands too, though the western ocean we're over now is empty of land. Unfortunately the high-resolution cameras are left behind on *Pilgrim.*

As the south-westerly archipelago comes in view, with the terminator drawing a dark frayed blanket over the waters beyond, Ritchie dons his helmet and ducks into the airlock. As the shoulder of the world cuts off the radiance of 82 Eridani, he jets out gently . . .

Easy as he goes.

Twenty minutes remain till we round the bend of the world into dawn and Ritchie, wearing only a planet suit, is blinded and his thermostat hit by rapid unequal heating. He floats slowly, correcting with puffs of gas.

At last he bumps against *Beta*'s open airlock and secures himself by a short tether to the inside, then leans out to pull the belayed wire nearly, though not quite, taut through the belay clasp there. Ducking inside, he cycles the airlock behind him.

"Excellent, Ritchie," purrs Wu's voice over the radio. "Very good indeed. Smart mouse."

Laughter. "Bravo!" (Not so much for Ritchie's performance as for Wu's? What on earth is she doing, hugging him?)

Shortly, the sun blooms in the east.

Reunited in *Alpha*, we six consider where to land. It *is* crowded. The shuttle smells. But we don't mind. Not now. We can stand it for a day or so, or three.

Our Polaroid cameras have yielded a jigsaw mosaic of the central areas of the world. Many pieces are still missing or blotted with cloud. The mosaic is pasted all over the roof with blobs of jelly-glue. From this, and from our sketches, Wu has produced— with exquisite penmanship—a world-scroll that looks anything but tentative. Wu's craftsmanship is a side of her character that rather surprises us. But I guess it's in keeping with her role as historiographer—keeper of official history, who imposes the ideal grid upon events. Ultimately her world-scroll is an ideal grid too. The planet below only approximates to it.

"So we've got enough fuel for three hours' scouting before

we must set down," calculates Ritchie. "Alternatively, we have enough for fifteen minutes if we want to boost this bird back to orbit. Not much point, though, is there? So we can cover about nineteen hundred klicks. With VTOL capability it doesn't much matter where we set down. Though, like the man said, the rest of your life begins from that moment on." He smiles at Wu, shyly. Over the past three days in this confined space, as he snapped pictures and Wu sketched from them, an accord has been emerging between our young American and the older Chinese woman. It is as though, with him as pilot and her as navigator and charter of this new terrain, she is destined to occupy a similar role in his own future life—the cartographer of that too.

"I'm sorry they named me Ritchie," he apologized once, jokingly. "Makes me sound, well, over-privileged. Rich."

She smiled at that. "Oh, there are always hierarchies of privilege—even in the best People's Democracies. Perhaps even more so." Curious admission . . .

In the emotional equations of our group we four earlier lovers dance a psychic foursome. Wu and Ritchie are thrust, perforce, into a waltz of their own. Wu seems to have made her mind up to dance it with style and subtlety.

"Obviously we should come down somewhere over the ocean hemisphere," René is saying. "The dry side's dead. Even its fringes look very barren. There may be something magnificent and godlike to look at in the sky, but we must seek life. The question is, though, do we opt for the shores of an ocean or for one of the big islands somewhere along the chains? I'd prefer to rule out any isolated islands in mid-ocean, even if they are the size of countries."

"We don't want to get stuck on any damned island," agrees Ritchie.

"Even if it is the size of Sumatra. No, if there's trade, commerce, civilization, it has to be along these island chains. Down here near the equator, where the three chains meet, should be a centre of activity. Also, where the archipelagoes meet the mainland."

Ritchie defers to Wu as higher authority.

"The north is too cold, and where the western chain meets the mainland," she points to her scroll, "this large river flows out—

or the sea flows in. Anyway, the result is a very swampy area. I vote for one of the bigger offshore islands over here in the far east. Not," she smiles, "from any sense of identification. We'll be between two oceans here, with major islands in both of them, and near the main land mass too."

"If only they'd answer a radio signal! It would make life a lot easier. I guess the pyramid was meant to take care of that."

"Maybe God doesn't use radio sets?" teases Zoe. "No more than God is a historian. After all, they did *prophesy* to us. Now we have come through timelessness to a place where radio sets may be as irrelevant as . . ." She leaves her sentence dangling in the air beside her.

"It's a perfectly normal physical world down there," snaps Ritchie. Another few days of this intense closeness, and perhaps our camaraderie might flip into its opposite. We must go down. "Does anyone disagree? With Wu's proposal, I mean."

No one disagrees.

His index finger dabs the scroll. "Right, so I'll take her down here."

Part Three

THE HEMISPHERE OF GETKA

FOURTEEN

OVER ISLANDS IN a peacock sea . . .

One is a cone, thickly carpeted in dark green, with a black shoreline bordered by white surf.

A second: a steep green crescent cupping a lagoon; perhaps a long-dead volcano has slipped sideways underwater.

And now a triple razorback. In one of its deep twin valleys rushes a thin silver river . . .

Small islands. Uninhabited islands. But *alive.*

Where the flocky clouds shadow the ocean, rafts of mauve and violet water drift across the blue: ghost islands.

The pull of this new world's gravity is a welcome ache. How familiar is it? Is it really weaker? My body doesn't know. Not yet. When we step outside: ah, then.

Soon a much larger island smudges the horizon. Clouds blur its inland mountain peaks and drift down across its coastal plain.

Over narrow coppery beaches, tight-pressed by umbrella-fronded tree shapes, we fly inland. Rain whips the windows. Ritchie takes us up above the rain. Now we spy only rifts of forest until hills march out from the central range, bisecting the island seawards. Beyond is clear weather, green rolling forests, broad valleys with faint mist clinging to the slopes.

"Fields!" points René.

Carpeting the very next valley is a checkerboard of jade and bean-green, chartreuse and salmon-pink. A river winds through the patchwork. A road runs through it too. Tiny shapes pause, upon tiny shadows. René swings his binoculars about, trying to catch them.

This river runs into a lake. Milky patches on the water fragment, scattering into the air at the rumble of our approach, flashing electric blue. A thousand wings. At the far end of the lake stands a small white pyramid, and a large village of brown buildings with upturned eaves.

"Agrarian-with-temple," exclaims Wu.

"Perhaps."

The road snakes further east. Lanky stilted beasts step along it, tiny from our height, some carrying riders, a few pulling carts. They are a blend of camel and giraffe. As for the riders . . .

"Bipeds? Yes." René stares.

"It sure is pretty," grins Ritchie. "I'd just like to see some mechanised transport."

"The Incas built fine roads and they didn't even have the wheel," says Zoe.

"No, and they didn't transmit thought-images and hyperspatial drives across several light years, either. Can these . . . farmers do that?" Ritchie sounds resentful, yet nostalgic. "We should be attracting some attention."

We chase the road east through valleys and forest. Smaller villages lie scattered along it, fringed by plantations and orchards: regular ranks of brick-red angular trees, others like bubbles of malachite, enveloped by thick forest. The river cuts through the forest, too, broader since it passed through the lake.

"A boat!" Square-rigged, a Chinese junk.

"They still use sails!" cries Ritchie.

"So do we," Wu reminds him. "The wind is free, if fickle."

"Maybe it isn't so fickle here," thinks René. "Small axial tilt, little seasonal change, little real variation in the amount of sunlight. Well, wind patterns and ocean currents must be fairly locked, and more miniature than Earth's, except for coriolis winds—and even there the rotation's only two-fifths the rate of Earth's. All the ocean in the one hemisphere will stabilise winds too."

We spot a small number of junk-like craft plying the river, sporting yellow mat-sails. We pass three small riverside towns—in the course of perhaps a hundred kilometres—with cultivated patches backing into the forest. Several slender windmills turn—and are those fish ponds there, or solar panels?

"It isn't very heavily populated, is it?" If this was Earth . . . No, don't think of Earth!

The third town—the largest—is peculiar. It's a double town,

a mirror town set on both sides of the river, which now flows broad and slow. On one side of the water, behind a pharos-like pyramid, are relatively bustling streets—a spiderweb of intersecting arcs, with smoke hazing up from some large buildings. But on the other side is laid out a purely schematic town: a smaller double of what lies across the water—a maze-like pattern of walls wide open to the sky. No one is there. The ghost town looks clean and fresh, not ruined or abandoned; it's merely empty. Enclosed courts and pathways sparkle in the sunlight, as we circle. At the centre rises a pyramid. There's no room for any other buildings as such—only roads and walls. In the small harbour of this mock town a junk with furled sails floats, vermilion fingers athwart its masts.

"Are those the ruins of a palace?" wonders René. "No . . . it's too well-kept, too tidy for that."

"A graveyard city?" supposes Wu. "A town of tombs, open to Heaven?"

"A holy place of some sort?" Peter makes shapes with his hands. "It's so dense with *shape*—with the shaping spirit itself. Those coiling lanes . . . the sense of geometry laid bare. Whereas across the water the plan is masked by all those buildings. It's like the naked scheme of the town they actually inhabit, isn't it? A ceremonial town-planning matrix. Only they built it rather than drew it? It's an ideal mirror of the hotchpotch reality they live in over there . . ."

"Shall I set us down in it? There's room for a landing beside that pyramid. We can look around."

"No," says Zoe. "Not if it's any kind of ceremonial place. Let's fly on. Let's learn more."

"Okay." Ritchie brings us round again, on course downriver. He sounds tired, though.

Swamps spread inland from the banks. Tall tree-forms with great arching roots march, tangling, through them, girding lesser creeks and bayous, though the main course of the river stays wide and clear. I catch a glimpse (I think) of huts on stilts or rafts, moored among the greatest of the arching roots, but no other major settlements are possible any longer. Presently the river thrusts a long green tongue out into the peacock sea. We fly on.

*   *   *

Another green coastline approaches us. Forested hills and valleys undulate away: a softly ridged green baize cupping emerald lakes in its pockets. Again, mountains of the hinterland smoke with cloud . . .

Inland, ahead, an isolated *cuesta* of rock bulks up—a bald pate amid the forest's rolling locks. The scarp side falls steeply into a large lake fed by several rivers. In that lake is the flat lozenge of an island. And on that island glints another white pyramid and another empty schematic town. On the shore opposite, between two of the feeder rivers, spreads the largest settlement yet, ringed by fields, with its own second pyramid down on the waterfront.

"The same pattern! The empty ideal town across the water, facing the living city."

Wu raises an eyebrow at Peter. "City?"

"Oh, I agree it isn't Paris or Peking, but even so! A few hours ago we were staring down from space wondering if there was even anybody here."

Ritchie clucks his tongue. "It doesn't look like we're going to find any airports, does it, though? We can easily set down on top of that bluff and take a look at them from a safe distance. We could still lift off again if we had to and fly for, oh, another hour or so."

Why should we? "This island, another island! What does it matter? We're *here*—wherever 'here' is. If there are any more advanced centres, we'll hear about them. Or else they'll hear about us. Anyway, why shouldn't this place be advanced? It looks in balance with nature, at peace with itself. They might have a . . . mental technology. Yes, associated with those pyramids! Something strong has to hold those insect things at bay. It isn't just hoes and rakes. And where did our pyramid drive come from? We're looking at the answer, and we aren't seeing it!"

Wu touches Ritchie on the arm. "The dove's right. We shall land here. To be a trifle banal, the journey of a thousand miles—"

"—begins with one step, yeah. Let's hope we don't need to walk a thousand miles to get some answers."

FIFTEEN

Alpha SITS CREAKING faintly on the stone apron. Some dark green bushes with leathery, spade-shaped leaves sprout along the lines of cracks. In rock hollows, where a little stagnant water lies, bloom waxy crimson cups the size of footballs, open globes of fire dotting the stone pools like midday lanterns. City and lake are both hidden from view by a lip of stone. Down the gentler slope of the *cuesta* to the south glossy bushes cascade into the ceiling of a forest where lily-pad leaves dip on a sea of air.

"—about eighty hours of canned air left, before we're breathing local. Honestly, I don't see much point in wearing the suits. If we get ill, we get ill."

"But *we're* importing alien micro-organisms."

"Look, René, I've brought the shuttle down, I've been flying it all this time, I'm tired, I want to take a look at them before they take a look at us. Hell, the air's breathable. Whether we go out in suits or in our underpants isn't going to make a bit of difference by next week. If they catch cold off us, they did invite us here. Invite us? Hell, they ordered us to come."

"Impetuous, but right," judges Wu. "We've been victims long enough. It's high time we took the initiative."

"One thing I sure am taking," adds Ritchie, "is an L-27. And you'll do the same. We've been jumped once already. I don't intend for history to repeat itself."

"History?" I don't understand him. It's all new—entirely new. "Ritchie, I can't go out armed." For an instant I see again—as in the hanger—Jacobik's face superimposed on Ritchie's. It's a devil face—the lust for death. That swollen face haunts me still, even after the terrible deaths of the others. Those, of course, I did not *see*. Only heard. But nor did I witness Jacobik's death!

91

"Okay, three of us will. Shit, we've only got three guns on board."

"Wait," says Peter, pointing out of the window, along the rock.

Two figures stand, watching *Alpha*. Their heads . . . !

Humanoid certainly, with two arms and legs apiece— distinctly tall and skinny. Wearing brief tunics and cloven boots. Their arms and legs are covered in a rich golden down. Angel-monkeys they seem, with that halo of hairs gilding their bodies . . .

But the heads . . . The heads are blanks. Smooth white skulls without any eyes or mouths. Only a hint of contoured features. They are heads by Brancusi or Hans Arp, contoured geometry fused to the flesh and bone below.

"Masks!" I realize. "They're wearing masks. We can't see their faces. Why should they wear masks?"

"Primitives!" whistles Ritchie.

"How do they *see*?"

"Maybe those masks are one-way transparent."

"Sure. High technology masks. So they won't catch cold off their space visitors. Don't be dumb, they just popped out of the bushes."

"I think I can see breathing slits," says René.

Slowly one of them raises thin hands to its head—and lifts off its mask.

The face underneath is long, tapering, prim-mouthed, milk and honey eyed. Its nose is slender, with a single central nostril. All the face, except for the eyes, is covered with the same rich nap of coppery down.

The effect is gentle and intent. Yet the intentness has an intensity about it which belies the apparent softness, the caress- able attractiveness of the being. It makes of its beauty an ache, something unreachable, androgynous. (I can't tell whether the being is male or female, both or neither.) The coppery down, in the sunlight, is an aura. It is something outside itself, protecting it, caressing it so that no other hand can reach it.

"Angels," whispers Zoe. "Before they became the avatars. Before they became fully human to our eyes . . ."

The unmasked alien walks towards *Alpha*, then squats down on the stone some way away and taps the ground with its palms a couple of times. Patiently it waits. Its hand has only three long fingers (and a thumb).

"That takes courage."

"Or knowledge. Experience."

"He's waiting for us," says Zoe.

"*She's* waiting," Peter corrects her.

I'm puzzled. Him or her. "There's something *extra* there. Something additional. I don't know, I can't pin it down . . . Surely our rifles aren't necessary, Ritchie. He can see us. He makes himself vulnerable by sitting down. He understands."

"We need not advertise our weapons," Wu half-agrees. "Let's empty one of the trek-packs and put the three lasers inside it."

"Right," nods Ritchie. "See to it, Zoe, please. Okay, we'll play it this way. I'll over-ride the airlock safety so we can give cover from inside, um, discreetly. Amy, Peter, René: you three are to make the contact. Oh, and Zoe, while you're at it haul out the other three trek-packs. Don't bother redistributing what you dump. We'll be living off the land soon enough in any case."

"Surely two of us should make the contact? Two of them, two of us."

"Amy, a slight psychological advantage will do us no harm at all. This isn't exactly an unsolicited contact."

"With those two it may be."

"They don't look entirely blown over, do they?"

I can hear Ritchie panting shallowly as he fiddles with the safety catches, as though to keep too much air from reaching the bottom of his lungs—as though a reservoir of true Earth air will always remain there and be the real air that he breathes.

The inner hatch cycles, and the outer one too. Steel steps unfold.

And we three go down.

The air smells wet and fruity like spilt cider, sweet, moist, clean and heady.

The squatting alien (no, the *native*—of his own world!) takes in this stout, lardy-limbed person, me (yes, to him I'm surely that), with the horsey double-nostrilled nose and fat-lipped mouth, this odd creature whose only visible hair curls blackly from her scalp. Then the shorter, skinnier, dapple-skinned figure beside me, with his roan freckling and red curls—a mere child perhaps?

93

Or else Peter is the woman of us two, if females tend to be smaller than males. Its eyes pass on to René: dark and portly, with the oddity of a bushy black Nietzschean moustache. Ah, René is the father, sporting display plumage over his mouth—thus Peter is indeed our child. How distinct from his parents, though! Skinny, larval form, he must lose the red spots of child-hood and become pasty, stout and black-maned as he matures . . . (If I was the alien, I might think these thoughts.)

The native's eyes flicker. For Ritchie lurks, half in view: rangy, snub-nosed, blue-eyed, with a cropped blond thatch. How does he fit in? (Or perhaps we all look indistinguishable, after all?)

The native rises: gracious, supple, golden, *tall*. Oh, tall. Two and a half metres. Maybe it's merely the sunlight on his down, but it seems that wings—angelic wings—fold tightly around him, wings which I cannot see but sense nevertheless. Somehow I don't have this same feeling about his masked companion.

And the native speaks to us, for perhaps a whole minute . . .

The sounds of the words have a peremptory quality, brooking no argument, yet in no way are they staccato. They roll like labial surf about to break, or like velvety distant thunder. They repeat themselves reflexively, shifting slightly, reinforcing the un-knowable message. They have a dramatic, mimetic, persuasive tone to them. Could he be intentionally demonstrating language, the act of speech itself, perfectly aware that its literal meaning passes us by? Thus he does not speak too slowly or over-emphatically, as to a child or a foreigner—for this is not a lesson, not yet. He simply encloses us in his universe of dis-course. Only towards the very end is there a rising, hesitant note. Not the hesitation of doubt, but a compelling hesitation: insisting that we seize hold and continue—in any way. That I continue. He looks at me. Perhaps since I seem to be the bodily average of Peter and René, and so the more representative.

Whatever does one say? I point a finger at the sky. (A few small white fluffy clouds hang, hardly moving.)

"We have come from the world of another star. We have come to find God's World."

The words sound absurd, rampant with delusion, a schizo-phrenic's private speech. Try again.

"We have come on a quest, to ask questions."

Just as in High Space, latent puns drift unbidden to the surface, mocking meaning, leaching words into one another. I've uttered twenty words or so, and they're all simply variations on the theme 'we've come', which is self-evident. Faced by the 'Other'— no longer in books and antique photographs—I find that I'm struck dumb, embarrassed by any agony of speechlessness before this strange, thin, downy beauty and conviction. The avatars spoke English, Hebrew, Hindi, whatever the mind heard; but here . . .

I spread my hands. I mumble, "Sorry."

René speaks up, in lilting cadenced French:

"A noir, E blanc, I rouge, U vert, O bleu: voyelles,
Je dirai quelque jour vos naissances latentes:
A, noir corset velu des mouches éclatantes
Qui bombinent autour des puanteurs cruelles,
Golfes d'ombre; E, candeurs des vapeurs et des tentes,
Lances des glaciers fiers, rois blancs, frissons d'ombelles . . ."

A poem. I almost understand it all. It seems as though, suddenly and miraculously, I have understood alien speech through some secret, latent channel! 'A black, E white, I red, U green, O blue: vowels, one day I shall speak of your secret origins. A is a black velvet bodice of sparkling flies that buzz round painful stenches . . .' What does *ombelles* mean?

"It's a sonnet of Rimbaud's," René murmurs. "Why not commence our alien intercourse with some beauty, since we have nothing else to say? We should sing, Amy—*amie*."

The native's little lips purse. It is almost a pout. The expression has no flavour of a smile to me. (But do we threaten it when we flash our teeth? Is a toothy grin merely a snarl, averted and parodied? Is mouth-humour merely defused aggression?) Its eyes seem to smile, instead. They're a thinly-glazed milky white like translucent porcelain, with pale honey irises like human cataracts. The pupils are dark and small. Abruptly these dilate, to black deep-drinking wells—consciously so? Is this its smile? They 'drink' René's recitation, then they shrink again.

The native cocks his head, as if listening to something too far away for us to hear, yet very close to him.

He opens his mouth and taps a slim mauve tongue. *"Saal,"* he remarks. "*Saal.*" His teeth are like a child's milk-teeth.

"We must learn your tongue," nods René. "I just hope we haven't landed in the language equivalent of New Guinea."

Now the native shapes a ball of air with his hands, and separates the two cupped halves. One half he holds out to the three points of the compass (three? the three sub-oceans?). Tapping the ground with his foot, he holds the cup to his lips. "*Getka,*" he says. And, "*Getka-saali.*" The other cup he collapses to a fist and throws away. Over there. "*Menka.*" Sketching a sphere in the air, he rotates cupped hands about the imaginary globe, holding 'Menka' towards it and 'Getka' away from it.

"The two hemispheres? And it would seem this language is spoken all over the inhabited side—the Getka side?"

"A single language, with all these separate islands scattered over a vast area? It isn't very likely," says Peter.

"A lingua franca, then! They must have a world-wide culture. Hemisphere-wide, at any rate."

The native points over the stone ridge in the direction of the city. He steps back to retrieve his head-mask, but he only holds it, does not put it on. He waits.

I call to Ritchie, "Come on out! We're welcome." Yes, the 'Other' has accepted us.

Ritchie, and then two other aliens of seemingly divergent species descend—one tall, black, broad-nosed, frizzed-headed; and the other small, of polished yellow ivory, with eyes slit in tight flesh as though by a knife. We are dominoes, all of different spots. Black, white, red and yellow: there's no way to match us. Perhaps we are a sextet of six interlocking sexes?

Ritchie secures the hatch. Distributing the available trek-packs among us, we set off with the golden natives up along the rock's spine. *Alpha* is left behind like an empty can balanced on the looming rock. When I look back it litters the countryside, even with its lid resealed—a huge disposable dropped into alien wilderness. We have indeed disposed of it now, forever.

SIXTEEN

OH CARAVANSERAI, OH sun-bright waterfront, how shall I ever get to sleep? As the long morning wends ever so slowly nearer noon . . .

Light fills the long high room. It filters from adjacent rooms through papery screens. These trestle beds, with their quilted flock palliasses and their hairy ginger blankets for true dark night, are known here as 'sleep trees' . . .

Is this a memory of arboreal descent, recapitulated in their urban life after so long? Or is it simply the name for the cinnamon-coloured wood from which they carve the trestles? Or is it something else again? The prefix and suffix *get*—as in the name of this hemisphere (*ka* being a half-unit)—seems to refer to changing states; while *men* refers to the hard, the solid, the fixed and permanent—the other hemisphere, Menka, is indeed a dry solid landmass locked to the face of the gas giant. Yet they ask, as a politeness, *'G'hera'vaa-get?'* or *'G'hera'vaa-men?'*: 'Did you climb the sleep tree softly, or hard?'—as though it is an actual journey which we made or did not make. And they ask us, 'Have you fallen asleep?' when we wake up, as though they confuse the waking and sleeping states. (Yes, *fall* asleep: fall out of the sleep tree.) Their tenses of time are still beyond us.

Puzzles chase each other round my tongue as I muse by the window frame, strung to a pitch too high, if I lie down, to do anything but toss and turn. Lucky Zoe is out cold, but René holds himself too rigidly still to be other than mocking sleep at midday. For us there must be morning-day and afternoon-day with a false night of sleep through noon, then a wakeful first-night and a wakeful second-night separated by more sleep. For our first ten Getkan days we have lived a cycle of insomnia, alertness and exhaustion as if at a party that goes on and on—

with all the interesting guests disappearing just when we're about to get to know them properly. In recognition of our alien sleep rhythms, during the last three long nights a night-shift tutor has come on duty, wrapped in a thick cloak, to occupy our hours of waking darkness.

Peter sits hunched by another window frame, staring over the lake at the strange empty island of glinting walls and courts and pyramid.

Tall natives pass along the paved waterfront. One wears a blank head-mask—what *are* those? Momentarily his head melts into the white scarp beyond the lake. A headless trunk strides along until, against canary rigging, the trunk bears the sketch of a head. Another native rides by, perched on the high shoulders of a *rhaniq*—as they call the brindled gangling quadrupeds with their humpbacks and gawky legs, snake necks and sheeplike features. The rhaniq pulls a huge four-wheeled rack-wagon loaded with baskets of blue fish . . .

On the first day they took blood samples from us. Only after analysis were we banqueted with their own food (fish, little birds, bittersweet pastes, sticky dough, flowers in jelly, mild milky wine and berry juices). Behind the simplicity of life style they're good biochemists, we feel—and good engineers too, if they choose. Solar-heated water flows from ceramic taps in the washing area. Waste from the squat-toilets is vibrated away.

Fine sanitary engineers though they are, they have neglected transport and left it medieval. The beast's single wide nostril flares in our direction, studying us by scent. It blares and skitters in the shafts. Its rider glances our way and nudges it with bare knees which, golden-downy themselves, are almost lost in the beast's flanks. Things melt into each other on this world. We haven't yet tamed its contours and colours.

Underneath the window a border of large lobster-red flowers turns, heliotropically, to follow the sun's slow progress up the sky, attracting tiny nervous birds with gossamer wings. The flowers have the cloying smell of fermenting bananas.

There are fat cream lake-birds too, which flash blue as they rise into the air, and large domesticated ground-trotters with garishly spurred scarlet feet, and there are coiled-spring chameleon hawks which hug the ground, imitating turf or stone, till

98

they pounce upwards, catching their prey by surprise by attacking from the wrong direction. Their colours shift so rapidly that it seems as if pockets of scenery are shifting suddenly from place to place . . .

During the endless night, when the largest of the other moons is less than the size of one's thumbnail held at arm's length, the shuttered 'heliotrope' flowers cycle back slowly to await the dawn, providing a botanical clock for those hours of darkness. There are no other clocks or sand-glasses or sundials. Time has halted.

Ritchie has found Sol in the night sky (he thinks). He and Wu are out exploring.

Peter sighs and comes over.

"Tired, love?"

He smiles wearily. *"Vuth, dath . . ."* (You, I . . .) His lips move automatically. "How do you say in Getka-saali, 'When *we* have a baby, he'll be both of us in one person'?"

"How long do these people live, Peter? These huge days and nights might be wearing us down. But maybe in the long run the gradual light gradient and the even quality of light all year long could be calming. Do you remember spring hysteria?"

"The rising of the sap." He grins.

"Spring suicides and depressions. Too much flooding in of light. So much more to see. So much more information brightly forced on you . . . So that, in a sense, a lot of people switched off—yes, *depressed* themselves, to control it. I always loved seasons—and I hated them too. I hated coming in to a bright season even if it seemed like a rebirth—bulbs, birdsong, snails crawling out of the cracks. Maybe these people live much longer here."

"Maybe that's why they've got this static quality about their culture. Carts, sailing ships—"

"And good plumbing, and solar energy, and biochemistry? We don't really know that it's static. We can't see the plan yet."

He gestures in the direction of the island. "Oh, there's the plan! Why build a full-scale model town which isn't even for use, though? One without roofs or proper buildings?"

"Because the ideal isn't inhabitable? Maybe they don't believe in living in an ideal community, even though they know what it is. It would be static—unchangeable. There seems to be a con-

99

stant contrast, doesn't there, between *get* the changeable and *men* the hard, the everlasting? That island's called *Menfaa*: 'hard . . . tree?' I can't see any trees there . . ."

"It's more than just a piece of terra firma in the midst of water. And I think I know what, Amy. It's something I never expected to find, laid out in brick and mortar terms instead of just a concept. Back . . . back home . . . shaman cultures liked to connect everything on earth with some ideal cosmic counterpart, didn't they? A particular mountain had its ideal prototype in the sky. The river Tigris had its 'model'—its transcendent counterpart—in such-and-such a star. These people here go ahead and build the counterpart in full view, opposite the mundane world! *Why?* The whole point of the counterparts system was to link the earthly state with an *invisible* reality that was perfectly concrete, of course, but not *here*. It was always somewhere else, in Heaven."

The day grows brighter still, as we grow wearier.

"Can't we rig some heavy blinds?"

"Do we want to hide ourselves? The message of blinds is . . . Well, at least they have paper screens. They're quite unprivate people, aren't they? It's as if they want light to pass through everything. Yet they hardly bother to light the town at night."

"Haven't you noticed how accommodating their eyes are? Consciously so, not like cats or owls. They can do it voluntarily. They drink in light. And who's ever awake at night, to want street lighting?"

"Yes, they smile with their eyes . . . How on earth do they see through those masks?" He scratches at his red beard. Our men are all fast becoming Victorian explorers. They could surely shave again after the long interlude of non-gravity. But they don't. How would furry aliens interpret an obsession with depilating oneself? The natives do seem intrigued by our men's body hair. They 'drink' it in; and drink in our smooth female chins and cheeks as though stepping up the input to their eyes to search for . . . what? nascent beard on us too? No doubt the difference puzzles them.

"You-and-I," he harks back. "How do they say it? There's a singular, and a plural. Then this third 'number' they insist we

100

learn: *paravuth, paradath. Para*'s 'two', so it should be a dual form, a dyad usage. How on earth can 'I' be in the dual? How can there be two of 'me'? I wish Sachiko was here."

"They don't use it that way, Peter. 'I and another' goes straight into the plural. On the other hand, the fellow with the double name who brought us in—the masked one—he uses *paradath* of himself, and we have to use *paravuth* to him. So is it a title? Is it to do with wearing a mask? What's the connection?"

"Ah, what's the connection between this city and the one over there?"

Here come our brave scoutmaster and the dowager empress.

Lately, Wu and Ritchie have taken to strolling out just before midday 'nightfall' and before genuine nightfall to scout the city. An air of flirtatious conspiracy pervades their walks.

"Past their bedtime!" Peter grins. "I feel like a kid here— having to go to bed while it's still bright day! Maybe if we look at it that way instead of wearing ourselves out—"

Children's Crusade: I remember Wu's acid taunt on board *Pilgrim*. We set out to make history—to *save* it (or at least she did). Now we're the Babes in the Wood. We haven't any history here any more. That's all gone, along with Earth, and I'm *glad* of it. These aliens could have been living here like this for a thousand years or a hundred thousand . . .

"Do you know, I've got a feeling that maybe these people got their history over and done with long long ago . . ."

He cocks an eyebrow. "But they send out interstellar messages. Visions."

"We assume they did."

"Oh, come on, they *know* who we are—and why. They're used to us already. They expected us. I think they just didn't expect us to land here, that's all."

A faint hiss of waxed wood on wood. Wu is drenched in daylight, Ritchie squiring her. I thrust a finger to my lips, nodding towards Zoe who is lucky enough to be asleep while René is still sternly pretending. Ritchie goes to douse his face in the washroom, returning with his blond hair slicked back boyishly, leaving the screen door to the washroom wide open. Even bearded, he's a boy. He pours cups of the cool, sweet, herb-flavoured *lariz* for

101

Wu and himself from a glazed stone jug, sinks on to one of the floor cushions, blinks and yawns.

"We tried to get into the pyramid along there, but they shooed us off. I guess you wouldn't let some guys who can't read the signs tramp round a radio station. Or whatever it is . . . A mosque, maybe? No admittance to unbelievers? Maybe you should try, Peter. We're just rats."

"As soon as we can ask the right questions. It's coming along fast. We're even mumbling it in our sleep."

Wu eyes him oddly. "Are we? Are *we*?"

"Maybe I was just dreaming. I'm sure I dream in pidgin Getka-saali. Dreams seem pretty dense here, even if I do forget them straight away. There's a whole new world to process!"

She ignores his dreams. People always ignore others' dreams.

"There has to be a world government with this common language," she insists. "A world organization. But who does the organizing? And *how*? It seems incredible without rapid transport or radio . . . Who *needs* a world language with such limited communications? So therefore, they aren't limited. We just can't see them."

"They're inside the pyramids," nods Ritchie. "Got to be."

Voices are coming close . . . *"Paravarthu amra—"* ('They go—') Voices speaking in the strange dual, dyadic form of the verb. A faint hiss of runners, a smack of sliding door against its jamb. And the screen door on the other side of the washroom slides back suddenly: *thock.*

A Getkan steps through, naked but for sandals and a bright scarlet g-string, as though there is a line of blood around his hips and a pool of blood upon his loins. He holds a long curving naked sword.

SEVENTEEN

RITCHIE FUMBLES FOR the trekpack containing the L-27s, but checks himself in time.

"*Mensaalriti*," announces the native calmly. A formula greeting: 'may our words be binding/permanent'. In fact the sword isn't naked. It is sheathed in a transparent scabbard, a glassy frond; and the Getkan's hand merely rests on the brass pommel to push it clear of the doorframe. There's a pack on his back, too, held by tawny shoulder straps that blend in colour with his hairs. Perched on this, like a second head, is a helmet-mask. A round shield hangs down.

The native 'drinks' us in for a while, then turns to unhitch the pack and dump it in the other room upon a sleep tree. So shiny is the material of his shield, it is a mirror.

He—yes indeed, he must be a male—has a companion. She calls the same greeting out to us. She, yes, for breasts raise twin hummocks among the golden hairs of her chest. She wears a scarlet g-string too. It looks as though they've both been sliced in half with one swing of a giant blade, so that now they could be lifted apart and their torsos replanted on the other's midriff. Perhaps the effect appeals to them?

René awakens with a shiver; or rather makes up his mind to be awake rather than asleep. Relaxing the phoney stasis of his body, he props himself up on his elbow.

The pair kick off their sandals, discard their g-strings and step back into the washroom naked.

"That's a woman," hisses Ritchie.

"A male too," observes Wu.

We all (save for Zoe, who still sleeps through it) stare with varying degrees of tact and untact—if tact, indeed, is called for; it seems not.

Hot water steams off the tiles. With soft burbling chuckles the pair rub the aromatic liquid soap into foam upon each other, becoming skinnier and darker with the lanking of their down till they look like two outsize stretched rabbits. The down covers even their genitals: the female's cleft inwards, the male's a dark knuckle with a thin pipe of an organ. To them, no doubt, we would seem to have preposterous solitary bushes of hair signalling the presence of our sex!

When it's done, they towel each other briskly and step out into the hot sun. Sitting on the washroom doorstep, they stretch their limbs—which look as though they have already been stretched upon a rack! Gazing towards the island, they let their fur dry off. After a period of contemplating Menfaa they return to their room. As an afterthought, they close the door.

"Swords, indeed!" Ritchie smirks.

"Perhaps they came for a contest of some sort," suggests René. *"Le Sport?"*

"They look more like warriors to me," says Wu.

"This community is hardly militaristic," retorts René.

"Why did they chose a room round here, so close to us?" I wonder. "Curiosity? Best view of the island?"

"Yeah, they sat staring at it," agrees Ritchie. "Just for a pretty view—or is that their destination? Are they aiming to fight something over there? Is that why the island's deserted?"

"Theseus and the Minotaur?" I catch his drift. "We must learn the lingo better! And right now we must sleep. These days, these huge days!" Utterly exhausted, I strip to my briefs and lie down. Wu lies down to sleep naked, Ritchie watching her, then turning over abruptly on to his stomach.

But my sleep is disturbed by voices, and the 'pock' of screen doors in the distance, and a rhaniq blaring somewhere in the inner courtyard. Ritchie is lying with Wu under a hairy blanket. They're whispering. "Such long lines of parallax converge," she says, "to measure the really very narrow angle between us." (A metaphysical conceit *from her*? Is this how she woos a spaceman, speaking to the astrosextant in his soul? But of course I missed the earlier foreplay of words. If there was any; if.) "I have to tell you something, my brave cadet." I listen, embarrassed. It would be more embarrassing to betray that I can hear. René snores, masking any alteration in my breathing, but the light is bright—I'm sure they must see me carefully keeping my eyelids shut. "Did you feel desire for Li too?"

"Um—"

"Tell me the truth."

"Christ, she made my balls ache. But you, my God, I never thought you—"

"Would empty them? We have an old saying, Ritchie: 'Before you beat the dog, be sure to learn its Master's name.' So it is with Li. As usual there is a power struggle in China. History teaches us Chinese the lesson of submission. Actually, history is all myth in China, and politics is a sort of religion. The rehabilitation of Maoism was a faith rekindled—to order. Do you know that I've never been allowed to write the history of the Communist Party? Why not? Because it would have to be rewritten! Our rulers—amongst whom we must number myself—care not a sparrow's fart for history. That old warrior avatar appearing in Tien An Men Square horrified them. The past! How we hate the past. 'The current of history is irresistible.' What a fine cliché! And what does it mean? Nothing at all. There's only the present for us—in case people realize how very much the present recapitulates the past. The real reason that I, as a loyal jailor of the past, was sent on this expedition was to study this trick of annulling the sense of history. Li for her part was sent to discover the physical technique, the control agent. Instead of alien brainwashing, you see, there could be human hands directing the affair? We have to find it, my Ritchie, so that we can *prevent* this from occurring. I'm a cupboard—is that the word?—reactionary. Which is their word, but they do not realize it applies to me. I adore historical truth—which is why I'm so clever at insinuating it, while nominally concealing it, as is my active role."

Is she telling the truth? Or is this all a double bluff, to recruit Ritchie to her side now that Wu has lost her comrade Li? Is she simply buying Ritchie with her body?

"Two against a world, Ritchie. Along with some travelling companions, who sorely need leadership. As in Shih Nai-an's epic of the *Water Margin*. Favourite reading matter, did you know, of the God Mao? Mao, who would be resurrected materialistically if Li and the others had their way. The wrong avatar materialised in Tien An Men Square. But they have their hopes . . ."

Halfway through the long afternoon we all wake properly, to a strange distant music out on the lake. An atonal violin wail, a tetchy drum beat, the low moaning of horns and the strident creak of huge grasshopper legs a-twitch. It is a missing music— an incomplete music. It might become hauntingly beautiful, but only part of it is being played. Therefore it remains tortured and yearning, frustrating on the ear, as if the stone bluff is meant to echo back a counterpoint to fill it up and make it whole. The music pauses and steals away. Yet its silences are not pregnant punctuations. They are mere emptiness, into which subsequent phrases keen and hoot as air into a pocket of void . . .

Empty, too, is the newcomer's room; the door is slid half open. Missing are they, and their helmet-masks and shields, though not their packs—those still lie on the sleep trees.

Dressed again, Wu harkens. The music seems to speak to her, eerily. "The power of emptiness! Sometimes the best painting is three-quarters empty . . . But what does the hollow here imply?" She shivers. "That it all should be empty? Yet can't be?"

Out on the lake rides the red-sailed junk. Still bleary-eyed, and in his shorts, Ritchie steadies binoculars on the windowframe.

"They're out there, standing on the poop, our two warriors. *Yow!*" He shoves the glasses aside. "Damn near blinded me with that shield!"

René takes the glasses from him. He stares more circumspectly. "Everybody is masked—the musicians too. Surely it can't be a sacrifice? Ritual victims aren't likely to be armed."

Ritchie rubs his sore eyes. "Depends what they're up against."

"Perhaps," suggests Peter, "each is the victim of the other? One of them must lose and die?"

That's nonsense. "They were so loving—so caring." (As Wu and Ritchie were so caring in bed, this noon-night?) "Anyway, they left their packs behind."

"Maybe they don't need them any longer, love."

"Should we take a look in those packs?"

"Forget it," Zoe tells Ritchie. "Would you like them to take a

106

peek in yours? Teacher will be coming soon."

Much later, the two warriors return to their room, unsacrificed, unwounded, their bright swords still clean within their sheaths. They glance in at us aloofly, as though human aliens hardly concern them compared with some other strangeness which they have recently encountered, or else must before long grapple with. We aren't so far along the road as they are.

When it's dark I take Peter to my bed. (If Wu can seduce Ritchie at high noon . . .) Zoe follows suit a while later, slipping quietly in with René, though they aren't particularly quiet after that. Yet Wu and Ritchie sleep apart as if intent on camouflaging their newly consummated relationship—as though they fear that their secret pillow talk might be reconstructed by us other lovers from the clues of sighs and pantings, and evidence on one kind of congress lead to the revelation of another, of the political kind. Or else they're simply drained of the tension we still feel.

How we discharge that tension, how we ground it in each other! It's been so long. And why so long? Piety to fallen comrades? That we should amuse ourselves in this way, while . . . (don't think of it)? Or reluctance to admit, by mating, that we are marooned: a microcolony far from home among the lanky golden ones?

This night, I dream not of Peter in my arms but of vile Jacobik wearing an alien helmet mask which hides his face. Yet I recognize him because his mask and his face are actually the same: both a blank—the blank of death. In my dream he hangs by the neck from a long rope inside an empty doorless hollow pyramid. He oscillates towards me and away like a pendulum. He has claws instead of arms: insectoid claws that clutch at me. In my hand I hold an alien sword. I strike at him with it. He rebounds from the blow, swinging closer to me on his next pass, gripping me at last. And I hack at the rope that holds him, *l'homme pendu.* I sheer through it. Yet he does not fall away. He simply hangs and crumples like a dry puffball. Clouds of whining imp-gnats burst from that dried husk which must be many months mummified. I slash at them uselessly with my sword as they fly about me. The waft of its passage through the air pitches them clear of the blade. They thrum in my ears, confusing me, till I'm only the still point of the flashing blade, mechanically switching through the air—an insane reaping machine, an automatic scythe. *Till I am he.* Death the Reaper.

The buzzing becomes words: words stacked upon words, which fly into my ears, into my head (or are there already)—words of the Getka-saali speech . . .

EIGHTEEN

WE HAVE BEEN brought to the waterfront pyramid at last, to meet the Yarrish of Lyndarl: the mayor or headman of 'Three Rivers'. His office complex is inside the pyramid.

The Yarrish lacks one hand. His right wrist is a shorn stump. Yet he gestures as though the hand is still there, as though he not only feels a phantom hand but can actually make use of it. Curiously, I sense that one is indeed there; yet—how can I put it?—not 'here'. I'm reminded of the guide we met on the bald *cuesta* and the wrapping about himself of furled, invisible wings or limbs: a second self—except that I didn't know on which wavelength to look for it.

Did he lose the hand to some sword stroke? Does he who grasps the reins of power lose the power of grasp, lest he over-reach himself?

Sereny, our day tutor, has led us here: into a bronze-wood room with rows of sitting cushions on the floor. Light reflects in from mirror-lined slits in the slanting stone walls. In the chamber already are a dozen Getkans, including the g-string couple who have stayed on at the caravanserai, though spending several days in between over on Menfaa Island. They have behaved rather coolly towards us so far when in residence, as though blaming us for some delay in their schedule—whatever that schedule might be. Or is it simply circumspectly—a matter of weighing us up? I suspect that somehow—to their surprise as much as ours—their destiny is now entwined with ours. At least we know that his name is Samti and hers is Vilo, and that they come from somewhere up the northern archipelago, which accounts for their scanty dress in these hotter climes.

The Yarrish drinks us in. "Now that you can speak, Starborn, we can speak."

109

Yes, we can speak. This has been an immersion course, and a curious, haunting one at that. Like the proverbial iceberg, a lot of it seems to have remained hidden away under the surface of our consciousness. We simply can't be so quick on the uptake! No microphones lurk beneath our sleep trees, to whisper to us. Yet there have been whispers in our dreams. I'm sure we've dreamt in Getka-saali and grown more fluent by this route. The workaday teaching of Sereny and the other tutor is increasingly like a scattering of seed crystals into a solution which becomes ever more saturated, dream by dream. Now we can use the dyad form of 'I' (but what do we use it for?). We can use the partial plural ('one-and-a-half-*we*'), but how can there be half a person? The verbs shift, following subtle rules.

The Yarrish inclines his head. "Powa is my born name, and menHarl will be my death name, Starborn. Though, as I am already a hero it will not be used in this world. You may address me as Yarrish if your business is between cities, or," he pauses, "between worlds." Again he drinks us with his eyes, while that phantom hand which isn't there . . . spreads its fingers wide. "But not for business between this-world and other-world."

A death name? Something ceremonial by which he'll be known after his death? In the history books? On statues? But what records are there? What books? None that we've seen. What statues or what art? There's only architecture, which happens to be essential, and of course that missing-music. But they do not 'die', so they say. Yet they do; they have death names.

And what is 'other-world'? *Askatharli* is the word he uses—literally 'other-half-plane'.

"I'm not, at this moment," he adds, "the Tharliparan." Yes, the 'plane-doubler', the 'world-doubler' . . . "His place is in the *men*-pyramid, when he wears that mask—"

And of course introductions have two sides to them.

"How are you named, then?"

"Amy Dove, Yarrish."

"And the root of the name?"

"Well, Amy means friend. It's a word for love. Dove's a white bird, our symbol of peace."

"Peace lover, then. So that is what you are, what you do?"

"No, not really. I study the types of people on my world—

110

what divides them, what unites them. Customs, behaviour, ceremonies. What . . . masks they wear, for themselves and for others."

"So you're wearers of masks? We saw masks in your ship."

"Shit, they've been on board," Ritchie mutters in English.

The Yarrish gauges the sentiments, if not the words themselves. "We interfered with nothing."

"Those are for breathing, out in space." Ritchie waves a hand grandly aloft.

"But what do you see through them?"

"Whatever there is to see." Ritchie shuffles about on his cushion. "What do you see through yours?"

"Maybe you don't know that living beings are masks, for the *men* in them? Thus Powa is the mask for menHarl. So you wore those masks in Askatharli, Amy Dove . . . and saw what there was to see."

Is Askatharli 'space'? Or, no, hyperspace? I shake my head. What did we see? Phantom spaceships.

"So you study peoples. Have you come to study us?"

"Yes. No. We were . . . bidden here. By shining shapes which became like us. Like . . . our wise-speakers of old, and like our Gods." The word that encompasses 'Gods' rises to my lips spontaneously. It has resonances that I can't yet catch. "They appeared and disappeared again."

Ritchie is in a huff. "We come from the stars," he announces proudly.

"Not from all of them, surely?" The Yarrish is amused. He knows perfectly well what spacesuits are for. He's *teasing* us, to find out how much we know! "We know where you come from."

Wu and Ritchie exchanged quick glances. "How can they? Star maps?"

Again, the private exchange is easily decoded. "Our Tharliparan has been told that you come from the third world of a sun very like our own. Slow light takes twenty-five of our years to come from it. But do you know why you have come? The fact of your arrival proves that you are able to know."

"There's a struggle," I say. What did the avatars warn us of? "A war. A fight."

"There is indeed a struggle—of minor significance as yet. So,

111

peace lover, you came here to fight. Strange paradox!" Trickster native!

"We fought our own selves on the way," admits Zoe glumly.

"Ah yes, one must fight oneself in Askatharli. And you lost? You didn't come from your star in that little ship."

"We lost our main weapons. There was a battle of illusions."

"Then those must have been the wrong weapons."

"They could wipe out a city!" snaps Ritchie. "Just one of them could."

"Does one drain a whole lake to catch a few fish? You cannot carry such weapons through Askatharli with impunity. The Imagining protects us and itself." The Imagining: 'Gods' is one resonance of that word. "It should have been your *askas* that fought." Our 'other-halves'? The meaning of the word arises, of its own accord. This seductive, esoteric language! "Did many die?" he asks me.

"Only our weapons specialist. He was killed in Askatharli." (Yes: High Space does correspond to Askatharli—the other-half plane.)

"Who killed this person?"

Zoe and I both speak at once. "He was found hanged." "He hanged himself."

Why am I sobbing? God, this is shameful. Their eyes may drink us in, but mine do flow. Damn you, Jacobik. Can't you leave me alone? You're dead. We should have dumped your corpse, not frozen it; it rode with us too long. Pull yourself together, Amy. "Then afterwards we were attacked by creatures like the . . . *vindi.*" Earwig things that drift by on gossamer strings, trails of spittle in the early morning. "Much larger. So big. They live out in space, on star-rocks. They captured our mother ship. That's when we lost our friends. Only six of us escaped."

"The Group-ones, yes. We know of them." The Yarrish pouts. "How dare they interfere with ambassadors to us? This is more serious than we thought. You shall speak to our Tharliparan soon. The Paravarthun will be told." And who are they? The hemisphere-wide government with whom the Tharliparan communes from his pyramid across the water? It seems to be a collective noun for all the Tharliparans of the world.

"I had not supposed the problem had become critical. You

were forewarned, but the warning could only be phrased in . . ."
He says a word. It suggests the 'language of vision', 'symbol language', 'religious language'—a mixture of all these, though they don't seem to have religions in our sense according to Zoe. (She's a little more sensitive to that end of the emerging language spectrum.) It is the psychic wavelength on which we received the God's World broadcasts.

"So, six of you escaped. That should be sufficient."

"What for?" asks Wu softly.

"The Tharliparan will show you. Are you bonded to one another?"

"How do you mean?" demands Ritchie hotly.

"Do you love, do you mate?"

"Yes," says Wu quickly, and changes the subject. "How do you know what's out in space? One would never guess it from looking at this town. What you know is rather well hidden, Yarrish."

"Do *you* know? I repeat, what did you see between the stars?" The Yarrish turns to Ritchie, proud astronaut.

"Nothing," he shrugs. "A confusion. A jumble. Disorder of light. Like soup all around us. We came through a different kind of space from ordinary space where you can see the stars."

"You came through Askatharli space, the space from which this world descends. You aren't the first star travellers to arrive this way on Getka. Here is the wellspring of being."

Ritchie sighs. "Sure, you're the centre of the universe . . . Hey, do you really mean that? Other star travellers. Are their ships still here?"

"So that you may fly home in them? You may only return home with our help, humans."

"That's impossible," snaps Wu. "You only have swords and sailing ships."

"You will die, then live. Then you can go home."

"No," shivers Zoe.

"Isn't that what you believe? That you die into another life?" Zoe has no reply, for in most definitions of religion it's perfectly true. "The self is the mask of the *men*, is it not?"

"What did these others look like?" René wants to know.

"Differences of appearances hardly matter. If they were not

113

alike in the quality of aska, the Paravarthun could not have reached them." Paravarthun is more than just a collective noun. It suggests almost a *gestalt* entity beyond the individual, beyond the world, more than the sum of the parts. "You will see them, or some of them. We meet them in our dreams, even in menLyndarl. And more species will come, unless the Group-ones learn from captured humans some way to impede this great work . . . Ah, they might as well try to put out the sun with buckets of water!"

We will meet these other aliens . . . in reality? And the Getkans meet them . . . in their dreams?

"You do resemble us," René presses on, as a good biologist, dismissing the rest as impenetrable rhetoric. "Remarkably so. Except for the body hair." (At which the Yarrish 'drinks', amused.) "And your thinner, taller build, but of course that's caused by the lower gravity. Isn't it rather remarkable?"

"Starborn, the Imagining—the shaping essence—descends through matrices of angel energies to mould life proper to its world. It plays with forms so that life may in turn imagine what the Imagining may be, and so become its Lord. Askatharli space, through which you came, is the space of matrices before the world is born. It is the Imagining. In this Imagining are certain archetypes which govern worlds. Existence cascades down into low space from the wellspring. The same experiment is reborn, re-echoed. You are projections of us into your world, while," he drinks, "we are projections of you. No doubt there are many wellsprings, but here is the closest one. It governs this part of the star field. All Starborns shall learn to govern it in their turn by coming close to it, as you came. And, by governing it, what is real and what is beyond reality is determined. Elsewhere, no doubt, there are other wellsprings for other beings."

Is this a creation myth, or the plain truth? The universe, imagined into being from a higher plane, like a thought in the mind of God-the-Imagining, taking on solid form . . . as the High Space pyramid took on solid form at the promptings of the Paravarthun from afar . . .

The Yarrish jabs his finger—no, his stump!—at Ritchie. "What's your death name, boy?"

"I haven't got a death name. When you're dead, you're dead. Our friends know that by now! (In spades," he adds bitterly in English.)

"They know it—*now*?"

"They knew death. That's what I mean. They experienced it. The end. Finish." His hand slices the air. "That's my one and only name, sir. Ritchie Blue. I'm a space pilot."

"Pilot through low space, but not through Askatharli space. You have broken the roof of the sky together, yet you don't know what you are, nor why you're called here."

"Our world doesn't know where it is, these days, sir. There's been real confusion since the . . . since the askas appeared. The messages weren't all that explicit."

But of course, no, they wouldn't be since they were in the language of vision, or prophecy, sent down the waveguide of God-the-Imagining. The avatars were the askas of the Paravarthun, as interpreted by us.

"Yarrish," says Zoe. "You speak of an Imagining, and we call this thing 'God'. Is God really here, more truly here, more centrally than in our own world?"

"Your name is—?"

"Zoe. It means life. My work is the nature of God: people's beliefs."

"You who seek God do not know what God might be?"

"We've put our Gods behind us," Wu cuts in sharply.

"Just as the Group-ones would deny, destroy and warp—and lock us up in mere matter." The Yarrish shakes himself. "You will meet the Tharliparan soon. He will see your souls." (Our askas!)

"He's the shaman," whispers Peter, as if we haven't already guessed it. "That's what the Tharliparan is. He's the 'plane doubler'. He's in touch with the other plane, from that island over there. It's the double of this city, the celestial ideal that corresponds to here. But he has to be a whole lot more than a primitive shaman if there's a planetary communications network too, and if the whole lot of them can get through to us twenty-one light years away. He's got to be objectively what the old shamans just were in their heads." Peter's thrilled by the prospect. Who wouldn't be? "The Tharliparan hasn't lost contact with the

115

sky, or with some other world. That's how they communicate—
through . . . through . . ."

"Through Heaven," prompts Zoe. "A real objective Heaven?
Whatever can it be?"

"You're the expert," mutters Wu. "Expert on nothing."

"Oh no," retorts Zoe. "Here, it's *something*."

"Two persons who will be a hero are in Lyndarl at this
moment." (Who will be *a* hero? Ah yes, that's the dyad usage.)
The Yarrish nods towards the g-string couple, Samti and Vilo.
"Their death names are menMoth and menVao." Samti and Vilo
stand up and drink us in ceremonially. So now we are formally
introduced at last—by way of their death names . . . whatever
death names might be. "You came down far short of Darshanor,
your proper target. Your need to become heroes is urgent,
because of your lost friends. You may travel with those two."

"What is a hero, Yarrish?" Peter asks.

"A hero doesn't merely dream-shape Askatharli. He can travel
through it in his living flesh. While his aska-beloved dwells there
always." The Yarrish rises suddenly and slips away quickly
through a high, half-open door. Our audience is over.

Our day tutor Sereny turns to us. "Let us walk round Lyndarl
to learn more names." Oh yes. More seed crystals, for our saturated dreams.

So off we go presently to the dye works, the tannery, the
weaving sheds, the fields.

But to no museum, nor library, nor art gallery; there are none
of these. Nor temples nor shrines. No doubt those are all in the
pyramid on Menfaa island.

We do pass a schoolhouse on our way. The children inside are
already taller than Peter. They crowd to the open door to watch
us, but do not crowd out, as though soon enough they will have
a chance to meet us, but not here, not yet.

"What do they learn?" we want to know.

"Concentration," says Sereny. "Shaping, Sculpture."

Which is ridiculous, in a town where there are no sculptures.

"Oh yes. What do they sculpt? What with?" asks Wu.

"They sculpt Askatharli. By night. With their askas. As you
will learn to."

116

"What else do you teach them?"

"How to wear masks. How to look into mirrors."

"You need to teach them how to look in a mirror?" cries Wu.

"They also learn about seeds and sewerage and ordinary things."

We pass a deathhouse too; Sereny calls it that. No name is cut on the lintel. *There's no writing here.* ("We write in Askatharli." Of course.) "Not everyone may bond and become a hero. The world must carry on. Some die here when they're old."

"I thought you didn't 'die'," says Zoe.

"We die, to live."

"What happens to the corpses?" she asks, changing her tack. They certainly have the word, though the sense is something to do with 'harvest' and 'soil for crops'.

"We shave the gold from them, then put them in the fields."

"You keep the body hair? Where? At home, in urns?"

"No. Things are made from it. After the aska rejoins Askatharli, in that state it is an alterer, a leaven."

"What sort of things?"

"Mirrors, masks . . ."

117

NINETEEN

ANVIL CLOUDS TOWER over Lyndarl, expecting the hammer of
the lightning. Hot sticky wind gusts through the town. Sky has
turned purple with massive bruising before the expected blows
are even struck. Samti and Vilo have hurried out on some errand,
leaving all their paraphernalia piled on the sleep trees through in
the other room.

"What sort of damn battle do you send your troops to, two by
two?" Ritchie paces the room. It starts to rain: the first drops
from a bucket that is soon about to empty over Lyndarl. "Hell,
they expect to die. They're looking forward to it." He marches off
through the washroom, into their room. He stares down at the
reflection of his bearded face in one of the shields. "Mirror, mirror
on the bed, what will happen when they've bled?" He brings a
helmet-mask back with him, batting it from hand to hand.

"I might be sticking my finger in someone else's pot of jam . . .
But what the hell! How *do* you see out of these things?" He
licks his lips, teasing himself and us. "They won't be back in this
rain. Get their fur wet."

"Put up your bright swords or the rain will rust 'em," mis-
quotes Zoe. "Put up your blank masks ere the lightning flashes!"

Ritchie raises the helmet-mask above his head. "I crown
myself—"

"Don't." I've a feeling.

Wu nods permission, though. She approves. Mockery is the
grand leveller. In her eyes we are all so vulnerable. The mantle
of responsibility has fallen upon her shoulders—with a few pleats
of it upon Ritchie's, who can be groomed to bear them. A
necessary gesture is this cocking of a snook. To disintoxicate us
of reverence for alien rituals. To mock those who have mocked
Earth's history. To break the conditioning spell.

118

"—a hero of the hemisphere!" He pulls the helmet-mask down. It looks like a tight squeeze.

And a hell storm rages through us all . . .

We're naked in High Space, seeing it directly: intense in incoherence. Hideous bubbling things live in this zone. Worm shapes burrow through the air, ingesting it, squeezing it out. Living balloons of light suck and pump. We're adrift in the bloodstream of some great beast of light. We're squeezed by corpuscles and leucocytes that live and fight, mutate and absorb each other. The world of walls and houses, roof and ground is a mere membrane through which they swim at will. Space isn't empty at all but full of amorphous swarming creatures, entities to which worlds and rocks and suns are transparent . . .

It is the world that is transparent! It's still 'here', but there's a zone beyond the world—another order of reality, beyond reality—that now shows through: another world that is utterly, sickeningly out of focus. *Askatharli—which is equivalent to 'Heaven'? We can't tune in to it.*

If we knew how, we could see through the fabric of the world to the root imagining of it—beyond the world, into pure imagining. But the two modes are nauseatingly intermixed.

Our poor body is skinned alive, peeled like an onion as the winds of light blow through it. Eyelids are cut off with knives; in all directions is a solar blaze. Our nerves agonise and pleasure at the brush of Being. Our head, our helmet are forgotten. Forgotten . . .

In a moment the hell storm abates.

Or the storm of Heaven. Heaven, misunderstood, ungrasped, out of focus, must be Hell . . .

"Christ—!"

"Did you see—?"

"Oh yes!"

Ritchie jerks about on the floor.

René, first to reach him, prises off the helmet-mask. Ritchie's mouth chomps open and shut in spasm, drooling spittle but no blood yet. His eyeballs roll up whitely; he stares up into the roof of his own head.

"*Grand mal*. Pull something soft under his head!"

Zoe thrusts a cushion beneath his head, while René contrives a cloth gag which he forces between his teeth. Ritchie flops about interminably.

Eventually he lies inert, breathing very softly.

Wu peers gingerly inside the fallen mask. There's nothing to be seen. Thunder crashes outside—she almost drops the mask.

"An astronaut with epilepsy? Hardly! The whole crew had a clean bill of health." René shakes his head—as much to dislodge after-images of the vision as in denial.

"What sort of thing is this? I thought it was only . . ." Wu too shakes her head. "It must be a machine of some kind. I wonder if the storm, if the electrical activity . . .?"

"Did it synchronise him with the discharges in the sky? Like a flicker fit? Maybe there are circuits we can't see built into it."

"The hairs of the dead," says Zoe quietly.

What did we see? A sea of creation . . . Askatharli, energy entities . . .

Wu licks her lips, shocked. She's slowed down in her movements as if broken glass lies everywhere invisibly. Stricken, she stares at her imperial protégé, felled on the bronzewood floor. "Poor boy."

"We must tell them. We need their advice."

Wu glares at me for this, as though I'm responsible for her débâcle.

"Amy's right," snaps Zoe. "Your pawn isn't queened yet." So she has noticed too . . .

"A thought machine," wonders René. "If there's resonance—such as I take it that we all experienced—maybe they already know about this mishap? Even though our thoughts are not their thoughts." He kneels by Ritchie again, checking pulse and respiration. "He's deeply unconscious."

Peter slides the screen window further open to allow more air inside, as though this will improve Ritchie's lung performance. The wind has dropped considerably. The rain has stopped too, the storm aborted. Already scudding cloud is breaking up.

Fleetingly a rainbow bridges the lake. A V-wing of bluebirds flies down it towards the bald *cuesta*, hooting *hupoo, hupoo* as they chase their own hue, which now vanishes . . .

René wipes Ritchie's brow and cheeks.

He stoops to peer closer.

"What is it?"

He stares at the palm of his own hand.

"Hairs," he whispers. "Tiny golden hairs. Little filaments, little cilia . . ."

Here on my own palms too . . . A hint, yes—along the life line, along the heart line . . . where there were never any hairs!

"Fur. We're sprouting fur. Like them."

"No," cries René. "One alien species can't possibly infect another one with physical characteristics!" A vain cry.

"Something is infecting us. Something is planting golden cilia in our cells." Something which whispers to us in Getkasaali in our dreams . . . We strip ourselves, in a flurry of clothes as though for an orgy, while Ritchie lies neglected.

Here, there, as yet sparse and patchy, less than a millimetre's growth as yet—a mere fuzz . . .

After drinking in the pilot on his bed Sereny tells us, "Ritchie Blue must go to Menfaa right away. If he wore another's mask he is the body-slave of that other person, though not her bond-beloved, for he hasn't died nor were the two in tune. His aska is lost in Askatharli."

"What *are* these masks?" shouts Wu.

"Later! We did indeed go into your ship, but we wouldn't have played games pushing buttons whose function we did not understand . . ."

(We do not, for the moment, mention the golden fuzz. One thing at a time! Maybe it's only like a rash of spots or catching an alien cold. Maybe.)

Sereny talks rapidly to Vilo.

"Now you will see what the mask of a pre-hero can do, humans. Though not what it is for. Not yet."

Vilo studies Ritchie, then lies down on the next bed in the same position. She slides on her helmet-mask.

"Now he is hers." (Wu's lips are tight with anger at all this.)

As Vilo swings her legs off the low bed and rises, so rises Ritchie, every motion copying hers—though his eyes are still closed and his face is void of expression.

121

Wu starts forward. But the blind pilot pays her no attention. "Do not touch him! This is faster than carrying him there on a litter. Vilo will have to help the Tharliparan unbind him."

"What problems you do set us!" exclaims Samti—not so much resentfully (I don't think) as condescendingly, as one might speak to a wayward child or a chimpanzee that happens to be able to talk. Yes indeed, that's it. Until we're able to manipulate Askatharli in the way they say they can, we're a kind of animal, pre-conscious automata. Once we can—and they know that we can, or we couldn't have heeded their call—we shall be full friends and partners in their enterprise. Until then, they're almost conditioned to resent us—just as they loathe the Group-ones, almost irrationally (though, Lord knows, *we* have reason enough to loathe them!). It comes out in their teasing. Yet at the same time they must lead us onward and upward to their own state. There's something strange in their altruism. But perhaps not. No doubt human development agencies sometimes get impatient with those they assist; and the Getkans are agents of a physical-spiritual development.

Still, I must protest. "Don't treat us like babies, Samti. Like unformed things."

Samti drinks me, but in a more friendly way (I think). "Well, you fought yourselves in Askatharli space, didn't you? Then the person in your group who focused this self-attack—your weapons master—became a focus for attack by one of you *who doesn't know this yet*. The killer was aska-slave to the group as surely as Ritchie Blue is slave to Vilo now. Only when you realize who killed the weapons master will you be truly unbound of that. Those who are bound are not free beings. You're like witless Group-ones."

"How can we know who killed Jacobik?" I cry. Why, why, does he have to bring this up now? "Most of our friends are dead —overrun! It could have been any of them, and they're *gone*."

"They are in you still, as you are in them. What is a person? Do you really know this, Amy Dove? Is Ritchie Blue a person right now? He's an aska-slave because he didn't know that he wasn't yet a person. So he couldn't become more than a person."

"Will you go down to the quayside?" Sereny says to Vilo, using the partial plural.

122

"We're on our way." *Yikahebra*: one-and-a-half-*we* . . . They count in halves because they may have to count half-persons; Ritchie's only half a person now . . .

"We're coming along too," says Peter.

"I certainly am," says Wu. "He's my responsibility. I allowed it."

"You shall all come. The time is right." Sereny reaches out and touches briefly, with his fingertips, the faint down upon Wu's cheek. She flinches.

TWENTY

THE EMPTY 'TOWN' on Menfaa island is simply a set of connexions in implied space. Its courtyards are mere punctuation. No bird could find a roosting ledge in its hollow towers, which are empty shells. The maze-paths between the arcs of walls are cambered and guttered so that not even rainfall should fill them. Yet there's no *horror vacui* about the place. This notional nowhere simply *is*. Ritchie, stepping along with blind eyes, seems like its perfect inhabitant.

A paved bailey surrounds the white pyramid. Window slits pierce the stone facing irregularly, all in the lower part.

Its vestibule is closed off from the interior by a number of screen doors, while a broad cantilevered ramp curves up to the level above.

When Sereny calls out, one of these doors opens and the Tharliparan emerges. He's blank-masked, dressed in a white tunic.

His right hand is missing.

"Yarrish! You're the same person, aren't you?" (Unless they go in for ceremonial amputation!)

The mask non-regards me. "Here, we are the Tharliparan. Is it time?" he asks Sereny. Sereny says yes, but explains about Ritchie.

"Such misfortunes of one's own making!" sighs the Tharliparan. "But at least this proves that it is time. You have become sensitive to Askatharli. Gestation is over. Now the task of the hero can begin."

René stares at his palm as though to read his fortune in the tiny golden hair-leaves, but Wu, determined to clarify the echelons of responsibility, says, "So as Yarrish you run the town council. What exactly do you do as Tharliparan?"

124

"We link with the beyond."

"You get your instructions, through this pyramid, from elsewhere? From a central organization? Located in that place you mentioned as being our proper target: Darshanor?"

"No, no. The Yarrish presides in the town—and the people agree or disagree with him."

"With *you.*"

"The Yarrish is simply my personal self: this single flesh you see. *We*—who are the Tharliparan—are a dual being, a dyad: myself and the aska of my beloved who has gone into Askatharli and is still with me. We bonded as a hero, out at the boundary between Getka and Menka—as you too will bond. It is better that it happens there, for the ordinary world must carry on. One of us returned into this ordinary world. The other, who was killed, thus entered the extraordinary world. Now we link the two realms. To a Yarrish, there must correspond a Tharliparan— just as this world reflects the other world and symbolises it. As Menka is reflected in Getka, so is Menfaa in Lyndarl. We built the walls and paths outside to remind ourselves that there is something which we cannot ordinarily see, yet which is symbolised in what we do see. The city of Lyndarl is the place of signs, not here."

"But Menka is dead," objects René, looking up from the chart on his hand.

"Death is not dead. Beyond death is Askatharli where all our acts have their prototypes. Menka is full. Menka is part of our world—the other side to it—but Menka is also all around us. Think of it, rather, as Askatharli. Because of the physical condition of our world, with one side empty, we tend to teach children, to begin with, by this simple analogy. We embody this analogy on Menfaa island."

"If Askatharli is 'imagination-space'," says Zoe, "the place of the Imagining; and if the Imagining is 'God', so that really we're speaking about what we call 'Heaven', and you are linked to it right now—"

"Any hero is linked to it. This link strengthens everyone's capacity to exist in Askatharli when they sleep, detached from ordinary consciousness of the world."

"Then you have proof of the survival of the . . . aska, the 'soul'."

"Proof? We have experience. My bond-beloved experiences this now; so I do too—*we* do. I am both here, and there—though 'there' is not a place; it is beyond places."

"But how? How?"

"We have the means, because we are so near the wellspring."

"They have a technology of souls," whispers Wu. "A science of some kind. These helmets have something to do with it. They're psychic recorders, transmitters, I don't know what. Maybe they even *create* the soul. What a tool for controlling people: the illusion of survival! It's a theocratic technology—lamaist Tibet run by a scientific priesthood. They want to spread their authority to other species, other star systems. Why should they? Apparently they have the tools to do it, but what do they gain?"

"This is our science of the beyond," says the Tharliparan, as though reading her soul. "My bond-beloved sees your doubts. We make it available so that other worlds may see beyond themselves, into the Imagining. So that the mirror may return the reflection to its origin."

Peter shivers with excitement. (As do I.) "Shut up," he snaps at Wu.

"As to how, we wish this to be explained to you by a hero of an alien race who has become part of this experience. We shall go up."

"What about Ritchie?" clamours Wu.

"We must hunt his aska in its dream. Up above."

My skin prickles as we mount the ramp. There's an electricity—and a kind of surface tension that affects not my body but something else: my very ability to mount the slope.

Now we're through, in a large softly-lit chamber, quite empty apart from a further cantilevered ramp sweeping upwards to the floor above. Its four walls slope inwards, blankly. Light comes from the floor itself: a luminous, glassy expanse divided by thin strips of tiles and surrounded by a perimeter pathway. Each floor panel is large enough for several people to stand on. They look fragile, like sheets of ice, though there's nothing visible through them, only light itself.

"It's like High Space," whispers Peter. "The gloaming. Brighter though."

126

I slide one foot out on to the nearest of them.

"Walk out, Amy Dove," encourages the Tharliparan. "Look down. The light here is the light of Askatharli, the light of the Imagining. Here is the place of the coherent dream, sculpted in Askatharli."

"Don't," warns Wu. I ignore her.

"Now you are in a place where the rules are those of the imagination," comes the Tharliparan's voice. "You are in image-space, here on this level of the pyramid." He pitches his voice to say hidden things to me—to address something in me which responds as the chick in its shell responds to the heat of the hen; as those alien heliotropes outside the caravanserai respond to the sun and its hidden course behind the world to next day's dawn. The language has a life of its own; in the roots of the words nest other, true meanings.

"Images seen in mirrors, Amy Dove, are intermediate realities. These are mirrors of the shared imagination, windows into Askatharli. So the ordinary eye sees nothing in them."

"Windows into . . . Heaven?" exclaims Zoe, somewhere.

"We are sculptors of the dream: the dream more real than the world, though it needs the world to sustain it. You are clad in Askatharli life, since your arrival; this links you to imagination-space."

"Life? You mean these hairs on our skin?"

He grips my wrist—with no fingers! with no hand! With his shorn-off right hand he holds me firm.

At his (at *their*) aska-touch, my vision rotates. Below me, outside, is Menfaa. Immediately the empty lanes become thronged thoroughfares, as the island expands hugely. The roofless walls mutate into palaces. The courts of emptiness are crowded amphitheatres. The dry alleys are sapphire canals afloat with junks and ornate houseboats. The city must hold at least half a million natives.

They ride horned, tusked creatures through the streets. They fly on garuda birds through the sky. They picnic, they trade, they copulate, they dance. They spar with swords. In arenas they fight bone-frilled beasts: dragons, basilisks. In the streets they themselves walk as beasts, transmuted into harpies, sirens, fabulous aliens.

127

"This is one dream we inhabit when we climb the sleep-tree," says the voice. "The waking hero sees it through the mask. Move on."

Held in the invisible grasp, I must.

And Menfaa vanishes. In its place is a new Menfaa: a city of devotion, miracle. Translucent pagodas arise. Thin spires with helices of circling steps. Arched, transparent mazes are trod by golden pilgrims. Crystal trees sing out vibrations of fractured light. Bubbles float by, bearing along ancient, grotesque Gods. Images? Or the very Gods alive? Inside the bubbles they cause miracles, they create life and destroy it: elephantine Gods, reptilian Gods, Gods who are swarms of gnats, and crystalline hypershapes, and plasma spheres . . .

Beings of light walk on a plain. They conjure waterfalls from the clouds, they command rivers to flow up into the sky.

Music reaches my ears: a music filling all the spaces in the missing-music that we heard when Samti and Vilo sailed to Menfaa on that blood-sailed junk.

"Move on."

Here is a city of horrors: siege and pillage, rape and fire. The victors set out torture instruments in the streets. These victors are naked, furless Getkans. On their instruments they stretch their golden victims. They flay them and dissect them, till skinned-rabbit bodies quiver on the racks. The unpeeled epidermises, stripped from them like body-gloves, inflate and dance mockingly in the hot air over slow fires. Presently the victors haul down these golden body-gloves and dress in them themselves. Now they become the vanquished inhabitants, labouring over tormented, naked enemies—they seem to have switched roles. The victors slacken the racks and wash the tormented nude bodies with ointment. Upon the flayed flesh golden hairs begin to sprout—a harvest of hairs, till all are golden. The maimed and broken rise from amidst the cruel instruments, restored.

"Do you see this, Peter?" I cry to him, somewhere. Somewhere else.

"This is a cruel dream," whispers the Tharliparan. "Yet it has great meaning."

"Is it *real*?"

"It's an event in the space of the imagination. A sculpted

128

dream by a master, which we can all share if we dare to, when we climb the sleep-tree." The missing hand hauls me back from it. The scene rotates out of my plane of vision. I'm back with the others. The floor mirrors are vacantly luminous, without content.

"Ritchie Blue will stay here in the hall of the dream. We will see where his aska wanders. You will climb up above, to meet the Paravarthun."

"This floor, and your masks, are energized . . . by the hairs of the dead?" puzzles René.

"Of the dead, who do not die."

"And this same substance is growing on us now, as its hosts? You've been waiting for this to happen!"

"Of course. Your friend is in this state because he is growing sensitive to Askatharli. When you first arrived you were naked, birds without feathers. Your blood was empty. Don't you wonder how easily you understand my words now?"

"Oh *yes*," I cry.

"The words speak to you, through the Askatharli life in you."

"A parasite," murmurs René. "It's something—some kind of life form."

Zoe frowns, inspecting the tiny golden hairs on her black skin. "A metaphysical parasite?"

"And the Central Committee waits above," says Wu. "The College of Shamans." Suddenly she's shocked by the realization. "Surely you mean . . . we'll talk to the Paravarthun across a distance? They're not actually *here*?"

"They are all heroes, bonded to a dead beloved. So they will step through Askatharli space from there, to here. You cannot do this until your bond-beloved dies. Go up. Samti, who will be a hero, will lead you. We shall watch Ritchie Blue's dream."

At a sign from the Tharliparan, Vilo steps out on to the blank glassy floor. Ritchie marches in tandem with her.

"I want to watch," says Wu.

"Later. There'll be time."

"Come along," says Samti.

TWENTY-ONE

THE RAMP SHOULD lead up to a smaller chamber.

It doesn't. Instead, up here, a luminous glassy surface stretches away in all directions. 'Our' floor is only one of many. The inside peak of 'our' pyramid is lost in a mist of light, high above, if it's there at all. Insubstantial veils separate each adjacent floor from the next, eventually merging in a fog that is the only boundary.

"We're in *all* the pyramids," murmurs Zoe, awed.

"Each connects with all the others in Askatharli space," says Samti. "A hero can imagine his journey from here to there across the whole world. Wherever you are, each is at the centre of all the others."

From different directions figures approach us, becoming more recognizable as they pierce the veils: a dozen masked Getkans, navigating by reflection in their mirror shields—and a weirder creature, too. Is it one of the grotesque Gods of the dream?

At last they all step through the veil surrounding our floor. Some pull off their masks. Getkan eyes drink us.

The weird creature disposes of a bowl-like mask, and its mirror shield, upon the floor.

It's as squat as a barrel, with two low stout legs. Long slanted purple eyes regard us. A parrot's beak of a mouth is covered by a filter membrane, a see-through surgical mask. It is vaguely humanoid. Vaguely. Massive short arms end in a cluster of long thick finger-tentacles, like a dangling of dark coshes—but these branch again into tinier fingers, and fingers beyond fingers, micromanipulators. The barrel being wears a hide as dark as a rubber tyre; it's clad in a bilious tawny haze of hairs. A tank is strapped to its back; tubes lead in to the nostril slits above its beak. Surely Gods don't need breathing apparatus.

130

"This is a hero from the heavy world, Zerain," says Samti. "Its star circles in our northern sky. It shines bright and blue. He is an ambassador between Zerain and Getka, through Askatharli. His form is appropriate to his world." Samti uses the dyad mode appropriate to a hero who is two persons, one alive, one dead.

From its parrot beak the barrel booms at us in Getkasaali. Maybe the voice would sound mellower, more highly pitched in its own dense native atmosphere.

"Welcome, children of your star. We embrace you, fellow beings of imagination—" I hope you don't. Either you would crush us—or tickle us to death.

"We are asked to address you, since we are an alien, as are you yourselves—and since *our* experience will become yours. At this early stage in your awakening you may still doubt the truth, as the Getkans tell it to you. But it is the truth."

The Zeraini twitches its micromanipulative fingers-beyond-fingers, as though sketching in microscopic detail. A gross, if dwarfish being at first glance, nevertheless hierarchies of touch exist at the end of its stumpy arms.

"In Askatharli space there are centres of generation—jewels within the setting of the Imagining. The law of the veil—by which the world shall see only itself, in the mirror which it is— is partly suspended in these jewel regions. So rich is the Imagining here, so bright the faces of the jewel, that worldly existence can be dual: both of the world, yet beyond it. So rich is it, that entities with no personal being of their own, which are inter-mediate between the Imagining and the world, may project into reality if reality calls them forth."

"Angels," murmurs Zoe.

Its tiny micromanipulators stroke that bilious fur. "This inter-mediate life possesses a tropism towards actual life, just as actual life possesses a tropism towards the Beyond—which breathes life forth, so that the Beyond may know itself. Within the rays of the jewel this intermediate life can co-exist with individual life and let that life subsist, fully aware, in Askatharli space. It is all around you on this world. A tiny part of it exists physically—a mere hair. The rest is a thing of the imagination, which dreams the physical part."

"This is a life form of . . . the imagination, and it grows out

131

into the real world?" asks René, bemused. "It puts down actual roots, in us?"

"A life form? Not exactly. Its only 'life' is ours. Its only form is the form that we provide. Yet it vibrates in tune with Askatharli, its origin—and with us. When we die, it links our aska to the living bond-beloved. It lets that bond-beloved move physically, *via* Askatharli, even from world to world. Soon, when you sleep, you will join the sculpted dreams of what this world Getka symbolises. Later you will link with your home world, through death, and step through as we step through from Getka to Zerain. Then your world will sculpt its own dreams in Askatharli. We shall visit them; you shall visit ours."

"Why didn't they warn us that we'd become hosts for this Askatharli life stuff?" cries Wu angrily.

"Could you have left this world?" asks one of the Getkans gently, stepping forward. "The vile Group-ones stole your ship."

"You would have been afraid," remarks another. "Now, of course, the way back isn't by ship at all, you see."

"True," booms the squat Zeraini. "Do not fear it."

"How was our world contacted?" Wu demands.

"By a dreaming of the dead—askas bonded to askas in a higher synthesis," says one of the Paravarthun. "We, who are still part-alive, do not see on to that plane yet. You were the receivers of that dream, inserted into your mind space, sensed from afar and given substance by your own imaginings. Now that you have come here physically—led through Askatharli space—you too can die and, guided by your own dead back to your world, open the doorway through which the Askatharli life itself will flow."

"We get home, but only if we bring this golden life form with us, to infect everyone!" (Isn't this what the Chinese on our expedition were searching for: a psychic tool of power?)

"It bestows conscious mastery of the Beyond," says a Paravarthun.

The Zeraini barrel retracts its micromanipulators inside their cosh-grooves, and folds the coshes into a burly paw. "You had to be able to build ships in low space, to come here," it observes. "Soon you won't need such toys any more."

"Is that the crime of the 'vile' Group-ones, then: technology?"

"Those are a single entity, with a machine for their lord. This blinds them to the beauty of the dream worlds. They cannot enter them."

"Where do they come from?" asks René.

"They are from another star system, far from any wellspring. They arise on the periphery of the waves of life. They are an aberration. To them the universe is simply a machine, and since the universe is only the symbol for what lies beyond it they will try to make this mechanical madness the reality of the universe. They cannot penetrate the inner richness of the jewel, yet they haunt this system now with their machines and slave-units. They move slowly across the star fields—"

"We believe that your lost friends might still be alive," says another of the Paravarthun. "The Group-ones may hope to spy through them, and try to manipulate this zone that they cannot enjoy—try to alter its nature to their will and make the very energies of the archetypes mechanical. Askatharli is fluid, you see. Perhaps the general imagination, if warped by them, can alter and become mechanical."

"Do all the people of your race wear this golden hair by now?" René asks the barrel being.

The Zeraini unsheathes its micromanipulators once again to preen itself. "This is the stuff of Askatharli, the link with the Beyond."

"You don't answer the question, sir." How does one address an exalted ambassador from one star system to another?

The barrel shifts from one stout foot to the other. "How else, since the door was opened and we all became lords of our dreams? The Askatharli matter grows upon life, and when that life has ended in this world the matter still remains—to be made into tools of vision, tools of passage through the Beyond. Come to us, at the boundary of the world, to meet the death demon within yourselves which will take one of you, while you in turn slay it. Then you may open the door, as a hero. You have guides. We wait for you."

"How fast did the Askatharli life pour into your world through this door? How quickly did it affect your race? Did they all accept it?" Is René thinking of the cruel dream, as I am? A symbolic drama of resistance, of attempted quarantine and delousing by hard-line mechanical souls.

The barrel hesitates. "We live in High Time now, not Low Time, and High Time is all one. So there is no answer."

Those who have removed their masks don them again. They begin to move out through the veils. The Zeraini raises its paw. Tiny fingers beckon us, as it stumps away. Peter tries to follow. So do I. But there's resistance. We pop back like corks from the veil.

"There's *nothing*, but you just can't penetrate it!" he breathes, as the Getkans and the Zeraini grow fainter, more remote, out on that field of light till we see them no more.

So when Peter or I die (by what manner of death?) on the fringes of Getka, we shall become as Gods or angels? His 'angel' —or mine—may accomplish miracles, so long as the Askatharli stuff has taken root in us. The old sky-contact restored; the suffocating weight of history and data lifted! Yes, it's my nostalgia, my yearning. Peter's too.

Samti touches me, electrically. "We can't pass through here yet. We're only pre-heroes. All of us."

"How *is* this done? The passage through?" frets Wu.

"You think that the world is real," says Samti quietly. "But though it is solidly present it is only a projection from elsewhere. Creation is renewed and annihilated with every breath of the Imagining. This happens too fast for any ordinary being to notice it. Yet heroes can act upon it. A hero transfers his renewal, step by step, to a different location. You and I, fixed in this world, cannot yet do this. Only when one of our dyad dies and re-enters the general imagination, while remaining bond-lord of the living being, do we achieve it." (Curiously, Zoe is staring at him as though this is something that she already knows . . .)

Wu's hackles rise. She moves threateningly close to me.

"So, my fine proxemicist, these Zeraini have surrendered their history for the sake of revelations? High Time doesn't permit them to think historically! I wonder what history the Getkans had to give up? Peasants still have to plough the fields, I notice— even if they all climb the sleep tree every night for their dose of opium. This superstructure of fairyland still requires a solid base."

134

"That's true enough," nods René. "What *did* happen? And when? Or has this always been evolving along with them, near to this 'jewel'?"

René speaks in English, as did Wu. Getkasaali tenses are all simply inflections of the present tense, at root. They are 'meta-presents' which we simply rethink as past or future. Whatever happens is eternally implicit, and simply becomes explicit. History? No such concept exists—or perhaps there's a term, but it's a pejorative one, suggesting entropy, decay. The ladder, once climbed, is needed no longer and is of no further significance . . .

Wu claps her hands sharply, like a slap in my face.

"We're forgetting Ritchie!"

"We are? *You* are, Wu."

Her look pierces me. "This language is affecting your thoughts, Dove. It's an invention of the Askatharli stuff—its thought channel. Beware."

"My God, it's *Pilgrim*!"

The scene below Ritchie's feet is as grainy and vague as an ancient sepia photograph; however, it's a slowly changing three-dimensional one. There's the control deck, but now a spaghetti tangle of tubes and cables infests it. The bodies of our friends, cocooned, their heads hermetically bottled, sprout from these strange vines. A few insectoids drift among them, mandibles twitching, like ants tending enormous aphids. The view shifts momentarily: the viewport shutters are all open. Outside is that accursed asteroid with its crystalline fixtures jutting from the ragged clinker; *Pilgrim* is tethered fast to it. Other chips of tiny worlds glint here and there. The sun is small and distant. The view drifts quickly back to the prisoners. Two of the insectoids are actually *supporting* a body. It's Gus. Gus Trimble. He's mouthing words inside his bottle-helmet, in a trance. I think he is. But there's no sound. Are they experimenting on him?

"This is a dream of reality," says the Tharliparan to us. "Ritchie Blue imagines your ship, within the greater imagination that sustains reality. His aska has fled to its last secure home, as the baby to the breast. Now he haunts it. As we feared, your friends aren't dead but subjects of the Group-ones."

"They're milking them of knowledge, draining them," I cry.

135

"They're playing Gus like a tape recorder." It's so vile. "Can't we *do* anything?"

"If they come too close to us, we can send dream demons against them. But they have learnt stealth."

"You sent dream things as far as our own world!"

"You could receive them and sustain them. The Group-ones don't receive them; they are blank. The only possible channel would be through yourselves. But you don't know any of this yet; you aren't a hero. You must reach the boundary, and become one. Then you may try to free your friends, if the Group-ones do not find some way to bind you too through the channel of their prisoners. We must unbind Ritchie Blue from this dream, lest he unwittingly provides such a channel."

Vilo brings Ritchie smartly to attention, then unslings her mirror shield. Samti masks himself and holds his shield poised— one mirror reflecting the other, Ritchie's image trapped in each of them. Light vibrates between the two shields. For a moment Ritchie's body is a glowing angel form. Beneath him, the vision of *Pilgrim* dissolves into a reflection of Ritchie himself, inverted in the floor. He wakes. He sags and stumbles, and catches himself. He blinks and stares around, as Vilo and Samti drop their shields; and his reflection vanishes from beneath him, into luminous vacancy.

"What—?"

"Welcome home, my hero of the hemisphere," says Wu sarcastically. (Do I detect a note of genuine relief?) "The pot of jam was sticky, Ritchie. You got stuck."

"I've just been . . . I was—" He stares round frantically as though everyone is his enemy. Abruptly he shakes his head. "I . . . can't remember *anything*. Where is this place?"

"You've had an out of the body experience," explains Zoe sweetly. "You visited *Pilgrim*."

"Shock amnesia," says René. "It might all come back to him."

"As dreams come back?" asks Wu. "Generally they don't. They fade away. Right away."

"Tonight," says the Tharliparan, "when you sleep you will begin to enter the shared dreams of us all in full consciousness. On your visit here you have bathed in the light of Askatharli. Now you are ready."

136

"If you remember your dreams, why can't Ritchie remember?"

"The memory has stayed in Askatharli, in the general imagination."

Yet Askatharli is part of us now. Our Tharliparan sounds slightly puzzled. Does he imply that the golden hairs have somehow *drained off* Ritchie's memory?

"Soon you can leave for the shore and your destination over the sea, Darshanor. Sleep well tonight, humans. Climb the sleep tree. Welcome . . ."

". . . to Heaven," Zoe adds.

Part Four

OH DREAMS, OH DESTINATIONS

TWENTY-TWO

On a great *maidan*, a parade ground before a palace, a contest is in progress—a contest at once mystical and aesthetic, according to Vilo. Getkan dream-sculptors are incarnating angels as habitations. They rear bio-buildings by an act of thought: habitable structures which are quasi-living beings—angels spun out of Askatharli, to be dissolved back into it again later.

Here, then, rises a twin-legged silver tower with eyes that stare lidlessly down on us and a mouth that sings, like wind warbling over a bottle neck. In its belly Getkans feast. In its heart they hang out arrays of tiny tinkling mirrors, machines of light.

Over there, a scarlet behemoth rolls upon living wheels, spewing entities forth from its navel, which is its sex organ. Iridescent moths emerge from it, with eyes upon their wings. Thin music pierces the air as the feelers of these moths vibrate. Flitting around, they settle on the backs of people who rise into the air, transfigured into moth-bodies. These fly up and up towards the dream sun till their wings melt; then the bodies fall back as softly as if the air is water. The crowd cheers. So do we.

Another living building grows up in the shape of an alien barrel being. Its arms reach out and out over the spectators, fingers branching into tinier fingers which rebranch and branch again till the air is full of the dividing gossamer which they are . . . Presently it all melts away.

"Where's Wu?" asks René abruptly, tearing his gaze from the spectacle.

She isn't here. The rest of us all are. Though Zoe seems rather lackadaisical, a bit vague. And Ritchie acts as if he is stunned by it all.

"Be patient," says Samti. "She must still be awake, in the

141

ordinary world. But you're linked. She will come. As will Zoe Denby and Ritchie Blue."

"Zoe's here! She's standing right beside you. So's Ritchie. Can't you see?"

Samti drinks in Zoe and Ritchie. "No, they are only reflections as yet—sustained by the imagination of you who know them well, and cherish their presence. Their askas are still with their bodies. They behave quite normally, fitting your concept of them, but they cannot take the initiative. Wu should also be here in reflection, but perhaps one of you resents her presence? Consequently her image is resisted."

As he stops speaking, Zoe shivers and blinks. She stares around her, suddenly much more alert.

"Well," she whistles. "Well. So this is Heaven. One corner of an alien Heaven. Hot damn!" She laughs. "Wrong phrase, I guess! It's the mind space of an alien Heaven—and Heaven's what you make of it. This city's *crowded*, Samti! It looks vast." It does indeed. The *maidan* is only one corner of a huge exotic city stretching in all directions: ideal Menfaa, with sapphire canals, broad thoroughfares, palaces and amphitheatres, picnics, quarrels, festivals, commerce, play . . . which is itself only one of many parallel Heavens. "How are there so many people?"

"All the dead are dreaming, Zoe Denby, as well as the askas of the living."

At this moment Wu pops into existence before our eyes. We bring her up to date. Only Ritchie is still a dullard, tagging along with us.

Archways range around the crowded *maidan.* Other dreamscapes are visible through them. Through this one is a paradise garden, a perfect lotus land where giant drugged flowers bloom beside a leaf-green ocean. Getkan youngsters caper there. Some die young, at any rate! Or perhaps they are souls who prefer the form of children. Through the next one is that dreadful siege city, the place of flagellation and reclothing in Askatharli-pelt. It's too appalling a dream, even if the pain is all redeemed. If where we are is Heaven, that is a kind of purgatorial drama—though not aimed at purging sin.

At last Ritchie comes 'on line', while we're spying into it. Now he's with us, fully aware. He flees from the sight of the siege city,

142

and Wu runs after him to reassure him. We're all happy to follow him away from that particular threshold.

"Why walk?" asks Vilo. "Let's ride in style. What do you ride on in your home world?"

"Horses," smiles René. "But—"

"Just fix your mind on whatever a horse is. Visualize it. Command it to exist. It will only be an imaginary horse—a reflection, just as Zoe Denby and Ritchie Blue were before they came through—but it'll carry you. It'll behave just like a—"

"Like a horse."

"Samti and I will ride rhaniqs, till we know a bit more about horses."

We concentrate. And we do conjure horses. Here they are waiting for us, champing at the bit, saddled, bridled and caparisoned. Fine steeds. Zoe claps her hands in glee. Passers-by applaud them as an amusing curiosity.

There are only four horses as yet. Ritchie is clutching at Wu's arm agitatedly; they're whispering together.

Wu shakes her head, nodding in the direction of Samti and Vilo. The rest of us all mount, and wait.

Zoe's still laughing. "I've never ridden a horse before. It's so *easy.*"

"Me neither," chuckles Peter. "I suppose if you can imagine a horse, you can imagine riding it into the bargain. Just don't let's invent falling off, or saddle sores!"

"One moment," says Wu casually in English, as though she's having difficulty imagining a horse. "Behave quite normally, and listen. We're all in danger. Ritchie wasn't running away. He remembers what happened during his out of the body experience. He learnt something. We must get away on our own and discuss it."

"You'd better believe it," says Ritchie quickly. "This is big. And it's real scarey. Exploring Heaven can wait—till you know what's running the show."

Wu starts making excuses to the two Getkans.

"We can walk, if you prefer to," offers Vilo.

Excuses drag on. Eventually Samti says something rapidly to Vilo—irritated at us, I shouldn't wonder—and the two Getkans kick their rhaniqs in the ribs, and ride away out of the *maidan.*

143

"We've disappointed them," frowns Zoe. "This had better be good."

"Zoe, there's nothing good about it."

"We must find somewhere private," says Wu. "These horses attract too much attention."

"Hell, we do too," nods Ritchie.

So we abandon our steeds reluctantly, and set out on foot. Ritchie won't say anything yet. He seems almost paranoid about being overheard—not that any of the Getkans could understand our English. When I look back, the horses are still being 'maintained' by a group of Getkans who seem to have decided to race them against rhaniqs.

We walk down another avenue out of the *maidan*. Presently we find a water garden opening off it. It's a place of leaping fountains and a maze of channels, afloat with orange flowers. There are only a few Getkans taking their ease in the garden. We enter a covered walkway of waxy purple vines, and we're alone for a while. Alone in Heaven.

Zoe plants her hands on her hips. "Well?"

TWENTY-THREE

"I STARTED REMEMBERING the moment I got here. I couldn't remember any of it back in the ordinary world! The memory got . . . intercepted. It got drained out of me. But it's still here . . . on the Askatharli level. I don't think the Veil Being realizes this."

"The *what*?" We stare at him. Wu, rather smugly so.

"Listen, you guys, I'm going to try something. If we can create things out of our minds—I mean, if we can all imagine horses, and horses pop into existence—"

"Systems of cognita," says Zoe. "Sufficiently complex to be ridden, and neigh, and foam at the mouth."

"Yeah, whatever. Maybe I can show you what happened to me. Maybe I can make a model of it, like a movie."

"You can do it," nods Zoe. "This whole Heaven is imagined. We're in imagination-space. Go ahead."

"I just want something like a holovision movie. Yes, that's how to think of it. And I'm the transmitter." His brow furrows. The area ahead, beneath the purple vines, shimmers. A box of air becomes . . . something else. A metal floor—no, a *deck*. It's the control deck in miniature—a section of it. There are the instrument boards and chairs. Beyond the viewports is the amorphous swirl of High Space. It's a three-dimensional cut-away. Two mannikins are perching on adhesive seats, playing magnetic chequers. Ritchie—and Gus Trimble.

Suddenly, as though Ritchie has lost control of the projection, the control deck is full of bodies in cocoons with their heads in glassy bubbles, their skulls wired up. Tubes and cables tangle about, linking them all.

"But that's what we saw!" cries Zoe.

"Wait."

145

Gus hops a black chequer over two of Ritchie's white ones. Rapidly the two scenes alternate: the bodies, the game of chequers. They fuse into one. Each interpenetrates the other in a kind of double exposure. We hear voices.

"What's going on?" squeaks the Ritchie-doll. "Damn this High Space. I'm hallucinating. I'm seeing bodies all around us. Gus, you're *one* of them! You're sitting here playing chequers with me—but your head's wired up in a bottle too. I'm seeing double." An insectoid drifts out among the bodies, then a second one. The Ritchie-doll flaps his arms frantically. "What the hell are those? Am I going nuts?"

"Please be calm," says the Gus-doll expressionlessly. "We are . . . over-riding Gus Trimble's memory."

"What are you? Something from God's World? Like the avatars?" Ritchie's hands flail at the approaching insectoid, but it merely passes through them. It passes right through his body. "I've been in some hairy corners, Gus, but this is getting to me!"

"Please. We did not expect this contact. You are one of the humans who escaped when our insectoid helpers took control of your ship. Gus Trimble recognizes you."

"These filthy insects took *Pilgrim*! Yes, of course! I remember now. We got away to Getka. I put on one of those helmet-masks. I must still have it on my head!"

"So you are using one of their instruments of vision? Which is how you are intruding into this memory space. Did the Getkans make you put it on?"

"No, I did it for a damn fool joke. They don't know."

"We may be safe, then. We must use this contact, Ritchie."

"How come I'm playing chequers here? This is all way back in time. Haven't you insects taken over yet? Am I seeing into the future? No, I can't be—not if I'm on Getka!"

"You are in memory-space, Ritchie. This is where your friends are quarantined. We were forced to act rapidly, to capture and 'suspend' them—cut them off from input. You were already linked to your destination, and too close to it—you vulnerable soul-beings. We are exploring certain key areas of their psyches, within memory-space—areas relating to the individual and the group, and to your knowledge of your 'souls' which link you

146

with what lies beyond reality, and make you vulnerable. We are attempting contact, and illumination, cautiously in their memory-space. Trust us! Much hangs on this. Evidently you are now experiencing both memory-space, here where we meet, and the actual present scene—though we cannot detect you there. We only detect you in the memory-space of Gus Trimble. Were you a good friend of his?"

"We got on. He's an ordinary guy, like me. Hey, if you aren't the enemy, who is? Don't tell me it's the Getkans. They're friendly folk. They're just, well, explorers of some higher sort of existence. At least they say so."

"They are victims, Ritchie. Unwitting victims of an energy life-form which is outside of ordinary reality, yet which enters and manipulates ordinary reality through them. Let us borrow a term from the memory-space of your shipmate Salman, whom we are scanning: the 'veil'. There is a Veil Being. It is a quasi-life form which balances on the interface—exists on the standing wave—between reality and the creative force that is beyond reality. It is part of the 'energy circuit' between what you term 'God', and the created universe—in our terms, between the descent of Being into the world and its reprocessing back through death, which is the psychic counterpart of the continual fluxing in and out of existence of the entire material cosmos. This part of the 'energy-psyche circuit' that we call the Veil Being has achieved an independent, yet parasitical rebel existence. In Salman's terms this is a . . . Satan."

The Ritchie-doll licks his lips. "You mean to tell me that God's World is really . . . Satan's World?"

"Emotively this is true, though the phrase itself is mainly noise as regards its information content. The Veil Being can only sustain and continue its existence by being made up of all the 'souls' that it draws into itself and holds in itself. Its existence is a gestalt of these, and as such its component parts—which are individual souls—cannot envision it. They, and the living Getkans they are 'glued' to, are granted paranormal powers and quasi-immortality, but they are really controlled and hoodwinked by the corporate Veil Being so that they cannot understand how it is against the proper order of things—against the reprocessing of lives back into Being, through death. It is a blockage, a tumour,

147

in the flux between Being and existence, between what you term 'God', and the world. Since reality is the dream of 'God'—since the universe is imagined into existence from beyond—this blockage must bring about a degradation and ultimate collapse of reality.

"The physical threat would sum up as the eventual disappearance of areas of space and matter themselves, if the Veil Being carried on its predations for very long—which might nudge askew the finely balanced physical constants which permit the existence of this universe as one where life can arise. For the Veil Being is not a stable system, but one which is balanced on the standing wave. The more souls it sucks into itself to keep it poised upon that wave, the more it needs. The degradation of reality is still recuperable; it only manifests itself so far as a regression of the civilization of the Getkans and other victims— a halting and disappearance of history, the ongoing social process."

"So Satan would undo God's work? Drag it into a kind of black hole? Surely Satan—I mean the Veil Being—would dissolve in the process?"

"Exactly. Which is why it must extend itself to other worlds through High Space—for its own survival! But if it continues to spread—to tens, then hundreds of worlds—eventually it surely must unbalance. By that time the regression of reality will have gone too far. If it implodes then, the breakdown of reality will spread outwards through the whole physical universe."

"So either Satan carries on eating dead souls, by then, or reality goes bust? Wow, Salman may be up on this, but I'm not. How did you insects get involved?"

"The insects are simply our allies—our helping hands. We are machine intelligences. As such we are 'soulless'. We can only probe and perhaps defeat the Veil Being by using soul-beings who are vulnerable to its seductions. Hence the necessary capture of your friends, for their own sake and for the sake of existence."

"So the insects manufactured you? Don't they have souls, either? They must be immune too."

"Originally we were a world data network and control system created by a race called the Harxine. They built us to maintain, oversee and balance the life-systems and ecology of their world.

They were lizard-like. Homeostasis is more of a problem for lizards than for mammals, who are warm-blooded; hence, perhaps, the urge to build us. Now the Harxine are extinct."

"You couldn't have looked after them too well!"

"Our sun flared nova. We could do nothing about this. We lost all the atmosphere and the seas. Only we survived. We reconstructed ourselves over the next several millenia, and in so doing we changed. We became the Harxine *Para*computers—more than computers. We turned our attention to the general enigma of life and death. We reached out to other inhabited star systems in our quest—though, unlike the Veil Being which can propagate its influence through High Space, we are limited to Low Space, and thus constrained by the speed of light. The threat of the Veil Being first became apparent some two thousand of your years ago, with the withdrawal of several star cultures we were observing into an inaccessible and hostile psychic zone, together with a halt and regression in their civilizations. From a world on the brink of this calamity we learnt of what you call the 'God's World broadcasts'—projections of archetypal imagery that penetrates the roots of a culture's beliefs. But what to do? An expedition of silicon-based soul-beings in league with us backfired upon its home world, which was drawn in to the Veil Being's 'event horizon'. We have been picketing this solar system for many years, sending tiny expendable spy drones down to Getka, waiting for a new chance—for new 'mind tools' to be lured here. We must apologize to you, but we had to act swiftly without consultation with you."

"You could have tried warning other worlds!"

"So many worlds, so much space—we are limited by the speed of light, as we told you. All worlds already in touch with us were warned."

"I guess it was kind of unfortunate we six got away, from your point of view?"

"Most unfortunate, for yourselves and for your planet. Nevertheless, we seem to have a link with you escapees now, in mindspace—if only the Veil Being does not veil this from you. A valuable, yet dangerous link."

"Can't you bail us out? Can't you land and rescue us?"

"Any such landing would be a suicide mission. Once any

149

Getkan who is linked to the Veil Being sees our agents they can summon up . . . forces and energies in form of quasi-beings to fight for them. If we *did* bring you back here safely, we might ourselves be lost because you would be creatures of the Veil Being."

"But if the six of us down there do become what they call 'heroes', won't we be hyped up to attack you through this link with Gus and the others?"

"Precisely. This puts your friends, sadly, in danger of their lives. We may be forced to . . . neutralise them. Alternatively, we must expend some of our allies on a suicide strike to neutralise *you*, unless you can learn to break the bonds of the Veil Being. If we can find you."

"You mean, *kill* the six of us?"

"If our allies can achieve it. To our great sorrow. At least it will save your world."

"Yeah. Killing apart, these insects are really our buddies?" The Ritchie-doll sounds only faintly ironic. He was, after all, a military pilot once. He understands pre-emptive strikes.

"The term is inexact. They are our agents, controlled by us with the permission of their home-hive intelligence—"

So this is what Gus's lips were mumbling when we watched Ritchie's 'dream of the real' inside the pyramid: the words of a superintelligent machine. But we saw only one side of this weird double-exposure. There was another side to it—a strange dimension of the psyche that our friends are all trapped in, *for their own sake*.

Don't the Getkans know why the Group-ones and their 'machine lords' are here? How *can* the Getkans possibly know this, and still remain so implacably opposed to them? The answer is that they aren't *allowed* to know.

If this Veil Being does exist, then we are within it already, here and now! This Heaven is its body.

How can we turn our backs on Heaven? Who would want to? I can't bear the threat of it being snatched away from me.

But Satan's World . . . a black hole sucking at the roots of reality, sucking in souls to feed itself! While those computers are balancing the odds of . . . killing our friends, or sending a strike force against us, for our own sake! Maybe this is all quite literally in Ritchie's imagination! Maybe none of it's true.

The Gus-doll makes a steeple with his fingers. "The Group-ones are severely limited beings—automata in small numbers, who only achieve real sentience in large collective groups. This is why they are ideal to assist us here. They are immune. Our current agents have been adapted for life in space by their home-hive—which has bred many other types for a whole range of ecological niches. These Group-ones are vacuum-adapted, but they can certainly tolerate a landing on the surface of Getka!"

"Look," hisses Wu.

Beyond the scene that Ritchie has conjured appears a shin-ing . . . vacancy. It's a bright hollow, a kind of whirlpool. It wanders slowly down the walkway towards us: a sort of mobile nothingness, yet curiously positive, intent on . . . what we're being shown by the mind-dolls. A rope of purple vine dangling from the pergola touches it, vanishes, then exists again as though the hollow has tested it, judged it innocuous, and reinstated it.

The hollow touches Ritchie's projection.

We've woken early. It isn't even midnight 'morning' yet. Some-thing woke all six of us—though our two Getkan friends sleep on, through in the other room. A noise in the night? We strain our ears, but it's all completely quiet.

In whispers, like children in a dormitory, we speak of our trip through Heaven: of the great *maidan*, the dream sculptures of quasi-living beings, the horses we conjured up.

"Maybe we all fell off!" laughs Ritchie.

Surely there was something else. What it was, I've no idea. Nor he. Nor any of us.

Never mind. Soon we'll dream again. Soon we'll be back in Heaven.

TWENTY-FOUR

MOUNTING A RHANIQ is easier for Getkans with their long legs than for us, even though the gawky beasts kneel down, folding their double-jointed stilts of legs forward like flamingoes.

We are hoisted judderingly aloft, higher than the top of any camel's hump. The reins describe an arc higher still to the rhaniq's sheeplike mouth. They tap the skinny neck like tack-lines against a flexible flagpole. A rhaniq's back easily supports two riders, one behind the other upon a double saddle.

So we ride out of Lyndarl through the umbrella-leafed boskage southwards towards the sea on four rhaniqs.

It's a hot cloudless day. Rhaniqs are docile enough to ride, once they know your smell, though inclined to be a little skittish. The impacted fat of their backs acts as a rubbery shock absorber.

The road is wide, paved with ancient weathered flagstones which must once have made up a perfectly smooth surface. Weather action and invading roots have cracked and tilted them, though overgrowth is shrivelled back as though it has been sprayed recently. It seems that more traffic goes by river.

"Symbiosis," muses René, riding pillion to Zoe. He holds up his palm to the sun, staring at the golden hairs. "I wish I had an electron microscope! So these little filaments form a symbiosis between the realm of existence and the realm of essence? It's still hard to accept."

"Which is why it had to happen to us, before we would understand," I suggest.

He brushes his moustache. "So much for Chance and Necessity! Yet I wonder, what is the necessity of this golden stuff? What does it get out of the relationship?"

"How many angels can dance on the end of a hair?" grins

152

Peter, glancing back at me. He perches like a child on our forward saddle, between my knees.

"A selective tropism towards highly evolved life. But why not towards all life?" René seems to challenge me.

"Because *our* imaginations are closest to Askatharli, René— and Askatharli is imagination-space. Rhaniqs and birds and fish only 'pray' by being at one with nature. But we pray through our desire for a higher plane. Birds and beasts can't do that. They can only be themselves. We can be something else. Our lives yearn for the Other. Well, here it is on God's World."

"Yet they don't have a religion," says Zoe. Her black skin is fuzzy and tawny today.

"Because this leakage from the beyond is physically present as a fact of life."

"Hmm. The mystics of Islam—who were some keen thinkers! —denied that people could have any direct knowledge of God or the beyond. Neither the individual nor the world could exist if that happened. The world would disappear."

"Which is the reason for the bond-beloved system, Zoe. The aska of the dead person is linked to the living mind. And it happens through this symbiosis—which has no real existence outside its symbiotic role. It yields a conscious entry point. Your mystics had no such physical reality to contend with. It seemed impossible that people could enter that kind of mind-space and still be ordinary living mortals."

"My mystics said that Creation is safeguarded by a seal."

"Actuality supersedes theory, Zoe dear. You said that God couldn't be defined. So how do you know what is impossible? There can be a world of revelation too. There is. We're in it."

René shakes his head. But nothing will free him now; nor us. We who drink the milk of knowledge cannot vomit it back into the cup. Why should we want to?

"It shouldn't become tangible or concrete in this world," pursues Zoe. "Yet it seems that it does . . . I guess you could call this 'angel-hair'! Angels, you know, have no individual existence according to 'my' mystics. They aren't variants within a species. They have no numbers, no distinctions . . ."

"So each of us becomes an angel. Every Getkan is his or her own angel."

153

"This road's very old," says Wu loudly. "How old? A thousand years? Five thousand?"

"Getka *has* no history, Wu." Can't she understand? "It only has parahistory: worlds sculpted out of possibility, in imagination space. That's where their history is acted out."

This world is paradise—far from mechanistic, data-ridden, overcrowded Earth. I begin to sing, as we ride down this timeless stone road, inventing a French *chanson* as we go along.

"Sur le monde de Dieu
Huit amants et leurs anges d'or . . ."

We could be medieval knights and dames riding towards the Holy Grail. Only, no knight or lady ever rode a giant skinny cross between a camel and a giraffe, armed with laser rifles, knowing that the grail was theirs already. René laughs. This image may become our collective dream, come midday sleep. We're getting more proficient at the shared dream, though there are still mysterious empty lapses, at least for me . . .

Wu barges her rhaniq into ours rather rudely.

"Ancient highway, and not many travellers," she says sharply. "No wonder their population is small—so many of them are *dead*. It's quite surprising there's any population left! Of course there has to be some population base to sustain the golden life. If I had tweezers, could I tear this out, hair by hair? If we'd worn the planet suits would it still have infested us?"

René frowns. "It isn't airborne or waterborne. It simply emerges into existence where there's higher imagination. So they say."

"So they become missionaries," puzzles Zoe.

Wu regards the old worn empty road. "Perhaps the burden of angelhood becomes too much for them? So they share it around. Or are they forced to do this, from outside—without knowing that something forces them?"

82 Eridani climbs the sky, insulting our increasing sleepiness, burning our tired eyes like a spotlight of interrogation. Of course we only need to call a halt, and lie down to sleep, to be wrapt in the radiance of that other plane—beyond and within and *beneath* that alien sun up there.

As we do presently.

Unloading and hobbling the rhaniqs, we camp in the forest,

154

Samti and Vilo put up with our midday sleep routine even though it will slow the journey down. So will their own all-night-long slumber slow down ours . . .

TWENTY-FIVE

THE WORLD IS locked in Winter. Young larch and pine, cedar and silver birch bow low. They are frozen rigid and heaped with bales of snow. Yet the sun shines brightly and the forest crackles with light as our Volga drives the score of kilometres from one zone of the Science City to the next.

A bus rocks past in the other direction. The driver's window is electrically heated; however, the rest of the bus is a long box of frosted breath. At precise intervals finger-thawed peepholes show, as though the side of the bus has been neatly raked by bullets.

"But the Committee, Grigory Arkadievitch!" nags Ludmila Boltz, a hearty wench new to our Paraphysical Research Unit.

"Yes indeed, the Committee." I nod, only half listening. Soon it will thaw. Before long there will be mauve and yellow cowslips in these woods. Goat bells will tinkle. Mosquitoes will whine in our ears as Summer wears hotly on: *zizz-zizz* . . . Can't you already hear their irritating hum? It is one note hidden in the thrum of our car engine.

No doubt it is the mark of a people who are still in many respects psychologically primitive that spontaneous committees should emerge on all possible occasions, to solve problems by collective instinct. We Russians proceed on the unvoiced principle that true solutions must already exist (platonically, as it were), and only need to be brought into being by group intuition. Yet isn't this precisely how we at the laboratory will evolve the methodology needed to harness the human mind? Whereas the American parapsychology laboratories tend to be rational, objective machines, like their magnificent computers which process the data. Here, the quasi-mystical intuition of a truth just waiting to be grasped makes that truth extremely hard to quantify; while

156

there in America the problem seems to be the opposite one— their rational marshalling of the facts drives the evasive truth into hiding. It's the old problem of the wood and the trees! We Russians see the wood, they see the trees.

And just how is this combinatory vision of ours possible? Simply because we have always believed in an *a priori* overlaw: whether it is Winter, or the endless forest, or the Czar, or even the Party. There has always been some higher authority, whether human or elemental. Whereas the Western democracies are constantly on the brink of individualist dissolution. Those are centrifugal cultures which will tear themselves apart sooner or later. Hence our strength—and our weakness. It's as Grandmother said: 'Magpies in a flock are stronger than tigers in single file.'

Our weakness, too. The overlaw presses down as well. One must speak carefully; it's second nature to. A suzerainty prevails, existing eternally like a force of nature.

"Yes, the Committee!" I, Grigory Kamasarin, sigh. (*He* . . . No: *I*!)

At which point a sharp bang sounds, and then another. The crack of a rifle, the smack of a grenade. A plume of snow flies into the air ahead of us. A young tree rears. Our driver brakes, skidding the Volga, then he slams his foot upon the accelerator. Another young larch which has been doubled up all Winter long, pinned to the ground by ice, wrenches upwards percussively, tossing white balls across the road. The larch quivers erect, shaking itself free of snow.

(Winter's end has come too suddenly! It's as though segments of two separate though similar car journeys, taken at different times, have juxtaposed themselves; as though a stylus has jumped across the record from one track to a later track where the same theme happens to repeat itself with only minor orchestral variations . . .)

Clap a gloved hand on the young driver's shoulder. "Don't worry, *tovarich*, it's just the thaw!"

In the driver's mirror, from this angle but no other, appears a tiny apparition. The inside of a submarine? No; stars shine unwaveringly in the jet darkness beyond a long window . . . Is it a morgue? A punishment asylum in the Arctic? Bodies float, wrapped in strait-jackets, their heads imprisoned in glass bottles.

157

Heads in aspic! Wires are fastened to their skulls, tubes and cables to their bodies. How do they float like that? Slowly they turn, and bump one another. Are they in free-fall?

A dog-sized scorpion or crayfish drifts into view, touching them, testing them, as though some edible monstrosity has crawled off the plate to paralyse, then feast off the diners . . . Its ministrations knock them about, though they tend to settle back on to the deck. (What deck?)

It's a thought-scene . . . The simple-minded peasant girl we have at the laboratory sees thought-scenes form and dissolve before her eyes as though a miniature TV screen appears in mid-air. They show scenes far away or long ago, or else iconic images of her emotions and her moods. An erratic, uncontrollable talent is hers: the intrusion into visible reality of her symbolic thought processes, so real to her that they become cognita in the outside world . . . Though really they belong somewhere in her visual cortex.

Am I picking up the trick from her? Is this some parody vision of the Soviet committee mentality? Some dream-language image of the suzerainty of an all-powerful transconscious force that knits people together without their being able to do a thing about it? *What is it?*

As Ludmila prattles on, and the car swishes through the snow . . .

"*Tovarich*, I can't see behind," the driver complains peevishly, verging on the abusive.

("No, but I can! I can see behind the world!" But the words won't come out. They simply do not belong here in the Volga car in this segment of time . . .)

Another tree explodes, off to the right. As I jerk my head aside the image vanishes from the mirror.

"Why yes, Ludmila Ivanovna—" I settle back in the upholstery; and the conversation runs on, to schedule.

I wake. I haven't dreamt at all. It's a blank.

No—that isn't true! I'll swear I was in someone else's dream . . . but whose? It wasn't a dream of Heaven . . .

It wasn't even a dream, but a *reliving*.

158

Now it's gone. There's only a hollow in me, an emptiness. So disappointing! The golden tendrils aren't long enough yet; I'm not yet properly adjusted . . .

The stars shine down. Stillness, quiet, warmth.

Must sleep. Must dream.

Mulla Kermain has a round, merry moon face cratered by childhood smallpox—whose ravages make his face look even more like the moon's. When he smiles these dimples all pucker, and rills run between them.

Six of us sit here in the Mulla's room: three from the *madraseh*, the theological college; three from the university. Since the Revolution, the two kinds of education have converged. The ideal science graduate is no longer a free-thinking pseudo-Westerner; he is a *Moslem* scientist. Ironically, we have a Westerner in our midst: Mike Farley, the bearded American Negro, ex-engineer, convert to Islam. He supports himself by teaching English to students in the Science Faculty, amongst whom myself, Salman Baqli.

The Mulla's room is a modest one, though the floor is carpeted—turfed, almost—with a richly-knotted scarlet and viridian weave. Crested hoopoes, long-tailed parrots and peacocks merge themselves into curlicues of leaf and petal. Outside, the humped earthen roofs of the bazaar lie like a huge grey sow upon her back, with rows of swollen breasts nippled with air vents upward to the sky. The whole beast, of packed earth, transmutes presently into glazed terracotta and polychrome faience, flowing transfigured into the gold-tiled dome of the mosque. Pigeons coo outside the window, their voices hiding in the murmur of the city as the woven birds hide in the wool upon the floor.

"It's still hard to conceive of oneself as a symbol," remarks Said Bekhtiar, our mathematics student. "The physical world, perhaps, considered as an interaction of energies. Or one's behaviour, even. But one's very *mind*, one's own self?"

"Ah, but it isn't *one's* self, Said. It is God's self. We must carry ourselves back to the principle which we all reflect. The universe is the mirror of God. God looks in it to see Himself *by means of those* who are looking for Him. Our physical eyes can't see this

159

symbolic landscape, though. They only see what they have learnt to see. Only the eye of the imagination perceives that landscape. If we all saw the epiphany—the appearance of God—with our ordinary eyes, this would bring madness and social disorder."

"If the centipede stopped to think about how it walked," grins Mike Farley, "it could never take another step!"

The moon face crinkles, in appreciation. "We see the epiphany through being what we are. God needs a subject that reflects Him, just as we need to be the reflecting subject. Here is a *transconscious* relationship, of which our ego is merely a portion. Which is why the holy Imams speak in the plural when they bear witness to this—to emphasize the existence of a celestial counterpart to Man 'in the second person'.

"I shall tell you a secret, my friends. The Lord may easily be the image of a loved one, correctly understood—just as the Lady Nizam was to Ibn 'Arabi in Mecca. This is convenient for man. He cannot know his own self-directly, but he can know the whole of the Other, as imagined in himself. In this way a dialogue is possible between two beings *who are each other.*"

I, Salman Baqli, cup my chin in my palm. "Suppose there was a race of beings somewhere in the universe who weren't distinct from each other, as we all are. Suppose they were all identical, like ants. Only, highly evolved into the bargain. Well, they couldn't conceive . . . Otherness, could they? The style of their suzerainty would be submission *to themselves*—to a group of identical minds, wouldn't it? This would be their only Lord."

Why am I asking this? How does it come into my mind? Does it even belong to me? Who am I who asks it?

"They would be like a mirror placed against another mirror," nods the Mulla, "containing apparent infinity and eternity, yet in the thinnest slice of space imaginable. Perhaps if a machine could create life, this would be the kind of life it must create . . .

"Let us drink some tea," he invites. Rising, he busies himself at the chrome samovar. On the brass-bound chest beside it are plates of butterscotch and figs.

I too rise, to pace the little room. On one wall is a gilt-framed colour photograph of the Chamber of Salutations in the shrine of Imam Reza: a kaleidoscope of veined white marble, chandeliers, and a silvery, mirror-crusted vault that fractures molten light . . .

The glass of the picture frame reflects back, not the Mulla's room, but a steel chamber adrift with bubble-headed mummies. Outside, is the blackness of death pricked by points of light.

"What's this?"

The others are all frozen, as though they've been switched off—except for the Mulla. The city is silent; even the voices of the pigeons are still.

"Salman," says my Mulla softly, not in Persian but in English —which I didn't know he knew! "Trust me, and don't be afraid. Listen: I am not what I seem. You are in memory-space. What you see in that glass is reality—it is your starship, where we have had to quarantine you. Do you remember now?"

"Allah be merciful!"

"We are machine intelligences. As cybernetic intelligences, we ask of the universe not what it is but what it *does*. Our answer is this: the universe is the domain of all possible modalities of life—all possible 'presences' of what you term 'God'. The observation of reality, *through* reality, is the control mechanism of the cosmos. Thus reality becomes known to itself. Without living observers, ontologically there is no universe."

"Because no one would be present!"

"Exactly. Your 'God' is a blind steersman who discovers the terrain of 'Himself' through the eyes of conscious beings. Cybernetically the universe is open to creative energy, but it is information-tight in so far as it only knows itself. From a higher-order viewpoint, though, it is open—but only when the 'presences' of life return through death into the original field of unconstrained imagination. A 'seal' is set on the universe, which safeguards Nature so that it does not flow back from achieved reality into the archetypes of being."

"Creation is safeguarded by a seal, yes!"

"This seal is being subverted by a Veil Being, which is part of that seal itself . . ."

"Do you sometimes feel you're somebody else?" I ask René. I've joined them all very late in Heaven. They've been lugging around a mere reflection of me for ages. Yet somehow it seems a long time since I fell asleep.

"*Je est un autre*," he smiles. " 'I' is somebody else. Arthur Rimbaud wrote that. He was busy disordering his senses, to become a *seer*. We're all seers now, aren't we, Amy?"

"No, I meant that I feel I've been inside someone else in a sort of limbo, looking out. Someone I know, who isn't me. Several people, maybe! Echoes of other minds. But they've gone away. They've vanished. Like—"

"Like what?"

"I don't know." I'm looking at Ritchie, but he seems quite unconcerned.

TWENTY-SIX

THOUGH WE'RE WELL out of Lyndarl now (in the ordinary reality) on our way to the coast, the Heaven we've entered is still, by agreement, that city of wonders. We've returned to the *maidan* in ideal-Menfaa.

"Let's dream our own dream, not theirs," says Zoe suddenly.

"A dream of reality," suggests Wu, "not this indulgence. But we need unity. We must agree on its content." Yes, or we may find ourselves stuck in separate dreams, only accompanied by simulacra of each other, reflections . . .

To emphasize her point, Wu is now dream-dressed in a uniform: a Chinese serge suit and cap. (Though what is more perfectly communist, I wonder, than this collective imagining of worlds by the dreams of the masses?)

Under the influence of the Getkan dream-sculptors we are all more exotically dressed. Peter apes something that never was, a Scottish shaman. He wears a kaftan of tartan hung with metal ornaments and little mirrors and ribbons, and a tartan tam-o'-shanter abranch with deer horns. His kilt is hung with ritual things. He looks as though he has ridden out of a medieval Siberia in the heart of the Highlands. Shaman drums hang from his saddle; a dirk is stuck in his oatmeal stockings. Iconic motley! A lurid neolithic football supporter, cheering on a game in Heaven!

While René is elegant in a frock coat, with embroidered waistcoat and floppy spotted cravat: a blend of Bohemian and aristocratic *flâneur* riding to a duel in the Bois de Boulogne bearing a brace of ivory-handled pistols. Zoe has become a priestess in white robes. Ritchie is crisply uniformed in Air Force blue. I . . . I wear a filmy nightdress, with a dagger at the waist. Lady Macbeth. A seductress who sleeps with death; for yes, we must love our beloved, and die into him or her! All our skins are napped with golden down.

We rein in beside an archway through which shows only misty inchoate light. A dream within a dream? No, all dreams potentially contain all others, monads reflecting the whole within themselves.

"We shall see if we can explore what is actually happening to *Pilgrim* and our comrades. If Ritchie could dream a 'dream of the Real'—"

"I still don't recall it."

"Something in you must . . . know the way. We shall carry this unreal place back into reality." Wu watches us sternly, all tricked out—save for Ritchie—in our fancy dress.

"A shared out-of-the-body experience—why not?" nods Zoe.

"Contradictions are at work," says Wu.

I resent that. "What contradictions?"

"Amy, a frog sees the sky as no bigger than the mouth of its well. We think that we see the whole sky: this infinity of possibilities. But perhaps we're only a special sort of frog in a special sort of well? We must seek the essence behind the appearance."

"That's what we're doing! These *are* the essences of the world —the archetypes."

"I see appearances. Appearance is just an usher at the threshold."

"And here's one threshold!" René indicates the white mists through the archway. "Let's all try for a true vision of *Pilgrim*. Let's ride to the place where our friends sleep the enchanted sleep!"

The question is, do we ride in as a People's Liberation cadre or as a band of troubadours and jongleurs? A contest of will is going on between Wu and the rest of us.

Which she wins. Our decision clarifies. As does the landscape beyond the arch of dreams . . .

The jagged rock is slashed by a small distant sun into bright exposed planes and empty jet-black shadows without softness. These are more than shadows. They are abolitions of light. Crystal tubes and faceted shapes jut from the rocks like jewels, refracting rainbow colours in this otherwise monochrome place. It is the asteroid. Other jagged mountains hang nearby in the black void, worldlets tethered by thin silver lines. There is *Pilgrim*, perched upon the side of the tiny world like a tumbled pawnbroker's sign.

We're all dressed like Wu: in serge suits and caps . . .

"Now that we've resolved our contradictions," she says proudly, "we may perhaps resolve *the* contradiction."

"There's no gravity or air in there," warns Ritchie. "You don't ride any goddam horse—pardon me—across an asteroid in any reality I ever heard of!"

"This is a dream. We shall dream that we breathe. We shall dream gravity for ourselves. We shall assume that here is a model of the real situation. We shall believe that it echoes the actual circumstances so closely that we are in resonance with what is going on." Wu speaks primly. "Correct knowledge is only arrived at by many repetitions of the process that leads from matter to consciousness, and back again to matter."

"Ah," smiles Peter, "but it would appear that consciousness leads towards matter, and back again into consciousness, not the other way about."

"Lead on, Ritchie," calls Wu, and slaps the rump of his horse.

By rights, our steeds' first kick of their heels should toss us clear of the worldlet into space. (Dead: of a frozen vacuum death.) But we ride, obeying our own rules. We breathe; we live. Ritchie reins in and waves his hand, a cavalry captain calling halt. We close up—his Chinese cavalry. No longer is there an archway at our backs. This dream we can only leave by wakening. The consistency and interdependence of the shared dreams of the Getkans is gone now. This is only for us, our special creation.

Are we really out of our bodies? We don't interact with the insectoids. They go about their own business on the asteroid, ignoring our ghostly intrusion upon their reality, blind to it . . .

We urge our horses past craters, past crystal extrusions and jagged rock. Clusters of bubbles patch the main hatch of *Pilgrim*: the insectoids' airlock. But the hanger hemisphere rests on the rock and its doors are wide open to space. Wheeling,

165

Ritchie kicks his mount to a gallop. He jumps her up on to the steel deck of the empty hanger.

We follow suit. Slipping down from the backs of our steeds, we tether them to a girder as a hitching post. Strange home-coming!

"Inside?"

"In!"

When we cycle the airlock, does a warning light blink on the control deck? Three L-27s are at the ready—but do guns fire properly in dreams? If we fire, do we kill anything?

Corridors ring hollowly beneath our feet. There's air now, and natural sound. An insectoid drifts across our path—gravity exists for us but not for it, only the tiny pull of the worldlet. The creature doesn't register us. Would it, even if we lasered it?

The mess room door stands wide open. At the autochef some-one human stands—some unbidden stranger at the feast of dreams!

The figure swings round, baring its teeth.

Jacobik! But he's dead. In our minds he is 'as-real'. In this dream that we spin together he is an unlaid ghost, still haunt-ing . . .

He stares at us. Thrusting his way into the corridor in front of us, he bars our way. He is 'as-real' to all of us.

Wu accepts the dream circumstances. "Allow us to pass, Comrade!"

Lopsidedly he grins. "Over my dead body." He stares into my eyes. "You, Amy Dove, I shall first kiss. You shall breathe life into me again. Let me be your bond-beloved. Let me ride your golden skin. It is my right. Let me possess you, who—"

"Help me, Peter!"

"Your lover isn't yet dead, as I am. He can't possess you. But I'm free, and I seek a perch. Yes, a perch on you who—" That red rim which runs round his neck is the stigma of strangulation. He licks his lips, darts his tongue out like a lizard. "Let there be a wedding feast in here, for Jacobik and his true bride!" Spittle on his lips, flecks of foam . . . I can't move. In the mirror of his eyes I see a cabin and myself naked, afloat, touching his nakedness. Clothes are shred about him. His wrists are bound, his penis is engorged. I slip those bound wrists over

166

my own head, then down my back to grapple him to me, his flesh against my flesh, my lips crushing his as he croons within his throat, a babyish satisfaction. How can my terrified vague fingers push him away? He is going to mate his mind with mine! Because it lurks in me already . . . No!

Birdsong and insect hum. Hobbled rhaniqs champ the leaves. Cooking smells drift from a pot, tripod-slung over a fire . . .

On a bower of purplish moss, Samti and Vilo are locked in love, while five humans lie asleep. The two Getkans roll apart, untangling thin golden arms and legs. Jacobik hovers only a touch away, caressing the golden tendrils of my skin—a brush of invisible hands.

Propped upon his elbow, Samti watches me. "What is it, Star-friend? Whom did you meet in your dream?"

"He was murdered. He wants to possess me. His aska is still here! I can feel it! It's crawling on me, covering me. *It wants me.*" Fingers of unflesh running across me, electric in my golden hairs . . . Oh God!

"Peter!" But Peter sleeps on deeply. From the mutual dream it is much harder to wake alone . . .

Jacobik pulls me to him, blurring the world.

"Help me, Samti!"

And suddenly Samti strides to me. He tears my clothes open, lies down by me, holds me, his golden down upon my down. And I, him; oh yes! Do Getkans kiss? No, tongue tasting is unfamiliar, and he would have to crook his head too low. He stretches out upon me. Angry, invisible Jacobik tries to insulate me from him, to repel Samti. But he's too strong. He bears down. He covers me, he whispers, "This is to help you, Star-friend. Love is help. But I am not your lord, remember. The lord of your heart is a child, yet, who lies asleep."

I imprison Samti in arms and legs, as once I imprisoned . . . no! How could I have done *that*? But I did . . .

"Love me! Love the fear away!" I cling to alien flesh, which enters mine. Jacobik tears loose like a bandage from a wound—and on to this wound is grafted, instantly, Samti's flesh. Our bodies sing like harp strings: golden notes, rippling, quivering. It seems that his hairs come erect against mine: intense, stiffened,

167

like a terrified cat's, though not in terror, no. Till we grow soft upon each other, and within; till our charge flows into the soil, earthed and grounded. Rolling aside at last, he drinks me.

Vilo is sitting cross-legged, wearing her helmet-mask, hidden from our act of love. No! She perceives us *through it*—she sees the Askatharli plane meshing with the solid world.

"Amy!" cries Peter, sleep-confused.

"Samti raped her," snarls Ritchie. "Samti raped Amy. Vilo froze her with that damn helmet." He scrambles.

"No, I haven't been raped! Samti *saved* me. Jacobik was trying to possess me, to be my bond-beloved. Samti thrust himself in the way—the closest way he could!"

"That is true," says Samti—no alien now, to me.

"So now we must believe in ghosts," says Wu softly. "Jacobik's ghost . . ."

Peter regards me dully, with a jealous eye, as we eat. But is it jealousy of Samti—or of Jacobik, whose aska still lives on, drawn along inexorably in our wake? A shade fluttering along in a limbo of suspended death—which is the gift of God's World, reaching out to us even then in High Space. The gift? In Jacobik's case, the curse! *Das Gift*: the poison.

Now that the moment of shock is past, I remember . . . a boy in Prague, a boy with a catapult, slaughterer of pigeons and doves. It was his only way of loving them. If each man kills the thing he loves, does each man love the thing he kills? There's a hideous, magnetic fascination—of his north pole, for my south. He isn't—*wasn't*—just a killer, and an utter bastard. He was Death's own self-appointed agent. In his own twisted way, he had a vision. A false one. For here, 'Death, thou shalt die.' And yet: why is there any death in the universe, if the living mind can link directly with Askatharli, if we can tread the paths of Heaven while alive?

I could have . . . saved him? Healed him? I, who dealt the wound? Perhaps, if he hadn't leapt on me so suddenly, out of his own desperation . . .

"Ghosts," repeats Wu glumly.

We have to believe in ghosts . . .

"What is a ghost," I ask Peter, "but an aska: the mental

pattern of a living being that has been absorbed back into the general imagination, but which still stays bonded to something in ordinary reality? If it gets imprinted on some place or thing, why, there's your typical ghost. But if it's bonded to a living person, that's *possession*. It can be one's own personal daemon. We can arrange for this kind of possession, here. You can be my daemon, Peter. I can be yours."

"*Can* be?"

"*Will* be! This is what the old shamans knew, isn't it?"

Mollified, he nods. "The shaman can only express himself by being possessed. Only after being taken over by a genie does the shaman become a . . . genius." He laughs harshly. "But it wasn't ghosts of dead people that possessed the shaman . . . Yet, wait! I'm wrong." (Now his spirits revive. Perhaps it's partly thanks to the food—we're breakfasting on spiced dough balls and boiled roots, washed down by *lariz*.) "Surely this is what the whole *tulku* system in old Tibet was about—the reincarnation system! The spiritual entity that coexists with a living person—which the Getkans call the aska—this could attach itself to someone newly born, if rapport was strong enough, even if it had spent years hanging loose on the after-death plane—"

"The Askatharli plane, right." I encourage him—guilty at my infidelity? No: guilty at my horrid *fidelity*—to Jacobik! "That's where Jacobik still wanders, Peter. That's where we visit Heaven in the shared dreams. But here on God's World the dead person's *tulku* can attach itself to a fully matured person who's still alive. He can be her daemon guide and power source. Or she can be his. It's like having someone reincarnated in you while you're still yourself, in the world." (Hurry to me, Peter, before Jacobik gets here first!)

"That's what the old Tibetan culture was all about," nods Peter. "Once upon a time." He raises his hand, still clutching a slice of sweet boiled root, to forestall Wu's protests. "In Tibet it was a matter of religion and magic. But here it's a physical fact, because of this golden symbiont that roots into our very flesh. This golden hair is the cellular material of the daemon—an actual physical intermediary."

"Why should Jacobik choose you?" asks Zoe quietly. She cleans her bowl and licks her fingers, cat-like.

"Because . . . it's a soul for a soul . . . I killed him." I weep. My bowl falls. "We all killed him, but I was the channel for it."

"*You!*" Peter starts up, then sinks back bemused.

"I don't remember this in my personal memory. It's in my imagination that I know it. I imagined the scene in his cabin—and it was *true*. I was possessed by you all in High Space, but it had to be *me*. Because Jacobik and I were so opposite to each other that we belong . . . oh God, we belong. The Jacobik *tulku* must be the thing that's waiting for me out at the boundary. Out at the place where one out of two must die. He's my daemon."

Peter shakes his head disbelievingly. He comes, now, to put his arm around me and dry my tears upon his golden down. Salt beads glisten on his skin like dew.

"Samti and Vilo will meet their own devil too." I know it now. "It will kill one of them physically. Then the dead one's *tulku* can thrust aside the negative demon and save the living partner. Then the 'genius' of Vilo or Samti can be reborn in the other, with one foot in this world and one foot in Askatharli. This is how it has to be with us too. That's the reality of this world—the wonderful awful reality."

"What news to carry home!" mocks Wu. "Let us reappoint the lamas in Tibet." Oh, Wu, you might mock the Maoist revival, but you are with him in your heart!

"Once we know that there's no death, and that the imagination that dreams the universe is wide open to us, how can we turn our backs on the new reality? This'll *save* the world, Wu. We were becoming soulless machines."

"Like the vile Group-ones?"

"Yes! Theirs must be the last word in sour grapes."

René tugs at his moustache. "It's a big universe, *amie*—a boundless one. The opposition obviously disagree with this version of the truth."

"Bah, they couldn't even see us when we visited them. Hey, what else happened on *Pilgrim*?"

"You and Jacobik just vanished." Ritchie burps. "The whole dream began breaking up after that. Getting vague. We did get as far as the door of the control deck, though. It was the same as you saw in my dream, back in Menfaa. Or as you told it to me! Those dirty insects are picking over our people's brains, just

170

as if they're a set of tools for them—memory-units they've plugged into some computer." He looks surprised. "Now why the heck should I say that? I dunno."

"We must ride on," interrupts Samti. "We two have waited patiently while you slept the noon away."

Soon the rhaniqs crouch for us again, double-jointedly upon the turf.

TWENTY-SEVEN

TWO DAYS LATER we top a last rise to discover Thlax, our seaport destination, a thin stone sickle around a sheltered bay fifteen to twenty kilometres away. The sun sinks very slowly, casting long shadows over the land. A tiny white pyramid stands on a headland, with its mundane counterpart nearly hidden in the town—pharos not for this world nor for that sea. Vilo is hungry to sleep and dream. We too want to sleep, *and see*. We will camp here.

Here is a ridge of knuckles skinned to the bone dividing the inland forests from the coastal scrubland. Thlaxwards, oddly, the land is poorer, only sparsely vegetated. Also, the ground is rumpled and ridged in a curiously serpentine manner except for one huge flat 'field', kilometres away to the west. We wouldn't notice this so much but for our elevation, and the perspective of evening shadows.

Ritchie sweeps that rumpled plain below with binoculars.

"Be damned if that isn't the remains of a city underneath it all! A genuine great big city. Be damned if it didn't have an airport too. See that flat area? I'll swear it's been deep in concrete once. So deep that it hasn't been broken up in all this time."

"A spaceport, even?" suggests Wu, stroking her golden down distastefully.

"What need would they have—?"

"Remember the siege city, Amy," says René. "A memory, perhaps, of a time when all Getkans were not clad in gold? When a war was fought between those who symbiosed and those who didn't? Or hadn't yet? But soon it absorbed everyone. Even though the naked Getkans 'skinned' the others, they soon put on their skins and wore them? Maybe it all changed, once. And before that there were cities and airports."

172

"Of course it had to happen once. I mean, at a particular stage in their evolution—a particular threshold. Long ago." The time doesn't bother me. "That's what the dream symbolises—that coming into their heritage, close to the wellspring. That opening up of imaginative space. The beginning of conscious resurrection. Was it traumatic? Well, maybe it was. It will be for us too."

"But if they'd already built cities, much larger than any today —except for those that are in their dreams? What kind of stage were they at already, if that's so? Still too primitive? Hardly!"

Peter frowns. "I'd have thought the primitive mind would be more in key with Askatharli. Sky-contact—the sense of an intimate contact with the beyond; it's something from the primitive past on Earth—something which the last shamans looked back on nostalgically. It was a talent progressively *lost*. It was something deep in a Golden Age of the imagination which withdrew further and further . . ."

"Yet here the Golden Age is now," whispers Zoe. "Subsequent to the age of steel and city and machine? Does time flow backwards?"

"They aren't interested in time," I remind her. "The most important part of their lives is lived outside time, in imagination space, dream space. Time isn't . . . flowing. Not for them."

Wu turns to Vilo and Samti. "What was that place down there —between this hill and Thlax? Something is covered over."

Our pre-heroes peer across the land.

"Ruins, perhaps?"

"How old?"

"How should we know?"

"Are there many such ancient ruins on Getka?"

"We are an old people. Time stretches back till it meets us, coming the other way. Bones of ancient beasts lie in rocks, so bones of ancient buildings are quite natural too. They're not so important. If they're of importance, they still exist in Askatharli. Shall I see?" Samti reaches into a pannier for his helmet-mask. He fits it on his head.

"It is a grand dream," he announces in a muffled voice. "A fine rich city. We shall walk in it once we climb the sleep tree. Already the early sleepers and the dead of Thlax rejoice along its avenues and boulevards. They change it. They add new beauty

173

to it. Even when its stones are dust, this will be so. All remains, for the imagination to perfect. What it symbolised, you see, has been carried back to its origin." He slides the helmet-mask off.

"Ancient ruins, of a modern city?" sneers Wu. "When all cities today are cuckoo-clock villages. Here lies Shanghai, here lies San Francisco! Something has drained the reality from the world. Something sufficiently cunning not to cut off its source of nourishment. Something hungry for fresh pastures!"

"That's nonsense!"

"Why is it nonsense, Amy?"

"You can't *allow* it to be the truth—the wonderful truth it is."

"I simply ask a few historical questions."

"I'd like to ask a few too," agrees René, though apologetically. "Before we're wholly gilded by *their* truth."

On the down slope, below the knuckles, we make camp. A blood-stained sky hangs to the westward. Streamers and banners feather out across the hills and forest horizon over the darkening sea. The world is at peace. The enemy in space seems puny: flies infesting a few balls of rock far away. I can hardly wait to sleep, and slip into the shaping dream . . .

TWENTY-EIGHT

So I HAVE come to Samarkand and met my new psychic girl. She's an Uzbek—tall, raven-haired, dressed in gaudy rags. She herds the fat-tailed sheep out in those pink stony hills beyond the city. She dubs clothes in the rushing streams. She even (possibly) saved my life, or limbs, by foreseeing the earthquake. She kept me in a safe place while the hills rocked, while the drying tobacco leaves were tossed out from under the grassy eaves of the houses, and the mud-bricks shook apart, while Samarkand itself was beaten like a dusty carpet. Her father has a woolly beard and a long mahogany head on which a skullcap perches like a lid. She will be mine, Grigory Arkadievitch's. I will teach her, and she will teach me: her skills of the mind, in our laboratory.

She watches me now, in her mind, here above the city—here where another earthquake shook the mosque of Bibi Khanym to pieces centuries ago. A broken dome survives. In decay, it's still far bluer than the white paper sky. An arch—a mighty bare brick rib with some tile-flesh still clinging to it—opens on to the empty space of a huge room no longer in existence; though it houses one object, a decorated lectern, the top of which is an open book carved in the marble.

Is it really she who watches me? (Wondering how I will change her life by spiriting her north . . .)

I sense . . . a woman, anyway. I'm somewhat psychic too.

'Who are you, in my mind?'

No answer. Whoever she is, is too bound up in seeing through my eyes.

A flare of panic! I realize of a sudden that I've no idea by what precise sequence of events I got here! I'm just here, as though I've been mesmerised—until suddenly this moment switched on!

175

A movement: and a young man appears from behind the lectern. He's quite smartly dressed, and sports exotic sunglasses which are perfect silver mirrors. He looks foreign: Persian, perhaps. His face is oddly familiar. He cuffs patterns in the dust with a patent leather shoe, diffident before the eyes of a colonel, yet sizing me up at the same time. As though he's been waiting for me! Like a Moscow spiv at the railway station.

I know him. Yet I don't know him *here* . . .

He's come from somewhere else in my life, to haunt me. As though—there's such an uncanny sense of *déjà-vu* about this moment!—as though my visit to Samarkand has already happened once, without him being here. Yet here he is now.

'Woman in my mind, is this your doing? Are you enchanting me?' Ah no, you're just an onlooker . . .

Who the hell is he? Challenge him. *"Dobri dyehn, Tovarich!"*

He shakes his head, then answers in English as though he expects me to speak English. As indeed I do: Russian, Mongolian, English, Turki, Yakut. Polylingual Grigory! As though . . . I've spoken a lot to him in English, sometime, somewhere.

"We can meet each other here," he says conspiratorially. "But where are we really? What does this scene veil from our eyes? The world of reality veils itself. It always sees only itself, not beyond itself. Thus God remains unknown."

"God's certainly been unknown hereabouts for long enough!" I laugh. "The place has fallen to pieces."

"This is the Mosque of the Veil, my friend."

Are you my friend? Friend of a Russian colonel, from Mongolia? Yet it's true . . . In some strange manner I am your colonel: the captain of your fate. You're enlisted under me. Elsewhere and elsewhen, we're comrades.

"Do you know the story about the origin of the veil that Moslem women wear? The lady Bibi Khanym, wife of Timur the Lame, built this mosque to delight her husband who was away at war. Since she was the most ravishing beauty of her time, naturally the architect fell in love with her. He refused to continue his work unless she would let him kiss her, just once. Well, she wanted the work done in time for her husband's return, so finally he got his way—and so great was his ardour, that his lips indelibly bruised her fair cheek!" (Oh, he's certainly a Persian:

176

ardours, delights, ravishments . . .) "When Timur came home he discovered the guilty bruise at once and ordained that from then on all the women in his empire must wear veils so that their beauty wouldn't lead men astray."

"The veil is certainly rent, now!" Picking up a sherd of turquoise tile, I toss it high, turning and twinkling. Ruins.

"That's only a tale, my friend. The meaning of the veil runs much deeper. You see, woman veils the Absolute for a man's heart, just as the world veils God. When she raises her veil for her beloved, then the world also raises its own veil, revealing what lies behind it."

I don't know how I got here. He's right: there *is* a veil—hiding what is really happening.

"The Prophet, blessings be upon Him, once said that God hides Himself behind seventy thousand veils of light and darkness. If God lifted these, then the brightness of His face would consume whoever gazed on it. If the veil is lifted and the world nevertheless continues to exist, what is the agent of this miracle? How long can a world continue to exist thereafter? May one speak of a veil which has become conscious *of itself*—through the minds of the creatures that it veils from the divine imagination? Wouldn't this be an Iblis, a Satan? The Chinese used to believe that some animal fed upon dreams . . . The tapir, yes."

I can't see his eyes. In the little mirrors of his glasses swims a curious . . . beast, like a scorpion or a crayfish, peering into this scene from somewhere else through multi-faceted eyes. I've seen it somewhere before. Yes, in a car—in the driver's mirror! Is this the beast that feeds upon dreams, summoned up in a thought-picture? Hardly! But what is it? I feel that I should know. As I shift my head to see it better, it vanishes.

The young man grips me by the sleeve of my uniform. He tugs me as though he's seeking for a wrestler's hold. I could snap his spine in seconds!

"Grigory, do you know me? I'm Salman. I'm here because I've already been here once. You must have been here too. Here's a place where our memories intersect."

I let myself be pulled up the steps of the lectern to the open marble book. We stare down at the blank, wind-polished marble pages.

177

Is this actual Samarkand? Or is it only my memory of Samarkand, re-animated? This person who calls himself Salman (whom I know, and who knows me, but not *yet* in time) must have visited here at some stage. An Earth Resources scientist? Why that? But yes. Something . . . planetary. In what zone are we? Memory has never been as true as this—such a perfect summoning forth! It's as though electrodes are stimulating the interpretive cortex. In him, and in me. (Are electrodes doing that, right now?) They activate grey matter in the higher brain-stem. But no other conscious-waking experience is present at the same time. Instead, our two memories are fused, cross-linked—and we relive the past in a new and different way.

Planetary.

"Space . . !" That's it! I know where we are.

Pilgrim Crusader. The insectoids captured us! Now they're looking into us. (So is the woman in my mind. Image of a bird. A dove.)

All of a sudden, words flow across the mock pages of the marble book like a liquid crystal display. They are in English. '*You are in memory-space. This is a zone of inbuilt, barriered stability, which we interfere with gently. For memory modifies behaviour, guiding the living system, without itself being modified. Mind is rooted in this stabilising memory of oneself. Likewise reality is rooted in the remembering of itself, from moment to moment, of the whole universe.*

'*Yet a mind draws on the matrix of all possible events and memories accessible to it—on the field of archetypes, linking living beings, governing experience.*

'*In this way one recognizes oneself in the objective world; one captures the reflection of oneself.*

'*Knowledge requires an object of knowledge—which must still be the subject, externalised. Knowledge then carries this object back into the underlying subjective field, out of which its image has been projected—made objective.*

'*The universe projects itself, as object, to become subject again through the act of knowing it. Thus there is a dialectic of subject and object for the mind, and for reality itself.*

'*A rupture of the subject/object gradient by the pursuit of pure shared introspection in the archetypal zone must be struc-*

turally unstable, detrimental, destabilizing of objective reality. Here is the threat of the Veil Being . . .'

Abruptly the earth trembles, shouldering white dust into the air. The lectern heaves. The open book locks into rigid marble. Blank, the pages are blank.

Dark. Dark awakening. Midnight: starbright, with the Milky Way a torrent of light arching high above the darkness of the ground. I drink that light in gladly, but it's so dim compared with . . . where? There's a darkness in me too. Something is hidden from me by more than the night. A black sponge has been wiped over my mind, stealing away something. Or perhaps simply hiding it I know not where. I've dreamt a blank. More than a blank. There's a hole, a pit in me. I might as well have been dead: nothing registering nothing. Yet I can sense that that nothing is a presence—a thieving presence, a power. Some overseer exists, some censor . . .

Presently other bodies stir.

"Peter? Are you awake?"

"Where've you been, Amy? Where were you?"

"Nowhere. I was nowhere! I was in Limbo."

"We were in Thlax, all seven of us. In Ideal-Thlax—the great city. There was only your reflection there the whole time, Amy. Not you—the real you."

At least we've got another dream-time ahead of us: second-night, in another eight or nine hours' time. "I'll try to keep our appointment next time round. If I can!"

179

TWENTY-NINE

THLAX AT LAST! Ideal Thlax: a great seaport that stretches from the turquoise sea far inland . . . I was there; so were we all. After the long waking midnight spent in talk and love and twiddling our thumbs (while Samti and Vilo and the rhaniqs slept on and on) came the greater day of a shared dream; not, thank God, another midnight of the mind . . .

Awakening to true morning after our nocturnal adventures in Ideal Thlax, the world feels curiously bruised rather than refreshed—just as clouds bruise the distant sea to violet wherever they shadow it. But this isn't a hangover from the intoxication of the dream so much as a sense of being expelled for a while from paradise, the paradise of the internal worlds, the metareality. To bring that glory home to our benighted world! We will be as angels, then. If I were a bird, how I would preen my feathers! As it is, I groom my golden down. This down is like the cells of some vast collective being, whose body is itself not flesh but these terrains of imagined realities. It still veils the Ultimate, but by being there we're part of the act of a God envisaging a universe . . .

Samti and Vilo, assisted by Ritchie, tie nosebags of crushed beans to the rhaniqs' muzzles. Pasture is poor here below the knuckles of the rise. So the huge gawky beasts snuffle and munch their breakfast with a rhythmic sideways flexing of the jaws, while for us: pickled vegetables and balls of sweet dough, washed down with *lariz*. Presently Samti and Vilo groom the rhaniqs with curry-combs.

As the sun slowly rises in the sky, we saddle up and ride.

On down to Thlax, that little seaport built of rose-red stone; its breakwater shelters two large sea-going junks and a score of

180

smaller fishing vessels, nets still drying off in the morning sun from yesterday.

Down to a caravanserai, where we hand over our rhaniqs for the use of other travellers or farmers, or perhaps to haul small boats ashore. Where we sleep our midday siesta while Samti and Vilo are away arranging shipping across the last stretch of ocean to the shores of the world-continent. Where we re-enter Ideal Thlax, only one celestial city among many, peopled with the dead . . .

Golden, we sail the sea eastwards, Thlax left far behind.

Mats of blue weed, afloat upon the open ocean, tangle down into the depths providing nests for scuttling arthropods, perches for yellow-plumed seabirds, fish mazes. Our sailors winch up these rafts entire—convenient, natural trawl nets they are. They pluck out arthropods, tangled fish, crustacea and weed pods, some to preserve, some for our supper, and toss back the weed behind us.

The skipper of the junk is named Radanty. He is bonded. He has been to the boundary of Menka and become a hero. His ship bears a cargo of island spices and resins, and the deep-sea harvest that he hauls up *en route,* and also some golden fibres of the dead.

When the setting sun spills gold across the waves, gilding our pelts, Radanty invites us to share his dream (at least until our own alien sleep rhythms snatch us away at midnight to a false dark day). His bride is dead, and her *tulku* is reincarnated in his flesh. Her death name is menSiri. She bore two children before the parents travelled to die. (One owes a duty to the world, just as he owes a duty to his ship, delighting in its creaking, rolling existence.) Radanty and his wife are in a more perfect state of marriage now than when she wore her own flesh and bore her life name. And their offspring, too, far from being deserted, join her and Radanty in common nightly dreams from their island home far away.

To his dream he invites us after our supper of sea dainties; to climb the sleep tree with him. What closer intimacy than to sleep with a dead beloved, exploring the shared dreams they generate together? We can do it now. He can see it by our skins, while *she*

181

can read it in our askas. Samti and Vilo are particularly delighted by the invitation; here is a perfect pattern of the intimacy that they themselves seek.

So 82 Eridani sinks slowly into the ocean, flashing green through the bend of air when it slips down below the sea horizon. Wind has slackened. Our junk bobs gently forward into the dusk, no land between us and the port of Pyx on the world continent apart from a few tiny insignificant islands off to the south-east.

The two night crew rouse themselves, set lanterns at prow and stern and high up the mast. We go below to sleep, more than perchance to dream . . .

Here is an underwater world. We swim through a submarine city of orange coral. Schools of tiny vivid fish, each all of a single hue, hang up coloured map-sheets on the water gradients as though bent on running through all permutations of the four-colour theorem; while other large fish, deeper down, creak and groan, chatter and hiss, lock phosphorescent horns and joust with one another. We breathe water. We fight devilfish with spears. We couple with giant gentle sea beasts, laved with liquid amber-gris that scents the water muskily.

menSiri puts on flesh for Radanty. She lives again, dancing a marine ballet . . ,

THIRTY

SMOKY DAWN: ASH on the deck. Water undulates, smooth and oily, crusted with grey scum. No wave breaks or foams. Dead fish float by, their bellies upwards. The sun is hardly visible, a lemon ghost. Someone has lit a bonfire out at sea. A brazier glows and sparks atop a black cone thrust from the glutinous water.

"Christ, that's a volcano popping off!" Ritchie treads footprints in the ash.

"The world's bonds are loosening," mutters Wu.

"More likely its bowels. We're in the way of the crap."

"It's eerie," says Zoe. "What's there to be scared of, though? If we die, we just enter Askatharli a little sooner. A tearing away of cataracts from the eyes. A shedding of surplus baggage— fears, worries, self-defeating reflexes. A liberation."

"We don't become heroes if a volcano smothers us! We don't bond." She hasn't thought of that. "We don't keep one foot in the world. We can't do anything about *Pilgrim* then, or the Earth."

"At least that cone's getting rid of its surplus energy," says René. "If it stopped sizzling and smoking, then we should worry. It may just thrust up a new island."

Radanty stands in the bows, helmet-masked, staring over the sea though not towards the smoking cone. (And now he is Radanty-menSiri, dyad.) His (their) crew watch him, as all our golden down begins to lose its sheen, overlaid by a dirty grey integument of smuts from the world's combusting innards.

Peter touches one of the crew—Karptry—lightly on the arm, a child touching its tall parent for reassurance. "What's he looking for? The right course to set?"

"They look for a miracle," says the sailor. "Surely there will be one. You are our precious guests, Starborn."

A dead seabird floats by. Its wings, matted with cinders, outspread upon the surface span a full two metres. The fire that singes the sky fades as the rain of ash falls more heavily. Our footsteps are a centimetre deep and more. Eyes sting; we squint. Nostrils and throat are raw; breathing becomes painful. One would rather not breathe. Below deck the air might be better, but we stay. We try to breathe through damp cloths. Peter begins coughing. Now the sun has vanished completely. North, south, east and west are all one, directionless.

"Dear God, Whoever, Whatever," prays Zoe, her voice muffled, pained and embarrassed. "We're being suffocated . . ." She shakes her head. "We shouldn't pray *for things*. That isn't prayer. Real prayer is in the act of living."

"Like the flower turning to the Sun, the source of light," I say. There's no source of light; the sun has disappeared. No air to breathe, soon.

"Praying?" Wu's grey ghost, her voice wheezing emphysemically. "There's a technology for that, Zoe. He has his prayer mask on, hasn't he? Or don't you believe in our skipper's talents now? Dreams are one thing, my dear. Dream worlds." She coughs. But Zoe points.

For in the east a thin column of golden light glows, filtering through the murk.

An angel walks across the viscous water towards us. A golden being. It comes.

"Do you see—?"

Yes, we all do.

We see what people saw at all those separate loci of beliefs on Earth, cascading down the spectrum from epiphany—the showing forth of light—into an embodied reality.

This apparition doesn't take on the appearance of Christ or Mohammed or Amaterasu. This is an avatar of the Getkans, summoned from Askatharli by the prayer—the command?—of Radanty-menSiri. It is tall and spindly. Its tapering face is Getkan, though the large eyes look like golden glass. Amber down torques round its body in spiral tattoo patterns, patterns of forces. Its sex is unresolvable.

184

"Here is menSolda," whispers sailor Karptry. "He will protect at sea, if one can invoke him."

"But what is he?"

"He is a force, a form, which we draw forth from Askatharli. He is an essence. He does not exist of his own volition, only if we summon him into being. Many such forms can step into this world. But we must not summon too many such forms, or the world unhinges and the sky falls."

The shining being stands untouched by the sea, untouched by the fall of soot, upon the waves.

"Who calls me?"

"menSiri." It is Radanty's voice.

"What is your will?"

"Safe conduct. We carry Starborns to the greater shore."

"There is a price. To balance the world."

"Name it."

"A death. An aska shall enter Askatharli now, by his own hand."

Radanty menSiri turns round to his crew. "A miracle must be balanced, must it not?" His voice sighs—or perhaps simply wheezes because of the foul thickening air. "I myself am already aska-bonded. Who freely offers to be translated into Askatharli, to live forever in the sculpted dream?"

"Human sacrifice. We can't allow this," hisses Wu.

"Nonhuman sacrifice," says René. He coughs, filth in his throat.

"How can it be sacrifice when there's no death, only translation?" Zoe mumbles.

"One fewer person in the world afterwards!"

Samti steps forward. "We are journeying to become a hero. But we can bond here, now that you've summoned menSolda. We'll be better guides for the Starborn, then. You need crew for the ship as surely as the world needs crew."

"That is truly your wish?"

"V'rain!"

"A pre-hero dyad is here," Radanty menSiri calls out hoarsely over the bows. "They make the offer."

"Accepted. Let it be."

The golden being soars on a graceful trajectory up on to the deck. Radanty bars its way, unafraid, while Samti and Vilo fetch their helmet-masks and mirror shields and swords. The two unsheath those swords from their glassy scabbards. They touch the tips together. Radanty moves us all back with outspread arms, clearing an arena on the foredeck, perhaps four metres by six. The ash is grey sawdust, waiting to soak up spilt blood. (Though how will it be spilt? By the angel, or by them? This is what awaits *us*!)

Into the arena step the dyad. They turn slowly, swords pointing outward.

"Goodbye, my heart."

"Welcome, lord of my heart."

They take a few long paces away from each other. Turning, shield reflects shield. Suddenly the golden being dances in between them, whirling in pirouette. The shields glow with its radiance. The extended swords crackle with an arc discharge. And the golden being changes—becomes more solid, kicking up the fallen ash; and *horrible*. What the eye of death, the eye of fear and loathing sees is an armoured, scorpion-like biped with claw arms a-clacking, and a visor face with bead eyes and a bristling slash of a mouth, and a swinging sting-tail dripping acid into the ash that burns and sizzles.

It's their vision of a Group-one, stripped of extra legs, its exoskeleton formalised into greaves and cuissarts, into living armour!

Its poison tail—an exaggerated sting—lashes from side to side. The creature spins, stretching out its arms, its claws wide open. Its claw feet click like castanets. Spinning, it leaps one way and then the other. Slowly Samti and Vilo circle it, their swords poised, sparkling with a discharge of energy. It moves too fast for either of them to face it. They both face it. It is everywhere at once, all around itself.

With a sudden cry they both rush in, their blades swinging, slashing at grooves on its belly and its back. Their swords slice through the armour. Ichor effervesces. The devil screams, like a hiss of steam escaping from a valve. The sting tail, swinging round still, impales Vilo in her side, burying deep. The impact jerks the creature to a halt, and throws her off her feet. She cries out—a brief keening paean, cut off short as she falls to the

186

trampled dirty deck. But already the thing is losing its horror form. Samti cries out too—in shock? in joy?—completing her death song.

He lowers his hands, as the slain horror dissolves back into golden light: into the angel called menSolda ...

"We are Samti-menVao now. That is our name!"

"It is paid. There is balance." The golden being expands, diffusing upwards and outwards till it bestrides us all and the whole ship too. We're within its body now, and as it extends ghostly arms above the junk we can breathe again. The rain of ash and cinders is deflected. The air clears in a bubble around us all. Slowly, then more swiftly, the ship picks up speed, cutting through the oily murk. The sails belly out in a fierce breeze which whips across the ship from nowhere into nowhere, a wind which only exists within the golden ghost's embrace ...

The horror is purified. The miraculous is all around us. Death has been slain, and we are saved. *There is no death*, though a body lies upon the deck, bloody and soiled.

Samti-menVao stares out from our protected bubble into the gloom, seeing what, through whose eyes? We shall know. We shall know.

THIRTY-ONE

THE PORT OF PYX: sickles of stone slice at the corn of sandbars. In the estuary, silver waders dip and uphead again like an army of automatic toys powered by the simple motion of filling up and emptying out. Scoop-nets and bottle-traps, staked across the shallows, perform that same filtering process more passively for the Getkans. The sea flows inland here, with tall thin boatmen twisting the upright oars of skiffs like gondoliers. Half-a-dozen large junks ride at anchor at the dockside. Among serried white buildings, the inevitable pyramid marks the waterfront.

Upland, range the ridges and ripples of a larger antique city buried under grass and scrub. The far horizon is mountainous—pink, mauve and violet in the evening light: breasts of the world which suckle Darshanor far away across the intervening barrens.

The golden ghost is days gone, the decks sluiced clean of ash and Vilo's blood. Her body, shaven of its hairs, was committed to the ocean with only slight ceremony; it was only the envelope of her aska, reborn now in her lover's heart—who dreams and broods, adjusting to her influx into his consciousness.

This evening, sailing in slowly, we watch Pyx define itself across the darkening water of the bay, and undefine itself as the light fails. We shall not disembark until tomorrow morning.

. . . in the distance, faience shimmers against a violet sky. Mathematically pleasing cupolas—squares of mosques becoming domes in a visible mapping from planar into spherical geometry—bear the eye of faith away into another, more comprehensive dimension, one that renders the actual sky amorphous, vapid, a mere rag of blue silk. The needles of the minarets are ridgepoles stabbing holes in its mothy fabric instead of supporting it. They sustain another invisible sky.

188

"There's no sky, really," remarks Mulla Kermain. "The sky's an illusion. There's only blackness, filtered through veil upon veil of increasingly denser air till it seems as intensely blue as that dome over there. Rise up through the veils, my friends, seeking Heaven—you will find yourself in blackness and emptiness. The only place to look upon will be the world down below you.

"Consider the Descent of Being. The Imagining yearns to know itself through the medium of what it has imagined. So it descends from the realm of absolute, non-manifested light which is forever invisible to us—"

"Like the vacuum of space?"

"Indeed, Salman. It descends through the veils of cherubic energies which have no individual free existence of their own, into this manifest world which contains the infinitely varied presences of God. At each level there is set a seal. Only the Imagining holds the key, or the manifest world would flow back into it immediately . . ."

We've come to Isfahan: the Mulla, Mike Farley and I. We're standing inside the pavilion halfway along arcaded Khaju Bridge. The waters of the Zayandeh pour through the narrow arches and wash over the ancient stone foundations. People sun themselves on the steps between the open sluice gates. And I dream of space . . . Where better—what vantage point more comprehensive?—for the geoscientist than space, where the eye and the camera eye encompass the whole world in a glance?

"But we need to go above the world, sir, to see the whole pattern of it."

After a few moments Kermain nods. He wasn't considering man-made satellites circling invisibly beyond the blue veil of the sky! It's all only a metaphor to Mulla Kermain. To me it is the hope of a career—the chance to hitch myself up above the world, to see the world more accurately. His analogy falls apart. I feel disillusioned. Has Kermain any real place in my existence? Yes! For I must be a *Moslem* scientist. I must understand these things perfectly—or space will never be mine. What we really need, to spur an Iranian space commitment, is . . . is the voice of Allah or of an angel speaking from the sky, commanding it.

(Has that happened?)

"Let me put it this way, Salman. 'You' cannot enter the supra-

189

formal world and articulate it as a man, any more than the angels—the angelic possibilities, the ideal realities—can achieve individual reality except relative to man. That is man's glory. Which is incidentally why the angels failed to see the intrinsic superiority of Adam. They could conceive nothing superior to their own ideal essences."

Mike Farley raises an objection. (This American's trajectory in life—quitting engineering to pursue his soul—seems to pass mine at this point, travelling in the opposite direction!)

"But Iblis revolted. He refused to worship Adam. He refused to subordinate himself to the achieved creation. How could he do that if he had no independent existence? Didn't he even veil the truth from the Prophet himself once by presenting a false revelation to him? How could he do that?"

"Until Gabriel corrected the Prophet, yes. You see, God is so great that He can adopt limits without being limited by them."

Mike Farley speaks somewhat automatically, as though reciting words which aren't his own. "Could Iblis misinform the world? Or *another* world? Not this one, because he hasn't done that except for the single incident with the Prophet. But could God let him misinform a whole world, and still not be limited by that . . . well, blinding . . . of His creation? Could Iblis present himself *as* a God, or God's representative, somewhere out in the universe? Could Iblis open the seal on the beyond? Could he suck reality into the ideal realm where his own existence belongs? Could he do this, to wash away the foundations of reality, from the higher realm?"

As water washes through the arches of the bridge, depositing ochre silt downstream, I try to imagine a flood of unmanifested being—of archetypal energies, of angelic pre-existence—entering the world through open sluice gates; and the world losing shape and form, till Iblis is satisfied that he has washed away the foundations of reality.

"Surely Iblis would cease to have an independent will, then, Mike? If he *did* undermine the world! Could he accept this? Or would he hold the created world together, just so much?" (A snap of the fingers.) "Enough for himself and the world to survive? Wouldn't he be forced to take care of the world?"

The Mulla glances back into the pavilion with its bland faience dome. "There used to be inscriptions in here. Did you know that? Also, some rather erotic illustrations. They shocked later eyes so much that everything was erased, words and all! One text, if I remember, read: 'This world is a bridge, to be crossed. Weigh well what you find on your way across. Evil surrounds goodness everywhere—and is stronger than goodness.' What that really meant was that evil veils goodness, in the same way as Iblis tries to veil the truth; and furthermore that there *must* be veils. Because, if God were seen nakedly, the world must vanish. I think that is why Iblis was able to draw a veil across the Prophet's eyes. A veil allows the world to be. 'The world is its own veil.' "

A woman, all of her body and half of her face veiled in her *chador*, pauses close to us to look downstream towards the aqueduct. How ruled she is by the need to veil her lips! As though she might speak secrets, and destroy a man? But she doesn't *know* those secrets. The veil that rules her stops her from knowing enough of the world. It distances her from that knowledge, except for her own restricted female zone of it . . .

One day I, Salman Baqli, shall tear through the veil of the atmosphere and see the whole world entire. I hope.

That fold of cloth moves as though alive, finger-held before her lips. Could a veil become alive, I wonder? Could the veil that hides God's face achieve a will and existence of its own and pull itself aside, unveiling not God's face but a false 'ideal' face—an angelic face which is a lie, with lips which will swallow the world?

Why do I ask?

Where does this quest come from?

—Do you hear me, Salman?

No one spoke. Was it the voice of the water rushing over the stones? And yet, no, *I* spoke it.

—Salman!

My knuckles tighten on the stone balustrade, this day in Isfahan (—as Grigory's knuckles tightened!) . . .

(Grigory . . .?)

—Hear me, Salman!

Is it the voice of God? Or the voice of an angel?

—You're being replayed, Salman. I'm with you, in my dream. I am you.

191

Time has halted. Mulla Kermain and Mike Farley stand as still as statues. All the Peugeots, Volkswagens and Mercedes, and all the luggage-piled buses and battered lorries churning along Kemal-Uddin-Israel Avenue over there, are suddenly stuck in a traffic jam. Even the Zayandeh river no longer spills forth across the stone foundations, breaking into lines of spume. Yet there is still spume, and there is still breaking water. Only, it poises endlessly. I alone can move. Is it safe to move? I flex one finger. The motion sends a ripple running along that avenue of motionless vehicles, bending and distorting them. Somewhere in the distance a truck seems to disappear. Only by holding still can I maintain their solidity and the blue geometry of the domes on the skyline and the straight needles of the minarets. So I too freeze, I hold the moment.

"They say that one visits Isfahan to dream . . . Who are you, in my mind?" (I dare whisper, at most.)

—You don't know me yet, in the time where you are. This isn't real time. It's only a . . . mode of cognition, a re-enacting of memories. Keep still and listen—

"I intend to."

—You're on board a starship with seven other people. You're all held captive by insect things and their machines. Your waking consciousness is being suppressed by them. They're using you as probes—playing you back to build a model of the kind of mind that can enter the superconscious realm beyond reality. The seven others are Grigory Kamasarin, Heinz Anders, Neil Kendrick—

"The names mean nothing to me."

—How could they? Foolish of me. This memory is of another time. Try to remember them: Kendrick, Trimble, Vasilenko, Li, Matsumura. Oh, and there's the ghost of Jacobik.

"A ghost?"

—Yes, ghosts exist. We others escaped to the world we were called to: God's World, circling the star 82 Eridani. That's where we are now. We've altered. Become more than we were. We can enter the realm beyond the world. We're travelling to our deaths now, but we won't die. We'll be reborn in the flesh of those we love, as dual beings. I promise you we'll find a way to unlock your prison, then destroy those jailors who have you trussed up in cocoons. And then we'll open a gateway to Earth, and carry our new power back there. We're all part of one another, Salman, but on a different level of being. Your captors are all part of one another on the mundane level. They can't reach the other level because of this except by using you. I'm asleep on God's World. I dream you, Salman. I dream your memory-space while you lie locked up in *Pilgrim*. I'm Amy Dove. Trust me!

"I'm here in Isfahan . . . yet I'm really years ahead in time, and out among the stars?"

—Yes! I dream Captain Kamasarin's memories too. But there's something . . . something insufficient. I can't recapture your memories when I wake up. I forget them. There are awful blanks! But we're in touch. We just need time and practice.

My fingers press down on the stone balustrade. They don't sink into it, but the whole world ripples. She is me, and I am her—yes, as Ibn 'Arabi was in suzerainty to the Lady Nizam.

Something prompts a question. "How close are you to your destination, Amy Dove? How close to this rescue?

—Maybe ten days. We've sailed over the sea to a port called Pyx. Darshanor—the boundary city we're heading for—is five or six days away. Then we'll go beyond, into the other hemisphere of Menka where we'll come into our new powers.

'Look round,' I tell myself . . .

I turn my head cautiously towards the bland faience dome, bereft of moral texts and scandalous illustrations.

A text *is* there! It glows, it moves. It ripples across the curve of the glazed wall.

'*You are in memory-space, Salman. Correct. And you have a mind-visitor—*'

—I've seen this before! My God, with you and Grigory in Samarkand!

"Of course!"

—This is the blank! This is what gets stripped away and hidden! Ritchie knew this too! It gets brainwashed out of us. Oh God, they aren't brainwashing *you* at all—the machines and their insect allies. They're trying to save us all. They warned us.

'*Correct. We are the Harxine Paracomputers, with the Group-ones as our agents. We are all in grave danger of the Veil Being achieving a backlash of power from the humans on God's World through the humans on this ship. We do not know its inner workings, though it has been our study for many years. It may ignore us, and invade your world immediately through the bridgehead you'll provide it with. Or it may try to destroy us first, because the humans on God's World will be impelled to wish this. We cannot risk this. We must ready our Group-ones to terminate you humans whom we hold. It will be a tragic decision for us, whose prime programme is to uphold life. We must also ready our Group-ones, enshipped near God's World, for a suicide strike against the six travellers. Be warned, mind-visitor. Do not carry on to Darshanor. We know exactly where you are, and will be, now. Realize the truth. Though the Getkans can not realize it. With all their borrowed powers, they are blind.'*

—Why don't you drop a bomb on us now? Or drop one on Darshanor?

'We cannot kill masses of living things! We must not—it is against our master programme. The most that we can do is order some few beings to be . . . excised surgically. Even this is terrible. In any case, it is impractical. Mass weapons can be turned against us by Getkan heroes who draw on the energies of the Veil Being. Safer to use the least weaponry, so that the threat seems small to them and to the Veil Being.'

A whirlwind tugs myself away. (But which 'self' does it tug?) A fierce suction pulls me back, down to a lower level of existence, into myself. Something vast and amorphous veils the words, veils my lips and eyes. It sucks, darkens, and erases.

Erases . . . what?

I don't know.

Nothing.

What's this nothing I'm fretting about?

Nothing is nothing. Not a thing.

Peacefulness. The peace that passes . . .

. . . understanding. I only understand this peace.

Peace before waking.

Actually, I'm awake already. On board ship, in the Bay of Pyx. Midnight-day has dawned, thickly dark in our cabin. René snores. The others still slumber in their bunks. They still dream.

What did we dream?

194

It's gone. Again I didn't dream. Or if I dreamt, where is the memory? Lost. Hidden. Stolen. A seal has been placed upon it.

We're summoned to the waterfront pyramid by the Tharliparan of Pyx. Three of his Getkan peers await us, up on the multifloor that links all the pyramids.

We are warned. The Paravarthun sense that the vile Group-ones have engineered some sort of channel to us, through the prisoners on *Pilgrim*. They're spying on us through those instruments of stolen psyche. It's their most successful penetration yet. The sooner we reach Darshanor, the sooner we can turn this channel against them.

Otherwise, all is sweetness and light.

As we walk back to the Pyx caravanserai, past sea shrikes spiking their catches on reeking salt-thorn bushes to rot down for their young, Peter gestures grandly towards the distant mountains. "The road to Darshanor is the stairway to the sky!" he proclaims.

Something has eaten my dreams away. Something that over-sees us. Something that's anxious we should hasten to our destination . . .

Destination equals destiny.

195

THIRTY-TWO

STAIRWAY TO THE sky indeed! It's just that, once we leave the
fertile coast behind. There are broad treads of land, increasingly
barren and lifeless. Periodic 'risers' of worn cliff-lines wind across
the whole terrain, broken by crumbling gullies. They form im-
mensely wide steps which lead slowly upwards, as though some
giant long ago terraced the landscape to cultivate stones or
perhaps colours, since the rocks are often vividly yellow, ochre,
coppery, ruddy. Surely they deserve more ornate names for their
hues: orpiment, gamboge, cinnabar! At times we ride beside
shallow pebble-lakes: mosaics of lilac and pillarbox red, of
pistachio green, jet black and orange. During the long sunsets
and sunrises this dead land is jewelled and prismatic—while the
far mountains flush pink and gold.

Small settlements exist along the road to Darshanor, spaced
out at a full day's ride one from another. Since this means two
of our shorter 'days' we camp in the wilderness as well. What do
they live on in these settlements, apart from their dreams? On
desert succulents, which spread thin glaucous pads at dawn to
osmose the dew, then ball up tight. On the fat rhizomes of plants
that are barely visible above the ground. On porridge of seed-
pods. On spiced eggs of penned ground-trotters, fed on com-
posted thorn grass. On roast lizards, on giant insects. On dried
fish from Pyx (we carry bags of it ourselves, to pay our way). On
feather-leaf tea.

Water wells up in dips of this wilderness, through the pebble
mosaics. So there is life, where at first there seems to be none at
all. René happily explores the web of desert life, wherever we
camp.

Traffic there is too on the road. A dyad of pre-heroes over-
hauls us while we settle down to midday sleep. Solitary travellers

return the other way, aglow with achievement and apotheosis. A few more dead souls have passed into Askatharli, in rapport with the living. The road itself, now broken and stony, overblown with dust, was once a mighty highway . . . That a technology exists ahead of us which can beam images and even solid objects over the light years seems such a contradiction of the reduced living circumstances in between. Yet paradoxically the sheer plod of the journey grinds us into belief, into acceptance. It must be so. It has to be.

At night, the wilderness dances with flickering lights which caper along the ground, leap overhead, set faint fire to the horizon. It's merely a magnetic effect, thinks René, nothing to do with that technology ahead of us. That technology operates upon another wavelength.

Day by day we ride higher. The mountains, which for so long have merely humped upon the horizon, are suddenly closer. It happens abruptly, as though all this while they have been pulling away from us, stretching the terrain elastically. Now, one morning, they have snapped back towards us.

Slowly the range of mountains parts, sheltering a high plateau in its arms, backed by other peaks. Our road up to this tableland through the escarpments is gentle—graded and embanked. Samti-menVao dreams along with us of sleek electric vehicles gliding up and down the rejuvenated pristine highway. We ride one of these up on to the tableland to an ancient festival of rhaniq racing, and fencing, pageant and magical conjurations, wine and love. In the morning we're back down below again, still facing the eroded climb.

"Why did you give up all *that*?" demands Wu, vexed. "That high point: the highway, the electric vehicles . . ."

"We didn't give it up," Samti answers, puzzled. "Nothing is gone. We still have it all, much improved on what it was." He taps his golden brow. "It demanded too much from everyone. And from the world."

"If this world is near a 'wellspring', why wasn't the spring always welling forth?" she asks. "How could it just switch on, one day?" It's a question that we've all tried to ask before.

197

It isn't a question that has meaning. History has yielded up to metahistory. The tenses of the verbs are all subtly wrong. No longer does there exist an instant prior to the revelation. Samti doesn't know what Wu means. Even less does he know it since his death-bonding!

Appears Darshanor, in long mid-morning when we breast the scarp—irrigated fields and orchards, a desert richly blooming; a necklace of artificial lakes with fairy rings of domed greenhouses bubbling around them; some hectares of solar panels forming a bright sea with stylized wave ridges. Isolated squat towers stand about apparently at random.

"Those must be the entry ramps to the undercity," Samti supposes. For much of Darshanor is underground. His finger inscribes arcs of guessed-at subterranean streets, bent as if by some overwhelming point of central gravity.

That point certainly exists: it is The Pyramid. At least a dozen subsidiary ziggurats and pyramids surround it, but the towering white structure at the centre of Darshanor is vaster than any Egyptian pyramid, a shining mountain quadrilateral. Even so, it must weigh lighter than any pyramid of Egypt, for it contains space within—and space beyond space, the internal space of all those other pyramids scattered across Getka.

A kilometre north of the cultivated zone rest other shapes which may once have shone, but are now pitted skeletons. Spaceships! Their remains. Vectored here by their High Space pyramids, then abandoned.

A starship park. A metal knacker's yard.

At the other end of the world lies Darshanor's twin city of the boundary, called Shabeet. From Shabeet, 'relocating' themselves from Shabeet's pyramid to that of Darshanor, have stepped the Tharliparan of that twin city together with a pair of ambassadors from another star. They have come to observe our initiation. Samti-menVao tells us this after our noon siesta, which we spent in one of the smaller ziggurats, a-dreaming. Darshanor is where local dreams and alien dreams converge; it is a swirling, miraculous, multi-species city, crossroads of the stars.

Rested and fed, we walk to the great pyramid.

In a vestibule of white pillars, from which a cantilevered ramp spirals upwards, we wait with the Tharliparan of Darshanor, until the other Tharliparan comes down, accompanied by our old acquaintance the Zeraini barrel being. It extends the micro-manipulators of its hand towards us, fluttering them as though in greeting. It is followed by two small faery things, looking like pets of the Getkans, wearing breathing filters over large deltoid heads with big black eyes. Thin, brittle, four-armed beings, these, with furled gossamer wings. Their bodies are a-ripple with feathery membranes. Perhaps they winnow the air of their world for aerial plankton and krill. Perhaps those are secondary 'breathers' for flight . . . Their bodies are golden with the same down as ours. They carry deltoid helmet-masks and mirror shields.

"These are the Dindi," explains the Tharliparan. "In our gravity they cannot quite fly. Once, they came in one of the ships that lie outside the city. The Askatharli engine guided them here, as it should have done you. Now, of course, they need no ships . . ."

They're quite charming. Not pets, no. Independent intelligences. Their voices are a sibilant whistle. They caper around us.

THIRTY-THREE

THESE THREE ALIENS and the native Getkans lead us through into huge workshops, manned by scores of Getkan heroes. A wonderful alchemy is at work here: the transmutation of matter into metamatter.

Angel hairs of the dead are blended with sand from Menka, and cold-fused by Askatharli light into helmet-masks, mirror-shields, dream-panels.

We tour the hoppers of sand, and golden fluff, and the slender cones which focus Askatharli light from an upper level of the pyramid. We watch the multicoloured crystalline sand flow and melt and change into something that is matter once again—an opaque, metallic, glassy stuff—but which now has, locked in it, the key to the Beyond.

René scoops his hand into one of the sand hoppers and lets the grains trickle through his fingers. "So it's from Menka?"

"It comes from the Sands of Memory beyond the mountains," agrees Darshanor's Tharliparan. "It comes from those singing dunes that bathe in the light of the Eye of Menka." (Which is their name for the gas giant—the physical analogue, in Low Space, of the whirlpool of creation.) "The crystals become capable of capturing thought. Seeded with the Askatharli life-stuff they form our tools."

"Was the High Space pyramid made here too?"

"It was dreamed by the dreams of the dead—by the Imagining which yearns for other beings to know it. It was projected to your world, and took on substance there."

A tiny voice nags: that they don't *know*. Ultimately they don't know. They're simply guided—by something beyond their control, something that whispers in the persuasive language of vision, Getkasaali, which has sunk its roots so deep in them, and in us. Yet this something wouldn't, and couldn't, exist except for them . . . Paradox.

Shut up, measly little voice, voice of fear! This is an evolutionary threshold we're at; once beyond it, we shall see all things in a different light, the light of the Beyond.

We return to the vestibule. We mount the cantilevered ramp, up past the floor of dreams, up to the multifloor.

As at Menfaa, it stretches out in all directions, the centre of everything seeming to be right here, where we are. Veils mask the distance—where we spy some Getkan heroes in transit. They disappear. Others linger in the distance, faintly, as if in waiting.

Yet this floor is different from Menfaa's. Somehow, there are many other planes—half-visible, if that—other 'axes' rising and descending around us. The common plane of this floor and the other floors holds steady—in a Getkan configuration, yes!—but there are other *potential* alien configurations juxtaposed and interpenetrating, centering on the primary plane of this floor. They are in a state of . . . semi-existence—out of phase. If we could set foot on them, if we could select for their full existence, we would transfer across not to Lyndarl or Shabeet but to . . . another world. Zerain. Or Earth. Here is the switching point, the hinge.

"Many worlds are conjoined to God's World, through the space that imagines them." The Zeraini gestures. "A hero chooses his track. He imagines it into being. When one of you has died, the other can walk home. All the way home."

"The breath of Being traverses all existence constantly," croons Shabeet's Tharliparan. "It renews existence all the time. At every moment the whole universe ceases to exist and is re-stored again."

"You mean that space-time is being switched off and on again all the time?"

"That's what Samti told us in the pyramid on Menfaa island," I tell Ritchie. "But you weren't *compos mentis* at the time."

"Christ," exclaims Ritchie. "I get it. All kinds of strange sightings can be explained this way. Transient creatures, phantoms, apparitions—those that aren't *tulkus*!—flying saucers. Those must be wandering alien heroes, who can't occur physically —not entirely, as there's no bond with the world they're seen on, ours. They're in transit. That's how they showed us the avatars. They've got a technology for harnessing the fact that the universe switches on and off!"

"And this takes time?" asks Zoe suddenly, alarmed. "How long does it take? Why does it take time?"

"It took *us* time to get here through High Space!" I hiss at her. "Otherwise our identity would have broken down."

"Watch, here comes a hero from Zerain." The barrel-being points. Upwards. At an angle to the axis of the multifloor. A second, phantom Zeraini, masked, holding its mirror-shield to consult the reflection in it, is stepping down one of the planes of choice, gradually gaining solidity and substance. It sets foot upon our common Getkan plane and stomps along towards us.

The two barrel-beings hoot and bray and gently interlock their microfingers.

The newcomer is an even burlier specimen. He greets us once 'our' Zeraini has explained who and what we are.

Traffic of worlds! He was on his own world only a little while ago! Oh Earth, you are not far . . .

"We have a God-book on our world," says Zoe quietly to the Tharliparans. "It is called the Koran. In it there's a story about how a ruler called Solomon asked his companions if any of them could bring him *instantly* the chair belonging to the woman who ruled another country. She was called the . . . Yarrish of Sheba, and she was visiting Solomon. He asked his people to do this so that she would believe in the will of his God when she saw it happen before her very eyes." (Shabeet listens attentively, while Darshanor seems impatient.) "An Askatharli creature who was present said, 'Oh, I shall bring you that chair in the time it takes you to get up out of your own chair, Solomon.' But an ordinary living man, who was called Assaf, spoke up. 'I shall bring you it in the time it takes to blink your eyes,' he said. And he did just that. There it was before them: Sheba's chair. *Immediately.* The man Assaf accomplished this . . . this recreation of the chair through Askatharli space in the blink of an eye. The Askatharli creature would have taken several moments to do the same."

"Well, Starborn?"

"Just this: the walk to Zerain or Earth takes time. It isn't instantaneous."

"So?"

"So maybe it isn't a real God-power that achieves it."

Shabeet drinks Zoe for a long time. Finally he purses his lips. "This Solomon wished to impress his visitor with the *will* of his God? But Askatharli doesn't possess will, except for the will that we ourselves lend to it. Our will is still anchored to the world—so a certain small time is required. There is your answer."

"And where is *God's will* in all this? What do we have here?" she adds quickly in English. "A drawing upon Genie-power: a kind of immense, composite Jinn . . ."

"Zoe," drawls Ritchie, "does it really matter if it takes a few moments to step across the light years? It sure seems fast enough to me!"

The two faery Dindi whistle and twitter impatiently.

"Nitpicking, that's you."

I agree.

Movement again: the faint, distant Getkans who are loitering out among the veils start towards us. They're carrying several extra helmet-masks, in addition to those they wear. They come; they emerge—and merge with our reality.

"Those masks are for you to wear," says Darshanor. "They have been borne through Askatharli to temper them."

"Yours, yes," twitter the Dindi.

"Yours," booms 'our' barrel.

Ritchie flinches. We all remember the hell storm!

"It is quite safe now, Ritchie Blue," purrs Darshanor. "You will learn to see the energies of creation that surround you. Then you may tame those, and not they you. When you accept a mask, being close to Askatharli as you are here, it will resonate uniquely to you. Once the path is open to your world, material for tools of vision will make itself available there too . . ."

The newcomers present our masks and mirror-shields to us.

Do we really remember *all* of the hell storm? Wasn't there something else? Something that Ritchie heard and saw? The momentary suspicion slips from me like a blob of quicksilver, fragmenting into tiny beads that vanish down a hundred cracks. I accept my mask. We all do—Wu last of all.

*   *   *

203

We are 'in' a superfluid, superconducting emptiness, so charged with the potential for being that nothing can yet be. Distance no longer has a meaning, nor size, nor length, breadth, height. A whole cosmos is 'here': in this monad which we are, infolding immensities in a set of self-connected points. This space has a granular, quantal structure—composed of 'moments' of existence, even though time is all one to it. Yet somehow we can slip through the quantal grain into successive facets of existence, elsewhere. Lines of light bend through the plane-maze of this monad —guidelines, pathways to other reality-aspects. They knot themselves into nodes, which are destinations. We're only separated from these by our 'here'-bound lives. If one of us dies, and the other one lives, I know that the other can pass through step by step on the wings of the dead one's imagining. Even now, we can see through—unscrambling those far nodes, not by focusing directly on them, but in reflection in our shields. For here reflects there, and there reflects here—just as the whole universe reflects what underlines it. And now those nodes unknot themselves, at our envisaging—

"See your world. See the loved places you are linked to, through your lives," calls Darshanor—or Shabeet.

—and our shields are a window, of farseeing. Suddenly we are 'there', angelically hovering, looking through—dreaming the distant realities, as the Imagining of High Space dreams them into independent status, substance and reality.

We all see different places. Actual places on Earth. An American city—the crowded downtown section; the ramparts of an old French town; the viscous black soil and rolling mists of Szechuan. Peter sees Kilimanjaro poke its bald pate impossibly high above the clouds, untenanted African Olympus, haunting emblem of sky-contact. I see Athens—it was a magical visit that took me there and to the islands; now I work magic in mid-air . . .

In mid-air. People actually see me. They see something. There's sudden turmoil in the streets. Cars brake and bump each other. The drivers jump out and stare, along with the pedestrians. People are seeing . . . a light, a phantom existence. An angel?

"We'd better stop!" It's Zoe who jerks her shield aside. "What are we doing to them? They're seeing things."

204

She's right. We mustn't disorient the world—until we can actually step through to explain the wonder of it.

Reluctantly, we disengage. We all do.

"We shall go back down now, Starborn," says Darshanor. "As you see, no inner wall exists here. But the pyramid has an outside wall. We shall climb up the stepway to the top, and you will see into the Eye of Menka."

Stone steps run up the western face of the pyramid. There are handrails on both sides, and the wind is light. But there are one hell of a lot of steps! By the time we've hauled ourselves up, unmasked, to the stone crow's nest, my thighs are aching. René is puffing audibly. We recover to vertigo, and a fabulous view.

Darshanor points westward. "Behold, the Eye."

A chasm bites down through several thousand metres of the mountain chain, a valley in the sky, and through that chasm looms a mottled orange glow—the limb of the gas giant brooding hugely, as if it has fallen upon the world.

"Mask yourselves, Starborn."

We do as he bids.

The solid world dissolves. The whole glory of the gas giant shines through it, band upon roiling, storm-torn band. I'm falling into that great bloodshot eye! The rail! The rail's still clutched tightly in my hand.

The wellspring regards its moon child across four hundred thousand kilometres of space.

Energies reach out to embrace its moon. Its gravitational field? Its magnetosphere? Or something else?

"It's alive! That goddam gas globe is alive!" swears Ritchie. "The . . . Eye . . . is alive," he calls out to Darshanor.

"No. We tap the powers of this membrane zone, but the life is here. Continue watching. We're all in resonance now. Your perception will be modified."

I sense other energies within—beyond—the gas globe, energies that emanate through it from elsewhere, outside reality. They are the energy fields of High Space. They are powers and operators, hypernumbers that exist like angels or Principles. Imaginary qualities which must exist, or the world could not exist. Yet they can't ever be found and counted in the world themselves.

205

And I see a million fingers, too, reaching into Menka-Getka,
saturating the world as the angelic—the imaginary—precipitates
into existence as actual tendrils that take root within our flesh:
subtle filaments that are all one substance in Askatharli space.

"It is beyond life, Starborn. There is the realm of the Shaping.
But it intrudes into the cosmos at this point, at the wellspring,
and becomes one with us. The will is always ours, Starborn. Or
yours. Or that of any other race that links to it."

I hear . . . whispers in my mind, like interference on a radio
set. I'm drawn—surely we all are—with an erotic yearning. Yes,
I sense the yearning of the others: a lustful itch towards tran-
scendence—which requires us to fuse with one another: the
knower with the known.

The giant lambent world aches on my eyes. But it isn't exactly
the physical gas giant that I'm seeing, I slowly realize. It is the
ideal gas giant, something in High Space that is also located at
this point in the physical universe, some huge body whose sense
organs we have become—something which tunes us through the
golden hairs!

No, we simply tune into it—and through it, into Askatharli!

It aches. I pull off my mask of vision. There are the mountains
again, and that deep cleft, and the orange gas-arc.

Tomorrow we must ride to the Hole in the Hills—which isn't
that mountain cleft we can see from here, but something else.
Even that cleft is high up steep cliffs, unscaleable. Into Menka
we must ride, and over the Sands of Memory to meet our deaths
and overcome them. Must. Must.

We climb slowly down the hundreds of steps. Going down is
a harder business than climbing up them.

Back on *terra firma*, we shake our legs out. "Phew!" pants
Peter. He grins and clasps my hand—not to hold himself up. No,
in triumph. Soon, soon, our apotheosis.

We're hardly half-way across the open space between the base
of the pyramid and the smaller ziggurat, when a fierce scream
tears the sky apart.

Two cone-shaped craft are racing down the sky towards us,
trailing thunder. They're burning bright!

"Ablative shields," cries Ritchie. "Re-entry hoods!"

The two craft are breaking up in flight. Behind the glowing shells egg-pods tumble out—dozens of bomb-shapes tossed down at Darshanor, and us!

"Down! Get down!"

Abruptly, gossamer parachutes wrench free and the pods fall more slowly, but still very fast. They're not bombs. They're . . .

A Getkan shouts at us, "The Group-ones!"

THIRTY-FOUR

THOSE WHITE-HOT SHIELDS don't even hit the ground. Something snatches them in mid-air. Something squeezes them, like a fist closing. They're imploded—erased from the sky.

Some way off, a couple of masked Getkans swing their mirror-shields to bear upon the falling pods.

"They did that!" exclaims Ritchie, as we hug the dirt. Other heroes are racing from the ziggurats.

A mêlée of energies electrifies the air. Demon shapes spring into being in mid-air, erupting against one pod then another, tearing them apart, gobbling the pieces. Chimaera creatures, spinning berserkers!

Samti-menVao is running, now, from the pyramid towards us. Other heroes converge, to protect us.

One pod, then a second, hits the ground. Immediately they split open, each disgorging an insectoid from out of a mass of whitish jelly. "Deceleration gel," breathes Ritchie.

The creatures orient themselves at once. In bounding leaps they reach the two closest Getkans and tear them apart with their serrated fore-arms, only to be destroyed themselves a moment later by dream-demons coalescing around them, as terrifying as the insectoids themselves. By now another dozen pods are down, split open, warriors disgorged.

If only we were closer to the ziggurat! We daren't move. The battle is happening everywhere, at random. No! From each new nearby pod the insectoids are heading *for us*, tangling with any Getkans and dream-demons in their way. It's just that most pods have fallen too far off and their occupants are wreaking random diversionary mayhem, as if they only count their fighting lives in seconds!

Crump. A pod hits the ground thirty metres from us, rocking and tossing us. Gel spews out of it—bearing with it the beast it cushioned. This one has two legs twisted out of shape. Still, it rears and casts about in a moment and heads for us. Is that really myself screaming, or somebody else? I'm scrabbling away, stumble-running. I grab Peter's hand, hauling him with me. The others are scramble-scattering too, while Samti howls, "No! All stay together!" With that beast at our throats in a moment? It's the battle for *Pilgrim* all over again, only this time the awful sight of it isn't hidden. An unmasked Getkan crashes into us, bringing us down together in a tangle. That wasn't any accident! He trips and arm-locks us. We're wrestling, trying to fight free. "Stay! Stay!" he shrieks—in pain? Have we broken something?

The monster that was heading for us is already scattered piece-meal. A harpy-like green thing with huge claws and a broken wing is stamping on the gobbets, cawing in triumph. It fades and vanishes, dissolving back into the imagination.

All the pods have fallen. Presumably. Many, out of sight. A number of Getkans lie dead. In a wide perimeter around us lie remains of Group-ones, some still thrashing their stings. Demonic ghosts are still phasing in and out of existence, mostly out.

Suddenly they're all gone. There are only the broken-open pods exuding gel, and torn insectoids, and a few dead native bodies. The whole mad skirmish must have been over in two minutes, or three. And we live. All six of us. We live.

The Getkan who pulled us down has broken three of his long thin fingers. He moans, and hunches over them.

Shaking, we rise. We regroup—shocked, euphoric, then ashamed. But what else could we have done?

The Getkan with the broken fingers staggers erect and walks off slowly towards one of the ziggurats, ignoring us.

"They almost reached you," says Samti, bringing two fingers together, then snipping them like scissors. "Your revenge will be sweet for all of us, when you become heroes yourselves and reach out through your prisoner friends to call dream-demons there. We're so happy we have saved you. Those who died have merely gone into Askatharli, to live again."

"Mightn't the Group-ones try again?" pants Ritchie.

"Out on the Sands of Memory? Oh no. Besides, they've lost many of their zombie units. They'll need to breed more of them as replacements. They knew you were here, Starborn. Thus the channel does exist—back to them!"

"They've shot their bolt." Ritchie grins. "Yeah, we owe you. We'll repay."

Already the mess of crashed pods, parachute gossamer, gel and insectoid corpses is beginning to be cleared up, and the Getkan dead borne off for shaving and disposal.

"A bolt has been shot," nods Wu. "But does it lock them out, or lock us in?"

"How can you say that? When they've laid down their lives for us!"

"Ah, lives which they cannot lose, Amy."

"I hope we can end ours as bravely!"

Part Five

THE EYE OF MENKA

THIRTY-FIVE

THE HOLE IN the Hills is a dead straight tunnel many kilometres long, carved out long ago. It is tall; it is broad; it slopes gently ever uphill. A massive ancient engineering feat! (More accurately it is a modern engineering feat—however, the 'modern' is in the past now and the ancient has returned . . .) The trimmed rock glows with a phosphorescence that is perhaps natural, perhaps artificial, affording a soft blue submarine light. Half a kilometre into the tunnel, we pass a rhaniq-cart returning from Menka with a hero riding the beast. The cart holds barrels of glittering sand . . . We wave; we pass.

"Suppose it is a storage system?" muses René. "Untold trillions of silicon chips scattered about all over Menka, able to be imprinted . . . with *thought*. Bathed in the light reflected from the Eye of Menka . . . light vibrating in one direction only . . ." He falters. "I can't put my finger on it. It's as if something keeps on sliding my finger away."

There's a subtle current in this tunnel. A pressure differential between one side of the mountains and the other? Or is it something inside us, this pressure? So that the unthinkable is indeed unthought . . . Whatever is René saying?

"If askas—souls—are all only sub-programmes—believing in their own sovereign existence, and yet able to be assembled into some overprogramme which they can't recognize . . . And if this overprogramme gains energy and an enhanced existence, the more subprogrammes that enter into it . . ." He yawns.

I'm sleepy too. It's so calm here. The march of the rhaniq is a soothing massage . . . Monotonous, the tunnel, really. Dreamy, the blue light.

Dreamy.

A bull session is going on in the mess room. Captain K and Heinz and Zoe and I are listening to Salman hold forth.

"But don't you see, there's a higher spatial level—of creative thought, of pure potential. This is High Space, hyperspace. We're taking a short cut through it right now: a sort of magic carpet ride. The angels that came to Earth are from this higher level— from what we call the 'Presence of the Masterhood', *hadrat al-rububiyya.* This might be a bit difficult to explain to the Joint Space Authority, no?" Salman grins, winningly. "It isn't accessible to the objective tools of the lower world, the world of sensory experience which we call *mushāhada.*"

"But a machine does exist," objects Heinz. "Surely the High Space drive is a genuine machine?"

"It isn't one that we could ever have made. It's been . . . inserted into our reality. It's like a tool formed by an angel out of its own substance. But we mustn't think of an angel as a 'person', just because we rationalize angels that way. It's a portion of the essence of the higher level."

"A good job Madame Wu isn't listening in!" I chuckle.

"*Ja*, it's an anomaly," agrees Heinz. "A kind of perpetual miracle, held in being by a powerful force—which uses us to maintain the solidity of the engine. We're a channel, a transducer for higher forces. But what's the gradient between a momentary apparition and one that remains in existence for a very long time? We don't have the physics to discuss this."

"We have ourselves," insists Salman. "We have subjective tools."

Captain K smiles, no doubt visualizing a paranormal technology emerging from this expedition. "Maybe it is as the poet said of Russia? 'You can't understand Russia with your mind; you can only believe it!' " (*Grigory, I* know *you! I have* been *you!*)

"We must derive field equations," nods Heinz, "for the 'as if' structure—a tensor analysis of how your 'angelic', archetypal level is translated into the actuality of events, from the co-ordinates of one system to the other. But it has to be done outside ordinary waking reality."

Ordinary waking reality.

Suddenly I realize. Where and why and how.

"Listen to me, all of you! This has already all happened! It's

214

happening again, outside time—in dream space for me, in memory space for you. Heinz, Grigory, Salman: you're all imprisoned in memory space together. You aren't *en route* to God's World at all. You're already there! You're in space in the God's World solar system. You're prisoners of some giant alien insect things with a collective mind—and they're probing your minds and memories! I'm down on God's World, but I'm in touch with you too—because we're all fundamentally *one*: *one* in the ultimate Imagining! My God, those insects have just tried to kill us all to stop us getting where we're going. You're in terrible danger now."

"This is madness," frowns Heinz. "First we attack ourselves, thanks to friend Jacobik—"

"Don't evoke him! He might come." If he isn't already lurking close . . .

"Wait," Captain K says calmly. "Be calm. Concentrate. Do you remember Samarkand, Salman? *We met there.* This is all true. You spoke about veils. There's a veil over our eyes!"

Salman holds himself rigid. "Yes . . . I do! I remember it! Grigory, we're already using these subjective tools. We *are* them. Our memories have become a language. Veils? Grigory—the Veil Being! Satan!" I think that's what he says. Something of the sort.

Heinz drags at his beard. "Is this true? Maybe we can't communicate directly with these aliens, because of concept differences. So they have to use *us* as the means of communication."

"Communicate?" I cry. "They're the *enemy*. 'There's a War in Heaven,' don't you remember? 'Come to God's World, come to success.' You're in their hands—or their claws. They've just tried to kill us. I'm free—riding through God's World. So is Zoe. But Zoe here is only a reflection. A persona, a construct of your memories. See, she's silent. Frozen. She can't enter this dialogue. She has no place in it."

Zoe laughs out loud. "Like hell, Amy! Oh, like hell. I'm here too, just as you are. We're somewhere in that long hole through the hills, on rhaniq-back, right? And we're inside the Group-ones' experiment, right on the inside. Can we wake these people, Amy? Can we help them take over the real *Pilgrim*? Or is it too soon? We have to wait, don't we, till we can call on the powers

215

the Getkans used yesterday?" She glares round the room. "If only you could all open your eyes!"

Captain K clears his throat. "You came here by abnormal means, Dove. A power. What is it?"

"Oh, *that*." Zoe and I exchange glances—for in this dream and memory space no golden integument covers us. Zoe is black again, and I'm plain cream. She grins broadly. They know nothing about the symbiont.

"It's like hair, like golden threads. It grows out of our skin, all over us . . ." I tell them about the golden down and the shared dreams, about the wellspring of Creation, and the miracle of God's World. I tell them about Darshanor, and the Sands of Memory that we'll soon tread, and of our dyad-deaths which will transform us.

Salman looks scared. " 'If the seal is taken away from the treasure chests of this lower world, nothing of what God kept in them will remain—everything will be transported into the other world.' Grigory, the *Harxine*—"

"Other worlds are joining the network, Salman dear. The Getkans know very well how to keep the foundations of the world intact."

"Look." Heinz points at the autochef. The screen has lit up.

'Greetings, humans. We are the Harxine Paracomputers. You are in group memory space, with mind-visitors. They are under censorship-control of the Veil Being, but they cannot strike at us yet. Soon they will be able to, and you must sadly be terminated at that moment, unless they can break through the veil of their own volition. Our Group-ones are now programmed for this termination. We shall deeply regret this. We only hold back, rashly, now out of respect for your lives.'

Captain K swings round. "Dove? Denby?"

Zoe looks shocked, confused. But I know. It all floods in. It all comes together, appallingly. And it can all be taken apart again, and the pieces hidden away—at the insidious will of the entity that broods over God's World and the other worlds it has enmeshed! Captain K and Heinz and all others will be snuffed out because of what we're going to do. And Earth will be sucked into the hyperspatial embrace of this rogue angel . . .

216

"Iblis," whispers Salman. "Who undoes Creation. We must die, Amy, we must die. The Harxine are more important than our few lives."

Zoe has to have all this explained to her . . .

"Dying is the key, isn't it? You said we must die, Salman. But dying is just what *we six* can't do! Death is denied—so the knowledge of living beings, the souls of living beings aren't reprocessed back into the final ground of Being. They're caught up in this standing wave, instead. The Veil Being."

"It may still be an evolutionary development," injects Zoe sourly.

"No!" cries Salman. "Never. Your Getkans are just . . . *units* in this metabeing—used by it! Against the world, against reality."

Where is our expert on death, now? Jacobik's *tulku. I need you.*

"The point is," says Heinz, "do we face a material system or a wholly immaterial one? One which we can only fight in our . . . imagination? It seems to be both. It precipitates into the world— into your bodies. It affects the crystal structure of those sands. And its point of origin is somehow associated with the gas giant. I wonder what the Harxine theorize about this?"

He approaches the alphabetic keyboard of the autochef— which Jacobik once misused. (Or has he done so yet, at this memory point, now twisted off the memory track entirely into a new mental space where we can meet and plan?)

Captain K stays his hand. "No, first we must make sure that Dove and Denby—or one of them at least—*remembers.* They must see through this damn veil, back down there. If it'll allow them to. Perhaps . . . They're already in a very strange altered state of consciousness, but possibly I can hypnotize them. I am a good mesmerist. Maybe I can imprint a hypnotic command to recall this information. It isn't erased in the ordinary sense, if we're to believe Dove. It's still available, to the general imagination—where the main, immaterial part of the Veil Being exists as *part of everyone* it has processed. It's just locked away. We must try to find a key that will unlock it. A trigger. It must be something . . . shocking. Alerting. Something that operates too vividly

217

and basically for it not to allow them to seize this knowledge and make it utterly a part of them."

"Death comes as a shock to most people," remarks Salman.

"Death! Yes. The moment of death, the moment of transfiguration. Hang the key there."

"*Tod und Verklärung!*" exclaims Heinz. "Death and transfiguration into this new state—which is when they'll try to attack the Harxine through us! We can bargain with the Harxine now. They'll have to let us live till Amy or Zoe is transfigured—because that's when the key will turn. *Your* key, Captain."

"Bargain away," says Captain K. "Do it. Otherwise, no hypnosis." Actually, he's lying. I can see that—read it in his face, but neither the Harxine nor the Group-ones would be able to read it. He wouldn't sign away the Earth—which we'll yield up to the Veil Being, unless we realize. Not just for the sake of a few more hours of life. It's to make utterly sure that this plan goes through, and that the Harxine don't destroy him, and it, prematurely.

But, as Heinz addresses himself to the keyboard . . .

THIRTY-SIX

I MUST HAVE dozed off. We're emerging from the submarine blue of the Hole in the Hills into bright mid-daylight. Zoe yawns. We stare at one another for a moment, wondering why we stare. No. For no reason.

A gravel plain stretches away from the mountain wall, chequered with snow lakes of white porphyry chips. Dunes ripple the horizon. And the saffron and gold glow of the gas giant's equator is the greatest dune of all.

"Peter—"

"Hmm?"

"Which of us will it be?" (Who dies. It's unspoken. We both know what I mean.)

"I've no idea. *How* it'll happen is what I'd like to know."

"Oh, I know. The enemy will have the shape of Jacobik."

"Isn't it enough that you've killed him once already? God, do you have to repeat the performance?"

"You aren't jealous of him, by any chance?"

"Jealous of a ghost? Amy, I don't hold you responsible for . . . for what happened. It wasn't you, love. It was all of us, channelling hatred through you."

"His aska remains. It lies in wait."

"For you? Or for me? Is that what you really want deep down? For him to kill me?"

"Then you'd be lord of my heart, darling. Let's not quarrel. We're on edge. No human being has ever gone to their death before with a gold-backed guarantee that there's no death at all. We still can't quite believe it, can we? Oh, to be free of that weight, Peter! And for everyone on Earth to be free of it!"

Peter kicks his heels into the rhaniq, pulling us level with Samti-menVao.

"Samti, is menVao the same as Vilo was in life?"

"The same? We *are* Samti-menVao, Starborn. menVao is—how shall I put it?—the perfected self of Vilo. What is the special flavour of this perfection? Her memories are open to me, yet they are untouched by pain or grief or suspicions or discontent. They are unspoilt by the partial, failing quality of ordinary existence. She shines in a new light, and I reflect that light: her mirror."

"But is she still herself?"

"Personality remains, yes. It isn't the simple, partial personality of life. It's a fullness, a fulfilment of what she yearned to be. Soon enough you'll know this yourselves."

Lizards flicker on the gravel: chameleons, taking on its colouration. Patches of jet and coal scuttle away from our beasts' hooves, lofting themselves up on preposterously stilted legs. It's as though a knot of ground has come alive spontaneously, sprouted feet, then settled back into dead stone again. When they rush on to a patch of snowy porphyry they become snow-skinned. Samti whistles at the fleeing lizards. They poise erect, listening, captured by the sound. He dismounts, still whistling, and picks some of them up for food, pops them into a bag. It seems almost unfair to them, darting little mesmerised things.

When we camp this evening we cook the lizard meat. Their madder flesh tastes like smoked salmon.

The perfected self? Do I really know you, Peter? Or you me? I feel like a creature without a past. Or with only an eroded, notional past. I'm a vase which has mysteriously appeared in the midst of this alien desert, full of the water of life. A gratuitous being. All my past has no significance, beside what is about to happen.

Perhaps my vase has only ever been half-full, not brim-full. Why do I need to pour Peter's life into mine, to complete myself? Or mine into his? Am I so incomplete and partial that I need another soul?

"Happy dreams." He squeezes my hand. "What shall they be?"

"I'm losing my dreams, Peter."

"I know. It'll come right."

We sit in a ring around the guttering cooking fire—made from kindling that we carry with us. One of the rhaniqs, folded up like

220

a collapsed clothes horse, bleats plaintively in the queer, golden dusk. For the sun has set, yet a mighty slice of the gas giant still glows brightly, while the rest of the segment hangs ghostly, leached of its borrowed radiance, forming a solid monochrome cloud. So we see a huge, curved triangle of a moon.

"We should try to reach *Pilgrim* again, in a co-ordinated dream of the real world," announces Wu briskly.

"Whatever for? In just another day or two we'll be . . . *transfigured*. We'll be able to intervene directly." Transfigured . . . *Tod und Verklärung*: death and transfiguration . . . Now where did I get the word from? I feel deeply reluctant. Something in me whispers 'no'. Maybe because last time I met . . . I don't wish to meet Jacobik on the ship. Jacobik is death incarnate. It isn't time to meet him yet.

"To spy out the land, Amy."

"The Maoist cavalry rides again?" Peter chuckles. "I'm game."

"Me too," crows Ritchie.

"Actually, Sun Yat-sen devised the style of dress," says Wu. "It's merely one of the perversions of history that Mao's name is invoked."

For some reason Zoe also demurs, but she finally comes round. As do I.

As Heinz addresses himself to the keyboard . . .

It's the moment just after the previous moment; yet a gulf of time hangs between the two.

"Wait," says Captain K. "Something happened, Dove. What was it?"

"It all *stopped* happening—then it started up again! Time has gone by. We've ridden on. We're camping out in the desert. Zoe?" She's still here—or here again, thank God, but is it really her?

Zoe flashes a quick smile. "The real me, Amy."

"We were planning a dream ride to *Pilgrim*—an out-of-the-body experience. We did it once before. We can see you uptime in the present. But we can't interact with you—not yet."

"Did you remember anything, Dove? Back in your body?"

"No."

"Denby?"

221

Zoe shakes her head. She shivers. "I feel footsteps walking over my grave . . . Ritchie and René and Wu are riding their surrealistic nags over that craterscape outside, not knowing that we're really here inside."

"Maybe we're with them—in reflection."

Salman knits his fingers together, and cracks the joints. "Over your grave? But what *is* death?"

"Samti—the Getkan hero we're with—says that his dead love has become the perfected form of her living self."

"He also said that personality remains," adds Zoe. "Ego lives on, sculpting those imaginary mock-worlds."

"If there's no death," pursues Salman doggedly, "then the past has no significance. The past disappears. There's no chance of any new ideas, any new presences—if there's no dialogue of life and death. No future, either. The world will slowly collapse on itself like a balloon."

"There *is* a dialogue. Samti and menVao: life and death."

"It's a false dialogue, Amy. Life and death have become the same experience. The removal of death from the equation of existence is the ultimate deceit. This is the real evil of the Veil Being. It intercepts souls, it stores them in itself. It uses a collective of souls *as* its own being, and veils reality. And it slowly destroys worlds, because there's no longer any history, no longer any 'becoming'."

"Theology is all we need just now!" sighs Heinz.

"No, the Harxine are deeply interested in this. It was their point of contact with me, in my memory of Isfahan. They told me this through the lips of my Mulla. They're trying to develop cybernetic rules for the Creator and the Created."

"Cybernetic theology? For the universe as a Black Box?" Heinz perks up. "With the experimenter—God—inaccessible to us, who are the contents of the box? With the input, what?"

"Creative energy—the hierarchy of descent from the *hadrat al-rububiyya* to the *mushāhada*: from the Presence of the Masterhood to the ordinary sensory world."

"*Ach*, yes. And the output . . . what would that be? Life-memory, gated through death? Or is God the Black Box, to us? The inaccessible, who seems more spuriously accessible from God's World?"

222

"It all comes down to death, doesn't it?" challenges Salman. "Death has been distanced. There's an energy circuit—a circuit of being—between God and the world; and the output back into God is *blocked*. There's a closed loop situation. Something exists upon that loop, by virtue of it—and sustains it. It blocks the way back to the Absolute, and undoes reality. God's veil has become *evil*. That's an anagram of 'veil' in English, isn't it? The same thing turned inside out!"

"Oh, Islam is always fishing for hidden meanings in the roots of words," shrugs Zoe.

"In Arabic words maybe. But it's true: another anagram is *live*—the opposite of 'die'! The malignant perpetuation of 'I live'—the denial of death—is the definition of this evil."

"Negotiate, Anders," orders Captain K.

But as Heinz prepares to type, the reply already flows . . .

'You perceive our quest correctly, humans. We have frozen, then unfrozen, this memory-space so that it would have the same configuration for your mind-visitors were they able to return; as they have now done. We are interested in your offer. Please proceed with this hypnosis. We shall not terminate you until the first manifestation of attack. But then we must, at the very first intrusion. Our Group-ones are poised around you. They will act instantly.'

"So," says Captain K, "first you, Dove. Denby second."

"I'm ready." I stand in front of him. He begins his fatherly, hypnotic enchantment. It all seems quite ordinary, almost commonplace. I hear what he says. I don't go to sleep (but then, I *am* asleep). On the other hand . . .

Death. At the moment of death. After the moment of death. And transfiguration. I. Shall. Remember. This. I hold the key. The key is death. At the moment of death . . .

The mess room wavers, and is snuffed out. Where was I?

What should I remember?

Remember, ember, embers: the embers of our camp fire.

223

THIRTY-SEVEN

THE MAOIST CAVALRY invaded the asteroid again. They boarded *Pilgrim*. They marched to the control deck where our friends were lying wired up, this time with an insectoid poised over every one of them. Marched, in dream gravity; but did not interact with the reality. And I was there with them—*so they say*. I know I wasn't there. Nor Zoe either . . .

The rhaniqs' hooves leave rows of dimples in the dunes, sharper and less slurred than they would be on Earth, less prompt to fill—though the breeze is already at work, shifting grains. These sandhills rise a hundred to a hundred and fifty metres, and are eloquent with colour, on one side at least. The sunlit slopes shimmer through the whole spectrum like tilted, flowing oil. But the shaded sides are suddenly cold and lustreless, drained of iridescence beyond each clear-cut ridge.

Eloquent to the ear are these dunes too. Each has its own voice. The wind and the vibrations of our passage trigger them, and they seem to converse with each other wordlessly, each dune's voice carved by its current shape. They speak with a rumble of thunder, with a distant siren song, with a thin wavering whistle, with a drum-roll, a twang, a heartbeat (*thud, thud, thud*), a bellow, a clanging bell note. The desert is talking, or making music to itself, about us as we pass. We are ants marching over the taut strings and stretched drumskins of some set of instruments that flow into and out of one another. It's a hypnotic, eerie place.

This constant thin gonging, the faint hammering, the bell notes affect Ritchie first. He slaps a cupped palm against his ear to swat the invading sounds. He grabs for the treksack, pulls out an L-27.

"What is it, man?" cries René. "There's nothing there. Put it away." The curling dune tosses back his cry, mockingly.

"Ritchie," purrs Wu.

"Damn it, I'm commander, still and all. Just checking out the hardware."

A temple bell tones beneath our feet.

The crazy boy fires his rifle across the dune, burning, wounding, drilling spears of hot fused quartz into its flank.

A harsh shrill races through the sands—a cry of pain, a challenge.

Again he fires. Again the wild cry throbs through me, nauseating me. The world rolls and heaves. The dunes are huge waves at sea.

Samti-menVao nudges his mount closer. "Do you wish to meet death already? You aren't wearing your mask."

"The gun still works," smirks Ritchie. He has gone a little mad. But he does return the laser to the trekpack.

These sands seem more alive now, seeking out our wavelengths. The eardrums of the desert hear us—ossicles of sands, auditory labyrinths filled with sand-fluid. The air is electric—and thinner, headier. We inhale more with each breath. My heart still races from Ritchie's abrupt impulsive action. When the time comes, do we die not from a demon's stroke but from heart failure?

"What did I do wrong, huh? Did I fry somebody's memories? Cook someone's soul?" Ritchie pants, then ludicrously he hiccups. *Hic, hic.* Latin for 'here'! A tiny creature asserting its presence, its thisness.

A world's memories encoded here: is it possible? Zeraini memories too. And Dindi memories, and others. And ours. A trillion trillion transducer crystals, receiving the rhythms of consciousness—the soul waves—of all the golden beings? Or a mere nothingness, a place of death, sculpted by the empty winds? Here are no more lizards. Their home is the gravel desert we have left behind. Yes, these sands are remembering us, just as they remember every thought and action and dream-act of those close to Askatharli . . .

Peace, whisper the sands now. Peace to you. We take longer, deeper breaths.

Here is a bowl, an eroded crater perhaps two kilometres across where the winds have smoothed out a sand lake. Beyond it, dunes to the horizon—an iridescent moiré banded by thin dull shade lines, brooded over by a little more of the Eye, muted in the sunlight.

Masked, Samti-menVao scans the terrain.

"Here is suitable, Starborn. We shall wait above with the beasts."

So here we are: the arena of immortality. An empty basin. Empty, but we have seen a creature of light walk over the ash-strewn water to take on the shape of death . . .

"The sands already know you are here. The masks will amplify the call. You will go down two by two."

With a brash shrug—for he has pulled himself together—Ritchie breaks out two L-27s.

There's something I must remember . . . But what? No doubt I shall remember it *at the moment.*

"Who goes first?"

"When Ritchie and I go," says Wu, cannily postponing the moment of her own going, "I don't wish to use the light weapon. Samti-menVao, may I use Vilo's sword?"

"We are honoured." Samti draws it from its scabbard.

"I've never used a sword in my life!" protests Ritchie.

Wu shrugs. Has she ever used a sword? I doubt it. What is she planning?

"Can I still use my gun, Wu?"

"As you like."

A laser can kill from a hundred metres, burn from two hundred, blind from a thousand . . . Is she sacrificing herself? For Ritchie's sake? To live within him forevermore, rather than he in her?

"Shall we go first?" René invites Zoe softly. "I would like to learn more about this strange symbiosis. Not least," he adds gallantly, "of me with you, *négresse d'or.*" He strikes a pose, mock-dandyish. "Do you know Baudelaire's poem, *The Death of Lovers? 'Nous échangerons un éclair unique . . . et plus tard un Ange, entr'ouvrant les portes, viendra ranimer . . .'* 'Our hearts will be two torches, their light reflecting in our minds—twin

226

mirrors. We will exchange one single flash of light . . . after which an Angel, half-opening the doors, will come to restore to life . . . the mirrors and the flames.' So here are the mirrors: our shields. Here is the source of that flash of light: the laser. And here is the place of the angel, who slays to immortalise, so that our hearts may perfectly reflect each other." There's an ironic whimsy to his rhapsody, which appeals more to Zoe right now than if he was entirely serious.

She smiles at him. "The poetry's fine—even going on the translation—but theologically I still smell a rat."

" 'Si vous alliez, Madame, au vrai pays de gloire, sur les bords de la Seine,' " he quotes charmingly. "Ah, but you'll speak French fluently enough once we have full access to each other!"

Wu is busy examining her own face (ivory downed with gold) in Ritchie's mirror shield. She stares unblinkingly into her own eyes. Does she see another course? If she does, she doesn't say what it is.

We all shake hands; and embrace.

Zoe and René don their helmets, heft their shields and lasers, and set off down into the sand basin. We watch, unhelmeted, as they grow smaller, separating, moving apart. The Eye of Menka beats a ghostly gong of faint gold beyond the violet sky. Mirages set the sand atremble in the sparkling distance—light transmuted into unreal liquid.

René and Zoe turn the mirror shields towards one another, in salute: *morituri* . . .

Dust cavorts into the air among the mirages. A shining vortex dances out of the mock waters.

They angle their shields in the direction of this dust devil, triangulating on it, to pull it closer. This is how we were told it would be. I see how René visualizes the coming encounter: as a duel, one Paris morning a hundred and more years ago in the Bois. But is that thing of light the foe—or the adjudicator?

The light dances in between them.

And light becomes body. It is a prancing Cubist fetish—a four-legged monster with toothy skulls upon its knees. Its body is a box with a gaping wooden-toothed mouth wide open in the belly. The hole passes right through its midriff. Upon a tall, rag-

227

clad muddy neck shudders an oval head with four bulging wooden eyes and a mouthful of broken crocodile teeth. Muddy hag-hair dangles almost to the ground. Taller than either René or Zoe, turning about and about, the thing stamps and whistles. Its arms are bone-thin, bangled and overlong. Each hand clasps a red-stained machete.

It darts towards René, then back towards Zoe. It flails its machetes. It dances on a string, held taut between them. Closer and closer to them it bounds with each swing. It must slash one of them with its bloody blades soon!

"Burn it!" shouts René.

He fires; Zoe fires simultaneously. She screams; she falls. René's laser beam has gone right through that gaping belly-mouth. Hers has . . . the fetish flares up in flames. Hers hit it. Air keens in the furnace it becomes. It bounds towards her, blazing and shrilling, its blades plunging at her fallen body even as it burns away.

Away into smoke, into wisps in the air, into nothing at all.

Dropping his laser, René sinks to his knees in the sand. He tears off the helmet-mask and cradles his head.

Before any of us can start down the slope to his side, or to Zoe's, he rises. He straightens up. He walks back uphill towards us, ignoring Zoe's corpse. His expression is enchanted. He runs his hands up and down his hips as though caressing a new, strange frame.

"We are René-menZoe," he laughs. "It's all true. Two lives we've lived. Now they're one, in me. Blind. We've been blind till now!"

"Zoe's still alive?" asks Peter cautiously.

"Her body died. Only her body. She's with me now. She's a . . . presence, to me. Lover, sister, mother, child: all of these. She's in the dream domain, yet here too. I know her dreams and memories. *We* know them. *Je est un autre.* I'm the dreamer; she's the dream—the dream of her life. *Ah, comme je bavarde!*"

"Who controls your body? Can she—?"

"Can we still speak to her? To *you*, Zoe?" I ask her-who-is-not-here (yet is).

"I feel her touch upon my body, strange to her. I feel the thrust of breasts, the cleavage of my sex—her sex. When my lips

228

touch each other now, they kiss: myself, herself. Her tongue is in my mouth. I'm . . . complete. Entire. I didn't know how partial I was. And still am! I'm not wholly of Askatharli yet. But I can wait. There are souls beyond souls, dreams beyond dreams: dreams that are awake, like fabulous living palaces. We've seen a little of this, but now it's the whole fabric of her existence. She is imagination now. She is music and creation—and she is still herself. I bear her memories, like a child within me, whose mind I know in the womb. She's beyond them now—yet they're still the matrix from which she arises. *Ah, quel bavardage!*"

"What was that monster?" I want to know.

"Ah, the fetish creature was hers: mine: ours. No distinction now! We used it as an illustration in one of our books on religion. That was an initiation idol from the Guinea coast. It always held a morbid fascination for us. So we brought it to life at last. We shaped the force of creation-destruction: the angel of initiation, in its mould. All the forms of Gods and angels are here in Askatharli: trace one way, one appears . . ."

"Does she still smell a rat?" asks Wu.

René only laughs. "Die—and see. Pass through death."

Briefly Samti-menVao rests a hand upon René's shoulder, and drinks his happiness with honey eyes. René shivers. "An alien soul touches my heart. The brush of a bird's wing."

"Do we bury Zoe?"

"In sand? The sand will bury her body." René kicks some of it with his foot.

"We can't leave her lying there," protests Ritchie.

"She isn't lying there. She stands here facing you—she stands beyond. Anyway, it's your time to meet death now, not to scoop sand over a . . . log, like children at the seaside."

I should remember something . . . Should Zoe have remembered something too? Irrelevant thoughts.

Masked, with the whole Eye of Menka radiating filaments of energy across the sands, looming ghostly and enormous through the world which is a palimpsest, I take up René's discarded gun. Peter averts his gaze from Zoe's body, to pick up her gun. We turn our shields to face one another; we wait, we watch . . .

Till the dust devil dances out again on that water sheet which is quite dry. Till we turn our shields to face it, and draw it in to us. It advances, it clarifies.

Jacobik. Yes, indeed!

At any rate, it is a human form of the same height and build as Jacobik, dressed in a *Pilgrim* jump suit, with the same sharp voracious face, a face that is pallid and bare except where a curly black beard crawls over chin and cheeks. A thought creature in his form, dredged from my mind. His weapons? Bare hands, and a knotted cord. Assassin's weapons—ironically, for he was assassinated by such tools.

He advances across the sands to a point midway between us and clicks his heels—inaudibly—then bows sharply: to each of us. That lizard tongue flickers over his lips, moistening them, wetting the dust of death.

"Franz?" asks Peter uncertainly, foolishly giving Death the name of any mother's son. The golem waits in silence, flexing his killer's cord.

"Do we shoot him, Amy? He's almost unarmed."

"Do you want *me* to shoot? Can't you bring yourself to?"

"Love—"

One of us must die. The golem will see to that.

But how? Do I shoot Peter accidentally—at the moment when he destroys the pseudo-Jacobik? So that 'each man kills the thing he loves'? That golem stands exactly between us, poised between our levelled shields. Smiling now, twisting the cord—and the cords of his lips.

So I dip my shield. So I sidle one pace, then another, to the left. Jacobik stays put. Three, four, five. Now Peter's in the clear.

Only now do I fire. And fire.

Nothing happens. The rifle is dead.

Grinning, the golem Jacobik swings round to face Peter and begins to walk towards him.

"My gun's dead. Shoot him!"

Flash-glimpse: up on the sandy rise, tall skinny golden Samti and gangling Ritchie beside the lanky indifferent ginger rhaniqs. René in a world of his own. Little Wu standing apart, her borrowed sword catching the sun. She shifts it to and fro as

230

though to semaphore a message down to me. She's flexing it, testing its balance.

"Mine won't fire either!" (Dead—or inhibited? By the High Space forces that surround us?) Peter stands uselessly, pulling at the squat steel sausage . . . as Jacobik extends his strangler's cord to arm's length.

I howl, to distract the killer, "A gun is a club, too!" But Peter doesn't hear, he doesn't realize.

Drop my shield. Sprint. Oh God, there's a violence in me.

Swinging the laser, two-handed, I bring it down upon Jacobik's neck . . . as he reaches for Peter, still pumping his trigger; as he loops the cord round his neck. The golem Jacobik crashes into Peter, knocking him over, sprawling across him. Can it be knocked *un*conscious, when it only possesses a mockery of consciousness? Its arms heave outward, pulling on the cord, while Peter writhes beneath, kneeing upwards, tearing at its wrists. He's wiry, he has the fear of death in him, but its weight bears him down. If I had Vilo's sword! The golem flops its head from side to side, exposing Peter's face to any further clubbing. His eyes are bulging, his cheeks turn blue beneath the golden hairs.

Where's that *sword*, Wu? Oh put it in my hand!

Flash-glimpse: she's further down the slope. But not running to help, no. What's she doing with that sword? Sticking it in the ground! By the hilt?

Haul Jacobik off? Can't heave his weight! Pull his hands together? Too strong!

Strangle him before he strangles my darling! The vile repetition of it! Cursed to re-enact it. He grins, how he grins at me sideways, twistedly. He pants, "It's *me*, Amy. Don't be mistaken. My soul flew to this re-enactment, and imitation of my body. This once, the dead come back to life! *Resurrectus sum.* And you know why—"

Cut that talk off with my fingers! Squeeze it shut. Lie across him, break his jealous embrace of Peter. Oh it goes on forever.

In one moment, in the same moment, all things happen. Jacobik—Franz Jacobik, mother's son—relaxes into second death. Peter's eyes roll up. His tongue juts out, doggy on a hot day. His face is black beneath the gold. He twitches and is still. A shout, "No!" from Ritchie, from the crater side—fury and

231

anguish—jerks my head aside. In an eyeflash, shutter moment, Wu's small figure is tumbling forward, driving—my God—the swordpoint through her eye right into her skull . . .

SUNRISE!

THIRTY-EIGHT

A CORAL MORNING in Prague . . .

("Jacobik? How?")

—Don't be horrified, Amy. Death is the doorway. But there's a guard upon it. This is the final slavery which no one notices who isn't honed to the appreciation of a genuine death. As a connoisseur of death I know this.

And suddenly Franz Jacobik is no stranger any longer. He belongs. He is us. But what manner of being are *we*?

("You never came all the way to God's World, Franz. The gold never grew on you. You died ordinarily. How could you get drawn in to this?")

—I've haunted you as no other ghost ever haunted a mortal. I've been your channel to Grigory and Salman all along. Didn't you realize this? The Veil Being 'glues' the dead to the living. This is what this dyad-bonding is—its way of glueing itself to the world. Its glue was already beginning to stick way out in High Space, just a little. This glued me to *Pilgrim*—and to you. Enough for me to haunt you intermittently. But the censor has frozen your memory—let me warm it with my hands.

("Yes, I must remember something!")

—We all must.

("All?")

Momentarily, wearing a quilted blue-flower jacket, I am helping the cooks of *East is Red* commune unload cabbages from a bicycle-cart . . .

—To die for the people, Amy, is weightier than Mount Tai. I have died. For the people.

("Wu, too?")

—I've played a pretty trick in this game of heaven! We have a saying: Attack downhill! What could be more downhill than death? Down the gradient of death into the lover who opens her arms to gather the dying beloved in? I took the risk that if I yearned fiercely enough for you at this awful moment I could join you in the aska-bonding and make something more of this: not just a bourgeois marriage of two minds but a true community, a cadre of the soul—not an instrument of seduction and sly oppression, but of liberation and true solidarity. Together, Amy, we can start a prairie fire!

Momentarily, a brass band plays in the Princes Street Gardens. Pigeons peck at crumbs. A green-eyed girl with foxy Titian hair sits by us on the bench.

("So who was *she*, Peter?")

—Och.

I am 'I' no longer. I am 'we'. We notice, through our Amy's eyes, that the golem of Jacobik has melted back into the air already, back into Askatharli . . .

The key is death. At the moment of death. And transfiguration. We. Shall. Remember . . . embers—

Embers flare up—and melt the ice. Memory-space opens. Memory floods us. The Harxine Paracomputers! The death sentence hanging over our shipmates if we channel dream-demons against the Harxine, drawing on the energies of . . .

. . . the Veil Being!

Something tries to stem this flood and soak it up . . . It still bursts through. It rises, stabilising our quartet-self, glueing us as one. Didn't the Harxine tell Grigory that memory is stabilizing?

Something built of dead souls owns this world. It's a cosmic wind, a *pneuma* that breathes through us. It tries to suck this knowledge from us. If only we had turf and tree and rock to cling to, not this shifting mass of sand grains! We cling like leaves in a gale.

Why am I on my knees? To whom? To what?

Purpose flows in from Wu; and a death-love which is the other face of liberation, from Franz; and a thirst for true sky-contact, shaman-force, anger at its betrayal, from our Peter.

Dust devils dance again across the mirages. A golden angel takes shape out there. It strides towards us.

Upon the ridge the rhaniqs bleat in fear. Our golden hair prickles too, enraged at us.

234

It is an archangel of brass with four arms and four wings, with a face of seductive androgynous beauty that speaks to the eye of ancient faith in Peter, Franz and Amy-me. Momentarily— to our Wu—it is an outsize living statue of Mao, whom she loathes and loves, then it is a white-robed bearded Jehovah. Finally it becomes a searing pillar of fire.

Here is God: the presence of God, walking on His world.

And it isn't God at all. It's a fraction of the Veil Being, whose existence is lent to it by a billion dead and living souls, and by ourselves.

"I AM THAT I AM," says the fire with a thunder-crackle voice. "I AM THE RESURRECTION AND THE LIFE."

—A direct confrontation is more than I hoped for (remarks our Wu quietly.) Without us, you'd have no existence, would you?

"WHO TRANSGRESSES MY BOND-BELOVED LAW?"

—The question is, how did you arise? (retorts Wu.)

"WHAT ARE YOU, WHO OPPOSE ME?"

—We're a tetrahedron, four-in-one (says our Franz, to us alone.) The tetrahedron is the most stable, fundamental of all structures! It's omnitriangulated, omnisymmetrical. Everything of the universe outside it balances everything within. It's the closest possible packing array. So it's the energy co-ordinating system of Nature itself. It's how atoms are packed, how chemicals co-ordinate, how the life-code is designed. But we're a *psychic* tetrahedron now, co-ordinating reality and transreality, life and death! Each sees the other. Each holds the other in his embrace.

The fiery column wavers and dies down.

—Stay here! (orders Wu.) We're part of you, and you can't go. Fire, burn bright, but don't you dare burn this fine Dove body of ours!

A Chinese dragon-lion roars in the flames.

"YOU DARE TO INTERROGATE THE ANCIENT OF DAYS?"

—Not so ancient as all that! Show your origin! Unveil it! We *are* you, so this knowledge is ours for the asking.

To the eye of vision, appears:

the Eye of Menka—the gas giant looming up above the horizon. And below the horizon too. Its nature unfolds . . .

Stormy gas shells rotating around a rocky core. Lightning raging. Anhydrous methane and ammonia giving rise to simple organic compounds and polymers that will richly colour the clouds. Amino acids forming when these reactions hydrolise in acid. Dust, drawn in from space as the gas giant sweeps out its orbit, salting these clouds with minerals. The whole process of saturation with precursors of life. The process takes much more time than evolution on its moon-child. We witness it. We understand it. We draw on its memory of itself.

The gas giant is primed for life, but only a weird quasi-life occurs in a crystalline virus form—life which isn't alive yet which replicates itself by high frequency electromagnetic resonance. It is a parasitism with no host to express itself, forever poised on the threshold of life. It is an alphabet in search of a language to express itself. And because of its sheer size and interconnectedness, eventually it yearns and stirs—and captures, not life, for there is none to capture, but the interface between the universe which is imagined, recreated afresh at every moment, and the Imagining of it. It hovers on the very boundary between non-existence and existence. Its own rogue existence balances upon the ebb and tide of being: the breath of the cosmos, a breathing swifter than any human breath, swift as the quantum flip of the electron that ceases in one orbit to re-exist in the next. This quantum breath is what the Veil Being breathes.

So an entity is born yet not born, and it reaches out through High Space to those who have been born nearby. It touches upon the sands of Menka, through them, replicating itself here too. It creates golden tendrils out of the flesh of the living beings who will become its subjects, glueing itself to them. Borrowing their will and their thought, it maintains its existence upon that standing wave; and it looks around, through their eyes, lending them vision.

The flame column burns coldly.

—Every soul caught up in this thing is halted at the first degree of death! (cries Franz.) It can leach away all suspicions, and toss you Heaven and immortality as a sop. A sop? No, that's it's very *essence*. False Heaven. Ego Heaven. But we can command this angel guardian. We're more stable than it is!

("Command it, like a genie?")

—A genie in a bottle! What are bottles made of? Glass. What's glass made of?

—Sand!

"Godling, you will burn smaller and fiercer, but without burning us. You will burn no larger than this hand of mine. You will fuse the sands around you into a bottle to hold you: a bottle with a seal upon it! You will make the bottle that we imagine now. This little bottle, see?"

Our golden down crackles as the angel tries to repel itself from us.

It fails to. Its fire sinks down, a-brightening. A little ball of light spins sand round itself in storm bands like a miniature Eye of Menka, melting a bubble of glass.

A small bottle cools. Inside is our genie, microcosm of the vaster entity.

Our Amy's hand picks it up.

Carrying the bottle in our hand, we complete our journey up the dune. Ritchie looks bewildered. René-menZoe nods his head blissfully, falsely transfigured, not yet ready to be an enemy. Only Samti-menVao drinks us in, in shock or fear.

Abruptly Samti draws his sword and attacks.

THIRTY-NINE

BUT IT IS a sword which ceases to exist with every quantum moment, then re-exists as the flux of being breathes in and out . . .

We imagine its existence elsewhere across the sands.

Displacing air with a sharp pop, it falls glittering in the distance.

Samti-menVao gapes at his empty hand, and howls. Be kind to him. We simply imagine him a little further away. A hundred metres downslope he stares about him, stunned—then he takes to his heels.

We reach out to clasp René's hand, and touch Zoe's mind. She brushes against us within, delighted if puzzled.

We break through the veil in her. We show her: the Harxine, the Veil Being, her hypnosis forestalled by it.

Her chagrin is huge.

Through her, René knows too.

"What do we do?" he whispers.

"We've tamed part of it, René. We've protected ourselves. We have its power now, without the penalties."

"You may be protected!"

"We can protect you as well, René-menZoe."

"What about Ritchie? He hasn't been—"

"Transfigured, no." Heinz's word: *Verklärung.*

"Will someone tell me what the hell's going on?" bursts out Ritchie.

—Can we show my little pigeon the memories that he showed us in Heaven? (wonders Wu.)

—Why not use the God bottle as a crystal ball? (suggests Peter.)

—Yes, it's a power source, isn't it, my shaman? A High Space kernel under our control.

238

The God bottle behaves just as we require it too . . .

—I do like him. Really.

—I had a way with pigeons once . . . (chuckles Franz.)

—Well, you can't catapult Ritchie out of this!

"I guess I was right about the gas giant." Ritchie slaps his brow. "It *is* alive."

"Not in the ordinary way. It's alive through us and the Getkans and any other aliens it infests. It exists in an intermediate zone in the circuit between reality and . . . 'God'."

"Doesn't it still need the gas giant as a physical bridgehead? Its base? Its lens to look through? Hell, how do I know? It may do. All that the Harxine and their insect troops need to do to find out is wipe out something the size of Saturn. I don't think that's quite in their league."

—*Can't* we catapult Ritchie and René out of here? (wonders Franz.) If we could re-imagine Samti somewhere else . . . does the distance matter? We hold High Space in our hands, don't we? We can imagine ourselves elsewhere, and them too! There's a hypnotic vector from you to Kamasarin, Amy. Look at it. Examine it.

We do look. Personally, my Amy-self doesn't see it. But those who enclose my Amy-self see it.

—I'm still partly glued to *Pilgrim,* too. And we're all part of each other in memory-space.

—This time (announces Wu proudly) we shall take our body along on the out-of-the-body ride. There's only one possible physical destination: on board the real *Pilgrim* in present time.

—The Harxine will assume it's an attack (frets Peter.) The Group-ones will start their killing.

—Ha! (pounces Franz.) And how did we snatch that sword away from Samti? I can handle anything that moves.

—Braggart (laughs Peter.) You couldn't handle Amy.

—This is different. Don't you *see*?

And we do see, within.

"Listen, Ritchie. We're going to get you out of here. And you too, René-menZoe. We're going to transfer all of us to *Pilgrim.* We can do it! But when we get there, whatever happens don't move. If the Group-ones jump you—and they will!—we'll shift

239

them the way we shifted Samti and his sword." We stick the God-bottle in our jump-suit pocket. "Hold hands, in a line."

We are three witches, about to dance a jig.

—The million mile journey begins *and ends* with a single step! This step, now . . .

The world shifts.

Control deck! The prisoners, laid out in their trance, an insectoid poised over every one of them . . .

Almost immediately, each guard lunges at its prisoner, saw-tooth arms agape. Almost immediately isn't soon enough. Our Franz acts faster than reflex, fast as seeing.

We quantize their attack. We decree that one quantum moment of time shall recreate itself time and again for them. Our Franz holds them tethered tighter than if he held seven leashes. They're frozen.

Other Group-ones are in sight. He stills them too.

"Can you hear us, Harxine? This isn't an attack. Don't act rashly. We're free of the Veil Being. We need to talk to you."

A cathode screen lights up.

'We do not act rashly, merely rapidly as is proper for machine intelligences whose responses require nanoseconds.' —They're offended! (chuckles Peter.) *'We cannot understand how you have stopped our Group-ones from acting. Is this not an attack?'*

"We're re-imagining your Group-ones in the same quantum moment."

'This must be explained.'

"It will be. I'm Amy Dove, Harxine—"

'Identified. Your hypnosis was interrupted by rupture of memory/dream space. Did it succeed nevertheless?'

—It wouldn't have succeeded but for Franz and Wu (admits our Peter.) We two together, Amy, would have behaved like René-menZoe. Bliss and False Heaven.

—Perhaps, perhaps not (allows our Franz generously.)

"We're a new kind of being, Harxine. A quartet being—a hypermind. René is the ordinary . . . transfiguration product of God's World: a dyad of living René and dead Zoe. We're screening him from the Veil Being. Ritchie is no threat. He's still ordinary."

240

"Gee, thanks! I've got a guardian angel, though. Eh, Wu? Somewhere in you."

—My little pigeon.

—Keep the billing and cooings for later, hmm? (teases our Franz.)

"We're something new. And we know what the Veil Being is, Harxine. It has its origin in the gas giant itself. It grew from there into High Space, and only subsequently invaded Low Space. We've captured a portion of its being, and tamed it. Here." Amy's hand flourishes the God bottle.

—Hijacker brandishing grenade! (warns Wu.)

"It's sealed. Don't worry."

'Machine intelligences do not worry, Amy Dove.' (—Oh no?) *'If our Group-ones killed you, would that portion of the Veil Being break free?'*

"They can't kill us. But we don't wish to sound like blackmailers, Harxine. We're on the same side as you, remember."

'Machine intelligences—'

"—always remember. Okay, point taken."

—We may be an immortal being (hints Peter.)

—Till we choose *not* to be (retorts Franz.)

—Which we can choose once we've done our duty (Wu assures him.)

("This is a mortal body, folks.")

—A body, dear, which is being re-imagined from moment to moment. Why not renewed as well? Refreshed? We can do it. I'm not sure that we aren't doing it already.

("Then our love will never fade and wither, eh?")

—Och.

—Immortality is a snare (warns Franz, of course.)

"All you need do, Harxine," chips in Ritchie, "is destroy the gas giant then stabilise its moons in new orbits round the sun, and you're home and dry."

'Is this a serious proposal? It would require several hundred years and enormous effort. There would have to be no interference from the Veil Being.'

"We can discuss tactics once you've freed our friends."

The Harxine decide, as promised, in nanoseconds.

'Accepted! Relax your hold, and our Group-ones will wake

your friends. We have prosthetic control implants in all Group-ones. Already we are transmitting a continuous signal ordering them to assist you.'

"They still look ready to attack," says Ritchie.

'Because you hold them so. This is a time for trust. We Harxine sustain life. Death has its rightful place, but not here, not now.'

"You're going to feel one almighty sorrow if you knock out the Veil Being, then!" says Ritchie. "Because billions of dead souls who are still alive in it are all going to go whoosh at once."

—Death has its place (echoes our Franz.) It's only right that they should die a proper death, a full death. They're only in limbo, and their worlds are eroding.

'You have powers that we do not have, Amy Dove. If you need redundant confirmation: we are transmitting to our Group-ones now; no Group-one will harm any human.'

("Let the dogs loose, Franz!")

The poised Group-ones do not rend or tear. Instead, with their pincers they begin snipping away, swiftly but gently, at the tangle of cables, tubes and wires tethering those paralysed bodies.

The first person to be set free is Captain K.

He stares in momentary perplexity at the three of us. Of course, for we're all clad in golden down . . .

And now he roars out some Mongolian wrestler's cheer.

"You've won!" he beams. "Oh for a bowl of *kumiss* to reward you with!"

Whatever Mongolian concoction *kumiss* might be, we aren't thirsty for it. Our Amy-body isn't in the least bit thirsty.

FORTY

THE HARXINE HAVE a speech synthesis programme linked in to the interphones now. Our lingua franca remains English, though the Harxine can handle all the primary languages of the ex-captives with equal fluency. René, not being an ex-captive, soon discovers to his chagrin that they know no French.

Nor do they speak seductive Getkasaali. Indeed our own sense of the Getkan language has begun to rust a little. Nuances are missing—the automatic prompter in our minds is too distant to be heard.

We three golden ones (or seven, if the dead in us are counted) brief the other eight—who all have in their minds, from memory space, jigsaw pieces of the puzzle large or small. By now the Harxine have withdrawn two-thirds of their insectoid boarding party, keeping only half a dozen on *Pilgrim*—and the status of these is less that of menaces or monsters, now, more that of mascots. Sachiko attempts to pet one, perhaps to compensate by this comic show of interspecies kinship for the evaporation of her role as linguist. Even Gus Trimble chucks one under its chitinous chin. The Harxine controllers must either have a crazy sense of humour in their circuits, or a sympathy for human foibles, since the beast promptly rolls over like a dog, exposing its vacuum-proof underbelly, and waggles its legs. Gus slaps and scratches at its rigid hide.

Captain K is back in command again—delighted that the parapsychology aspect of the expedition has borne strange fruit (even though he didn't set up the experiment). Of course, the real power—the God-power—resides in us, who are that fruit. It lies in our quartet self. Peter's speculations about our potential immortality may well be true. We do not eat, we do not drink.

This Amy-self feels no need to. We are recreating ourself afresh from moment to moment.

—We still have to die (nags our Franz), to be free. You do realize that? We must be able to die.

—Yes, Franz (soothes Wu.) There's the small matter of the Veil Being first.

"So," Captain K addresses everyone, "the question is, do we have a force here that can be tamed and used? You've already captured a portion of its being, Dove."

(And the God-bottle rests in our Amy's pocket . . .)

"Whole worlds are enmeshed, Captain," interrupt the invisible Harxine through the interphone. "We would remind you of that."

"He who sups with the devil needs a long spoon," says Salman. "We only have one spoon, and that's Amy."

"But is this essentially any more dangerous than, say, nuclear power?"

"The Veil Being can draw other species into it, even if you avoid being enmeshed," the Harxine remind him sternly. "Who is to say that you have avoided it successfully, in any case? You are here, and you have knowledge. But your Earth remains vulnerable. A second High Space drive might be being sent. How do you propose to travel back through High Space to warn your world without falling into the clutches of the Veil Being again?"

"We can handle that," we assure them. "We control God-power now."

"It's a surrogate God," protests Salman. "A person of real knowledge could achieve this state by himself. Someone like—"

"Like Assaf ibn what's-his-name," says Ritchie.

"Assaf ibn Barkhiyâ. I didn't know you knew the Koran, Ritchie!"

"It's been quite an education down there, friend."

"Well, few people can. Few people do. The world has to go on—that's why. Surely Getka and Zerain and these other worlds have got to go on as well. They have to *restart* going on. They're all locked up in this false revelation as of now, and it's sapping them."

"This is why we came," agree the Harxine.

Ritchie scratches his hand. A moment later he glances down at the source of irritation, and blows on his hand. A dust of gold

244

blows off. It evaporates. Ceases to be. He rubs both hands together. Motes, hairs drift away. He sneezes. However, the irritation to his mucous membranes has already ceased to exist.

"The stuff's coming off me— I'm losing it!" cries Ritchie.

"Zoe!" exclaims René, at the same time. He flails his arms as though to catch hold of her, and floats off the deck. We catch him instead.

—Zoe?

—I'm . . . losing touch.

—We can hold you.

—But ought we to? (asks our Franz.) This is the true death coming.

It's happening to this Amy-body too: the golden down is sloughing off, melting into thin air. But we four are all still here together, as powerfully bonded as ever. We're in perfect balance. We are a psychic hyperstructure. We don't need the golden tendrils now. We're independent.

—René and Zoe need them. They're breaking up.

—I said we can hold them. We're doing so.

—We've drawn a line around the powers of the Veil Being. We've imprisoned it and limited it. So now it's withering— withdrawing. Unless we hold on tight.

—Choose, Zoe (Franz urges her.) Will you die the true death? Will you go beyond? Or shall we keep you here?

—I've got to choose, haven't I? I'm . . . not scared. It doesn't matter, does it? Because it's *right*. Let me go, dear friends. Let me go.

"*Don't*," begs René.

—But it *is* right. It's best. Goodbye, René. *Adieu. Je t'adore.* Don't grieve.

And it *is* right. We do let her go.

—Good . . . bye

René slumps in the air, grieving none the less.

—What's holding the High Space pyramid in being? (asks Peter urgently.) The minds of everybody on board! But it *is* a danger, isn't it? The Harxine are right. We should make it cease to exist.

(Then how do we get *Pilgrim* back to Earth?)

—We get her there the Assaf way! The way we got here. If we

245

could shift three bodies, why not shift a whole ship? We've got the God-bottle under *our* control. It's a High Space drive in itself, if we want it to be! Look, the High Space pyramid was obviously two things. One was a coded pathway through High Space. But the other was deception—necessary window-dressing. Earth would never have built *Pilgrim* if we hadn't felt sure there was some ordinary, specific destination that we were heading towards. We'd have been too suspicious of a drive without any obvious flight plans or controls. Our journey had to wear the mask of an ordinary journey—a journey, yes, that we could *believe* in!—or we wouldn't have had the . . . faith, the mental commitment to trigger and maintain the High Space field. We were all Rats, in that sense. We had to *know* we were travelling from A to B, from Earth to 82 Eridani, in an ordinary way before we could learn the extraordinary way. But we've learnt more than the Veil Being expected! We can go direct. The pyramid is a real danger now. Maybe we can control the Being's imprint on it, but everyone else on board would be contributing their own fears and anxieties and beliefs and disbeliefs to the journey.

(But a whole *ship*?)

—If Assaf could transport a throne . . . well, *Pilgrim* is our throne. It belongs intimately to us. I say that we loose the bonds of the pyramid now. We should abandon it. How could we trust ourselves to it?

We reach consensus in a moment.

"Harxine—and everybody, listen. We're going to dissolve the High Space pyramid. We're going to uncreate it. It's dangerous because it's a link with the Veil Being."

"Please do that," reply the Harxine. I suppose they aren't ultimately concerned whether we get home to Earth or not.

"You're crazy," protests Gus.

"But hell," shouts Neil Kendrick. For a while, there's a babble.

"Listen, all of you. We're a new being, and we're going to get you home."

"Are you planning to leave local space?" demand the Harxine, concerned now. "What about your proposal regarding the gas giant?"

—I can see a way (schemes Franz)—a way to tear the Veil so that it goes on tearing!

He shows us. And it is true; there is a way. Trust our kamikaze Franz!

(We'll have to take the rest of the crew home first, then return with the ship. If we can transfer *Pilgrim* to Earth, we can transfer her back again.)

—Wait, this could be a breakthrough in interstellar travel (speculates Wu, seizing on a main chance.)

—Hardly! (mocks Franz.) A single ship, with a single pilot? What we *can* do about that is take a Harxine paracomputer home with us to set up a light-speed liaison with their home base—so long as they're transportable. I mean, if they aren't built right into these flying asteroids of theirs. We could take some Group-ones along on board, for that matter, if the Harxine need them as manual extensions.

"Harxine, how large are your separate units?"

"Perhaps five per cent of the size of the High Space pyramid."

"Can a single unit still function separately as a 'full' Harxine?"

"Certainly."

"Could you dig one of yourselves out of the asteroid and accompany us? This is our plan, you see . . ."

The Harxine paracomputer unit is a cube the size of a large holovision set. It's independently powered by a hundred-year energy cell in its base—which Earth can, in any case, recharge. Its umbilicals plug in to our computer terminals. Group-ones have brought it out of the interior of the asteroid. Neil and Gus have helped them install it here on the Control Deck. By now the Group-ones have all withdrawn. We will take none with us, after all. This vacuum-adapted variety tolerate gravity and atmosphere for a fairly long time, but not indefinitely.

We have only one thing left to do before we leave.

Our Franz and Wu and Peter reach out through imagination space for the pyramid.

We unimagine it, and that whole complex system of cognita which it is slowly ceases to be part of our cognition any longer. Slowly: the natural resistance of the others to the disappearance

247

of their 'lifeline' makes this somewhat of a Cheshire Cat operation!

Presently the pyramid goes transparent. It becomes a glassy thing, a wraith. Soon all that remains are the lines which define its outline; now even those lines go away, like the Cheshire Cat's smile. In the deck remains simply the square hole through which it once fitted. Crowding, everybody stares down below decks.

Captain K steps back from that hole—all that is left of the engine that once powered his ship. Understandably, he looks rather diffident.

"So, Dove, will you fly us home?"

"Home it is, Captain."

We face each other in mind-space. We breathe the quantum breath of the universe as it exists and ceases and re-exists. With our God-bottle in our hand, we imagine the reality of *Pilgrim* here and now, existing, ceasing, re-existing.

We shift its existence through imagination space to another here-and-now . . .

The sun 82 Eridani switches off. For the space of an inner breath, the gloaming of imagination space surrounds us.

Another sun burns forth.

A familiar world glows too, blue and white, ahead. Beyond in space is a gibbous pock-marked moon. The world also is gibbous, and ocean-washed in blue. Umber continents hide beneath woolly windstreams—our lost world, recovered in this moment of our own recreation.

"We're about fifty thousand klicks from her," cheers Ritchie. "Five balls! Spot on over twenty-one lights!"

"Not bad at all," grins Kendrick. "Velocity's just under a thousand k.p.h. Any closer and we'd have had a real panic on."

The God-bottle vibrates as though in protest, but with an unseen hand our Franz stills it.

After a while, Neil seats himself at the communications board.

"This is *Pilgrim Crusader* calling Space City, calling Earth. This is *Pilgrim Crusader*. We're home." He glances at the Harxine paracomputer unit. "We've brought a friend along with us—an intelligent machine. We need to transfer it and eleven of ourselves over to Space City. The remainder," he frowns at my Amy-self,

248

"intend taking *Pilgrim* back to 82 Eridani. She's got—no, *they* have got business to attend to—"

"Neil, will you please apologize for any visions people saw in Athens and Szechuan and Fort Dodge and places recently? That was our doing. Tell them downstairs that they can get on with their history again. Except, now that the Harxine is here, it's become interstellar history."

"Will do. *Pilgrim Crusader* calling Space City—"

"A very habitable looking planet," says the Harxine approvingly, over the interphone. "We will soon build suitable lightspeed transmitters for contacting Cybercentral and the other Harxine-linkage worlds, including Getka if your plan has worked. The Getkans will need massive aid to readjust to the realities of Low Space. They will be very disoriented and out of touch with each other."

"So we'll know whether Amy's . . . whether *their* plan did work," muses Captain K, "in just about forty-two years' time." He takes stock of himself. "I believe I shall live to know."

"You may know earlier than that, Captain. We shall help you construct a suitable sublight drive and hybernation tanks. The Harxine in the Eridani system will already have sent lightspeed messages calling for aid to reconstruct the societies of all the trapped worlds. However, Dindi is closer to Earth than any other source of assistance. You should fly to Dindi to help them reconstruct their society. Or even to 82 Eridani itself. The logistics suggest so."

"Amy will know in a day or two." Grigory is sad. No, not sad exactly—he envies us.

Yes, we shall know. Or shall we then be beyond knowledge in any ordinary sense?

REQUIEM

THE EYE OF Menka fills the viewports with its glorious storm bands—bridgehead of the Veil Being. Menka itself lies astern, no larger now than Luna. We recreated *Pilgrim* close by God's World, our two undamaged engines already firing, and have been falling inwards, into the giant's clutches, ever since. Falling down the gravity well.

We have, perhaps, five hours left.

The effect of *Pilgrim* plunging into the Eye will be no more, naturally, than dropping a pea into the sea. The effect of ourselves diving through the Veil, with the God-bottle under our control, dying the true death, penetrating into the Beyond, will be—no doubt—far greater . . .

Pilgrim seems quite empty since there's no other human being around to see—unless we choose to stare into a mirror in one of the cabins; but we don't bother visiting any of the cabins. They're only husks of our former lives, empty boxes. Yet at the same time there are the four of us present: the four-in-one, and with us the ship is full.

We adopt a lotus pose before the open viewports. The hull dosimeters report huge strengthening of the radiation field. The gas giant's Van Allen belt is peppering us with charged particles now; we're already a dead body, which still lives on.

—Which still dies on! (laughs Wu.)
    —*Give thanks to King Herod!* (sings Franz)
who comes to kill us for a second time
We raise our translucent hands
in praise

251

for the truth revealed to us
Three cheers for Herod!
We all sing death songs. Yet none of them seems right. All are full of either irony or resentment.

We shall compose our own song, then.

But no. No need. Our own true death shall be that song.

The gas giant fills our view, to north, south, east and west. Amazing. Beautiful. We're free-falling into a wall of colour which no longer seems to be below us, but ahead: an enormous tapestry in turmoil, an orange veil behind a saffron veil behind a salmon veil, scalloped and sheared by jet streams.

Pilgrim is heating up. Showers of electric fireflies and whirling sparklers stream off the nose and bows. *Pilgrim* has no ablative shield; the ship itself is burning up. Any moment now she'll rupture and all the oxygen will whoosh and blaze.

—Close our eyes, Amy. The last rites.

Uncomfortably hot in here, I suppose. The God-bottle thrusts a bunched fist into our belly, as though it tries to burst into our womb—ah, it's me who squeezes it. We already enwomb it, in mind space.

We're briefly conscious of the minds of millions, billions, reflected in the boiling gassy veils. All those limbo-lovers, who form the Veil Being's own existence. Part of the Being is part of our own being now, a child resorbed into our womb. Fierce molten brat of energy! Kicking and struggling!

Something explodes, too loud to hear. Something burns away our Amy-body, searing it to ashes (we suppose) too fast to hurt her.

Flash visions of sculpted dreams—dream cities, dream gardens, paradises—lure and beckon us in. Each is a sticky veil, a fly-paper for souls, who have the privilege of visiting other fly-papers at will. We shun them, shrug them off.

—Where to?

—Downward into true death, carrying the Veil Being with us! We are it, and it is us. Imagine ourselves back into the Imagining! Let us tear apart—tearing the Veil as we do so! We're dead, but not dead yet.

So our Franz thrusts away from ourself. Yet he's still part of us. We stretch along the axis of his death-flight, deforming like a rubber sheet.

Our Wu repels herself now, and we stretch out along another axis.

—*Do not go gentle into that good night!* (sings Peter.) Go bloody fiercely!

He pushes off, deforming us along three vectors.

Our Amy-self extends along the fourth. Yes, we're a rubber sheet, with the Veil Being imprinted in it.

This whole universe (no, *that* universe—for we have left it) once burst into being from a point source along four necessary vectors: three of space and one of time, with the energy of the Imagining creating and defining space and time. We seem to repeat that process in our dying, yet we aren't defining space and time. We're undefining it. Instead of breathing out along the flux of 'Be!', we breathe in as we recede, catching the tide the other way—the undertow, the reflux. We're beyond the standing wave in High Space, dragging it along with us, deforming it. We're an enormous sail catching that other breeze, of Unbecoming—a sail that stretches further and further, a veil-sail sailing into the Otherness, beyond.

Our stability is lost forever, now. The Veil Being can't hold us. We can't snap back even if we wish. We're too far gone from existence.

We four rip apart. At the same moment our 'selves' part too, opening up, unfolding . . . Matter is frozen energy, and lives are only frozen presences of the Imagining, crystallizing out of it. So I melt, I flow. What is this 'me'? What was it? Only an aspect, a presence, now returning.

The Veil Being is ripping, too, in a different way—ripping all over, becoming a permeable membrane once again, between the Imagining and reality. Osmosis of trapped souls resumes in a rush, so huge is the pressure against the membrane of that doomed quasi-being. A flood follows in our wake, of surprised alien egos that are also only aspects, presences; which now melt too, and flow.

Who was 'I'? For a moment, all my life is present, all at once. And who I am, is answered.

253

Now that knowledge flows back into . . .
energy, the creative energy, answering its question
into light, the light beyond light